SLIPKNOT

SLIPKNOT

A SHERIFF GAVIN PRUITT MYSTERY

Gary McKinney

Special thanks to Ice Nine Publishing for kindly allowing the use of Grateful Dead lyrics.

Cover design: Karen Parker © 2007.

ISBN: 0-9723706-5-X
Library of Congress Control Number: Pending

Kearney Street Books
Slipknot
First KSB printing (November, 2007).

Printed in the United States of America

Kearney Street Books
Po Box 2021
Bellingham, WA 98227
360-738-1355
www.kearneystreetbooks.com

Please note that Elkhorn is a made-up place. It may look similar to the area in which I was raised, but the places writers were raised don't often fit a fictional rendering. So, like writers do, I unapologetically made it fit. Thanks to Sgt. Dave Richards, Bellingham Police Department, for the excellent law enforcement advice. (Any errors in police policies and procedures are the author's competely.) Thanks also to Alan Trist, Ice Nine Publishing. Special thanks to Meredith Cary, Chris Halpin, Margi Fox, Sara Stamey, and Kate Trueblood. RD oversaw this project, as he does all the projects those of us who knew him produce. Dedicated, of course, to my family—Karen, Morgan, and Fallon—but also to the Grateful Dead, not so much the band per se, but what they embody for those of us, whatever age we may be, who have grown and changed with them.

PROLOGUE:
NOVEMBER, 1994

The fog was wet, thick as cotton, and the headlamps were next to useless. Might as well have been penlights. The road no help, either, one switchback after another—appearing without sense or warning. Who'd engineered the damn thing, a road builder or roustabout? The idiot in the back moaning like a sick cow, garbled noises through the tape over his mouth. A fine state of affairs…a helluva state. Should never have come to this. A little shoving around, sure. That part had seemed inevitable. Some people needed physical intimidation; there was nothing savage about it. Yet the man had remained obstinate, proud of his arrogance. Matters could have been settled easily enough—but no. A next step had to be taken, then another, and now there was all this, a place beyond the furthest point imaginable, instinct taking over somewhere along the line—though where was unclear. Yes, the power remained, but focus had blurred. This damnable road! This maddening fog! If the ridge didn't appear soon all these actions taken so confidently would be reduced to memory, embers dying as quickly as the fire had burned hot.

Then around yet another switchback the fog broke. Just like that! As if surfacing from a deep dive, an interminable ascent, lungs about to burst, then the deliverance of sweet, life-giving air.

Above the fog line, the full moon burnished the stump-strewn logging operation a bluish white. In the surrounding ravines, banks of fog had settled over the adjacent ridge tops, spreading into the distance like black islands on a gray sea. Here was a magical kind of beauty that few ever saw, the art of pure nature—moon, landscape and silky fog.

The yarder lay ahead—by comparison, a jarring vision of technology. Yet incongruous as it might have been, it was where the driver steered, legging down on the emergency brake before reaching a full stop, jostling the idiot in back.

Bam! he kicked with bound legs. Bam! A desperate man now. He'd damage something if he wasn't attended to—no time to savor the transcendent beauty. Hatch door hoisted up, body rolling out like a barrel, falling funnily, a bark of pain—muffled by tape.

"What to do?" the driver muttered, though the answer came quickly. The knife was available, as was the pistol, but something more interesting, too.

The captive wore a coat with thick shoulder padding and the driver grasped him there and began dragging him toward the steel spar pole. Under the spotlight moon the coupling lay brightly lit a few feet from the yarder—where it should have been left by a competent crew.

Now if there was only rope…

CHAPTER ONE

By the time Sheriff Gavin Pruitt negotiated the last switchback on the logging service that forked off Nalpe Road, the fog that had blanketed the valley during the night had lifted. Unfortunately, as if turning over in its sleep, a high screen of stratus had taken its place, which would soon thicken to deliver a consignment of cold, heavy rain and in the process wash all the physical evidence right down the gullies. Pruitt's hope was to finish the site investigation before the deluge began.

At the crest a motley collection of orange and yellow equipment appeared, settled on the ridge like a homely bird clinging to a muddy branch. Pruitt parked next to Willapa County's evidence van, stood from his car and took a deep breath. The air was clean as line-dried laundry up here—fresh air something he needed sorely after his first duty that morning, sorting out a child molestation charge. The interview with the abuser had nauseated him. The interview with the victim, a nine-year old boy, had made him want to cry. Then the call for this: a murder apparently. A long strange Monday, all right. And he wasn't even in uniform yet, but rather still wore the clothes he donned for child abuse interviews: a cable-knit sweater over a cotton shirt, tan slacks and brown oxfords. Lee Wilson, Chief Deputy for Investigations, had secured the crime scene with a ribbon of yellow tape strung between tree stumps, but before approaching it, Pruitt traded the oxfords for the mucking boots he kept in the trunk of his cruiser.

As Pruitt neared, Wilson self-consciously ignored him. Nearly two years had passed and he still hadn't forgiven Pruitt for trouncing him in the election, even though the real reason for his defeat had been Wilson himself, who may have been an expert in forensics but was too coarse of speech and too insensitive of manner for the PR side of the job. None of the Willapa County constituency could imagine Wilson as Grand Marshal of the Fourth of July parade or as a goodwill ambassador in the elementary schools.

As a case in point, it appeared he'd unmercifully grilled the crew, skulking a few yards from the crummy in their hickory shirts and stagged pants, glancing at Lee as if they'd enjoy getting a piece of him, out here where grievances could still get settled man-to-man. Yet mostly they were staring at the victim. Pruitt, too, lifted his gaze, John Carpenter's unnaturally long-looking body swaying from the telescoping steel spar pole, head hanging at a strange angle, ankles swollen around the tops of the shoes, the hands blackish-blue.

Pruitt sighed and thought of The Grateful Dead's *Franklin's Tower*, invoking under his breath the four winds to blow this poor man safely home. It wasn't much, but the necessity of a spiritual thought in the presence of such horror was overpowering. *Roll away the dew*, please. Allow John Carpenter's soul a joyful glimpse beyond the stage scrim of physical existence.

Yet there was also the practical side of what this was. Or the debacle. One of the most celebrated ecologists in America dead in Willapa County. Pruitt already with his hands full keeping loggers and environmentalists apart from one another. Deadlines nearing, nerves fraying. Everybody waiting for Carpenter to complete the assignment that had brought him to southwest Washington State in the first place: deciding the fate of Black Bear Ridge, fifteen-hundred acres of privately-held old-growth timber smack in the middle of Pruitt's jurisdiction.

For eighteen months he'd gotten an earful. Environmentalists demanding protection for the wildlife, the owls, birds, and bugs; loggers claiming they needed protection, too. What about their jobs? Their families? It amazed Pruitt that the middle ground got displaced so quickly. At some point, his personal politics had taken a completely practical aspect: cut the trees or don't cut the trees, people. Please just cut the crap. Which, of course, wasn't about to happen now. Not with John Carpenter swinging dead from a spar pole.

Pruitt strode up to Glen Hampton, a bandy-legged man who was both the crew chief and a police reservist. Glen didn't even bother with formalities. "What the hell do we do now?"

Pruitt said, "Grok it."

"Grok? Isn't that something pirates drink?"

"Sorry, Glen. It's a sixties term. It means scope the scene. Get the smell of it."

Hampton said, "All I can smell is that damn loader. When this is done I gotta check if there's a leak in the fuel line."

Addressing Lee Wilson, Pruitt said, "What do you make from the statements?"

Though investigation was Wilson's reason for living, he slumped against the truck's fender as if he couldn't care less. "They drove up, it got light, there was the body." He thumbed to the knot of workers. "If you believe this mangy pack."

Just before he heard the sound of an approaching vehicle, Pruitt would have sworn he heard a collective growl emanate from the knot of men Lee had slighted. But probably it had been the vehicle, which Pruitt hoped was assistance, the ambulance or other officers, but was instead Pat Crowley, head of logging operations for Saginaw, Inc., whose logging show this was. Pat's idea of assistance would be to bury the body hastily behind a stump and get the crew back to work. After sliding his pickup truck to a stop on a slick of yellow-brown clay, he bolted from the cab.

"What the hell, Gavin?" he called as he approached.

Crowley had short black hair that tufted out from underneath his orange hard-hat, and wore a plaid wool shirt, chinos, and work boots—though there was no mistaking him for a laborer. In spite of the working man's costume, he had the unfrayed, unsullied, tucked-in look of management. To dispel any notions to the contrary, he lit into Pruitt the moment he reached stage-whispering distance. "This has ramifications I don't need to get into, do I, Gavin? Or do I?"

Pruitt toed some dirt. "Let me see if I can figure this one out, Pat. The crew's down, which is costing you money, and a man's dead, which is going to cost the company's image a few points. That about cover it?"

Crowley glared at him. "This crap attitude of yours is wearing thin. All this touchy-feely nonsense in a police force, for chrissakes. You should have locked up all these greenbacks months ago, instead of turning'em out as fast as you take'em in."

"Pat, you're the kind of person all in favor of trampling over people's rights until those rights happen to be your own."

Crowley continued glaring. "Two years from now," he said, "we're going to run your liberal ass the hell out of town."

Pruitt said, "Two years from now you can try anything you want. Right now you can step back."

"I'll step back after you tell me what happened here. I've got to call in this frickin' disaster to the home office and explain what the hell is going on."

Though a turf war with Crowley was counterproductive in every sense, Pruitt was about to back the Saginaw manager down—forcibly if necessary—when Lee Wilson stepped in between them, hoisted up something disgusting from his throat and spat it on the ground.

"Start with your basics, Pat," Wilson said, wiping his mouth with the back of his hand, then wiping his hand on the back of his trousers. "His fly's up, and there's no stroke magazines lying around, so you can rule out an accident by depravity—unlike that pervert last year out near Bay Center who tried to coordinate hyperventilation and popping a load and got himself hung dead for his trouble."

Under different circumstances, his deputy's reference to the Bay Center incident might have been construed as civilian harassment. Since he'd gotten Crowley to shut-up, Pruitt gave Wilson rein.

"Then you gotta notice that face. Christ, you can practically see the petechial hemorrhaging from here. A face like that you gotta figure he went up alive and kicking. I'd say whoever strung him up not only wanted to make him suffer, they wanted to enjoy the show."

Crowley pressed his lips together, yet could not seem to take his eyes off the body.

"So if it ain't an accident, and it ain't natural causes, then we're left with either homicide or an act of God."

With that, Wilson hocked up some new disgusting article from his throat and spat it on the ground. End of lecture. Pruitt wondered if he emphasized his points similarly in the classrooms at the Washington State Criminal Justice Training Center, where he gave quarterly seminars on evidence collection and preservation.

Pruitt said, "Thanks for the input, Lee. I'm sure Pat understands our predicament a little better now."

Crowley seemed out of rejoinders. He was looking a little pale besides.

Wilson said, "You going to do stills?"

"I sure will," Pruitt said, and turned to walk back to his cruiser for his camera—accompanied by Pat Crowley, who finally regained his voice and whose overriding theme was as Pruitt assumed, adverse publicity. "All these environmentalists," he said. "And the media. Like a pack of dogs. We're bidding for the rights to log Black Bear Ridge, too, you know. They'll blame us first."

Pruitt opened his trunk. "Does having Carpenter dead give your company an advantage, Pat?"

Exasperated, Crowley said, "How could it?"

Pruitt pulled his camera out of the truck by its strap. "You're a big company." He slammed the lid. "Whose logging site was unfortunately singled out for this heinous crime." He slung the strap over his shoulder. "I'm sure you've got people who can write a decent press release." He stopped moving and engaged the corporate man's eyes directly. He wanted badly to quote *New Speedway Boogie*, ask him to stop trying to dominate the conversation when he clearly had nothing new to add to it, but knew the waste of quoting the Dead to a man like Crowley. Rather he said, "As long as you've got nothing to hide, you've got nothing to fear."

Crowley said, "What the hell's that supposed to mean?"

Pruitt had hoped getting under Pat's skin would get him to blurt out a morsel of useful information—for instance, that he'd overheard one of his crews talking about getting Carpenter up to a site and teaching him a thing or two about trees. When nothing came, Pruitt said, "You have something personal against John Carpenter?"

Crowley's eyebrows knit. "Hell no. Why would I?"

"He's probably got family that's going to miss him. Have you thought of that?"

Crowley read him for a moment. "Screw you, Gavin."

Pruitt relooped the camera strap over his shoulder. "I didn't think so."

CHAPTER TWO

When the deluge began, the ink identifying the plastic evidence bag with the crime site photos—a stack of Polaroids, two plastic canisters of 35-millimeter, and a video tape—had barely dried. Was this the *Box of Rain* that Robert Hunter, the Grateful Dead's lyricist, had been thinking of when he wrote that song? If so, a change of title to barrel of rain might be more appropriate. Even in his slicker, water was soon rivuleting down Pruitt's back, dripping off his nose and chin—cold, yet cleansing in a way unmatched by bath or shower. When he ran his hand over his eyes and cheeks to clear his vision, his skin literally squeaked.

With the advent of the downpour, all pretense at collecting forensic evidence was dropped. The only job that could not be avoided was getting the body down.

Proceedings stalled while Glen Hampton, the yarder operator, threw up. Although a police reservist for some ten years, he'd never witnessed a murder scene and it finally got to him. Then Carl Pulkkinen arrived in time to get into an argument with Lee Wilson about a trauma found at the back of the dead man's head. Over the downpour, Pulkkinen, who served as both Prosecutor and Coroner, said, "Pre-mortem."

Lee Wilson dismissed the notion. "He got whacked after."

"Before," Pulkkinen insisted. "It's obvious. Knock him out and string him up."

Wilson said, "Carl, you don't know shit about this kind of thing."

Pruitt said. "Let the autopsy settle it."

Water dripping off his nose, Pulkkinen said, "Your deputy's pushing insubordination. This time I'll charge him, too, goddamnit."

To Pulkkinen, Pruitt said, "Carl, I'll take your concerns under advisement." To Wilson, he said, "Lee, put a clamp on it," adding a look that said he meant it. Then he joined others in a dash for cover, muttering to himself about grown men still acting like kids in a school yard.

Pulkkinen accompanied Pruitt back to his cruiser where they would confer and map strategies. Once safely out of the cloudburst, Carl undid his coat and got comfortable. Like a slowly filling balloon, Carl's midriff had been expanding relentlessly in the five years Pruitt had worked with him. "What you got," he said, "is a local, pissed off as all hell, who finally decided to do something about it."

Pruitt was jotting down notes, trying to ignore the cloying smell of Carl's after shave. Reactivated from exertion and moisture, the fumes had found their way to the back of his throat like a warfare chemical. "There's a lot of money involved," he said. "You got Saginaw, the other timber companies, not to mention the Japanese, all vying for that forest."

Pulkkinen undid his tie, which never stayed fully knotted much past ten in the morning. "Those companies aren't going to kill anybody for it, Gavin."

Because he respected Carl—his intelligence and occasional wit—Pruitt always heard him out, even knowing beforehand that the Prosecutor trusted corporations implicitly, and blamed nearly all crime on bad genes. "I don't know what those companies are capable of, Carl. Any more than you do."

Pulkkinen pushed a strand of his thinning, wet-slick hair back over his balding pate. "See it how you want, Gavin. To me this looks simple: A logger finally killed a greenback." He chuckled, though not with good humor. "The Grand Poobah of greenbacks at that. What a story."

⊕

As Pruitt drove away the torrent reached its apex—the rain coming down in buckets. Visibility was negligible, wipers slapping frantically, the trip back down the treacherous switchbacks torturously slow. Then in a wanton display of Northwest fickleness, the storm abated as suddenly as it had arrived, the cloud cover changing from a fierce roiling smoke to friendly cotton balls, the stinging downpour of only moments ago now a swath of mist as soft as dandelion puffs. Now, too, there were breaks between clouds and shafts of bright sunlight, searchlight narrow and probing.

Fifteen minutes later Pruitt turned onto Rutsatz Road, which threaded a path along the Nawaikum River, and drove until he saw Raphael "Raphe" Jones' police vehicle parked off to one side. Jones had been his second hire and, on the tails of his first hire, Ing Yen, a Laotian, had earned him the nickname Equal Opportunity Pruitt. From the less liberal of his constituency he'd heard grumblings that once he gotten his hands on power, Pruitt's true rice cake-eating, Grateful Dead-loving self had begun bleeding through his forest-green uniform in shades of commie-kissing pink, and that his first term in office would be his last if this was the new breed of cops he was bringing in.

For his part, Pruitt had immeasurable confidence in his new deputies, and was certain that by re-election time they would be political assets. Competence won people over, and both of them brimmed with it. Take, for instance, the way Jones had positioned herself for this simplest of stakeouts. The Rutsatz had no shoulder, so she had found a long-forgotten turnaround near the backside of a bow-shaped curve about a hundred yards short of the property Pruitt had sent her to keep an eye on. With her cruiser backed in, its nose but little else was exposed. Not only had she found the most unobtrusive location from which to baby-sit her charge, she'd made sure not to present a traffic hazard.

Pruitt, on the other hand, could do little but stop in the middle of road and hope nobody would drive by for a few minutes. Hearing the crunch of his tires, Jones tossed the dregs of the coffee she was drinking from a thermos cup into a bush, where it steamed off the leaves as she trudged over to greet him.

Ex-Navy and college educated, Jones wore her brown, blond-streaked hair in a French twist and used enough make-up to put the conservative public of Willapa County at ease, but not enough to make her feel uncomfortable if she had to sweat.

"He hasn't moved since I got here. There was a slow but steady arrival of cars between 7:30 and 8:00. Since then it's been quiet. Nobody's driven out."

Pruitt thanked her and relieved her of her duty, worrying as he did about the dark bags under her eyes—a look that had spread like flu to all his deputies, getting by on a minimum of sleep while working all the overtime hours. Tired people struggled to work cautiously, even as cautiousness, in the current crisis, was what the sheriff's department needed most.

Pruitt had directed Raphe Jones to watch over David Spoor, the leader of ANGER, a radical environmental group whose acronym stood for A Noble and Green Earth will Remain. When the heirs of Bernard Henry Hickson had announced their intention to sell the fabled Black Bear Ridge old-growth, David Spoor had been one of the first to leap to its protection, going so far as moving to Willapa County to stay close, renting the older two-story house just coming into view, where from a round, steel chimney snaking up an outside wall wispy smoke drifted, sharply fragrant in the still morning air.

Pruitt pulled up behind a string of vehicles using a tamped-down patch of lawn as a parking apron. As he climbed out of his car, a dog tethered at the front door rose up off its haunches and lowered its head, growling in warning. Behind the dog, a curtain pulled back, then, shortly, the front door opened and David Spoor stepped out, bearded and wearing cowboy boots, jeans, a corduroy shirt, and large-framed, burgundy-colored eyeglasses. Others appeared behind him, long-faced and clearly displeased with Pruitt's arrival.

After silencing his dog with a faint hand signal, Spoor called, "Sheriff? Can I help you?"

"Morning, David," Pruitt called back. "Got a minute?"

After turning to say something to his guests, Spoor walked out. He was younger than Pruitt by a few years—a hard-core radical politicized by Vietnam, where he'd done a tour as a grunt, and though toughness was a part of his rhetoric, Spoor himself could be charming. At a conversational distance, he stopped to lean against a car. Behind him, his compatriots spread themselves about the porch as if it were a city stoop.

"This some sort of police harassment?"

"Yes, David. I'm standing here in your yard harassing you. Which is my style, as you well know."

Spoor held a hand up. "I'm a little busy this morning, Gavin."

Not about to turn on his famous charm this morning, Pruitt noted. "I know you listen to police bands, so I'm assuming you've heard about Carpenter."

Spoor nodded that he had.

"What I want is for you to call everything off for a few days."

Spoor guffawed. "Gotta hand it to you for balls, Gavin. Why the hell would we do that?"

"The point," Pruitt said, "for both of us right now, is to keep people from getting hurt."

"That point has been reached and gone beyond, wouldn't you say?"

"Neither one of us knows what happened out there. You're thinking rednecks, but maybe I'm thinking it's one of your people."

Spoor said, "That's absurd."

"A small price to pay, don't you think, to create a martyr the likes of Carpenter? Think of the PR: ignorant red-neck, logger militants kill godly ecologist, protector of Thumper and Bambi."

Spoor snorted. "Nice scenario, but nobody in ANGER would have killed him. We're pranksters, man." He smiled. "Just handing out invitations to the Acid Test."

Pruitt had to gaze off towards the Nawaikum, rushing loudly this time of year from fall rains. Like everyone, Spoor knew Pruitt was a Deadhead and rarely passed up an opportunity to razz him about it. But this just wasn't a time for levity, and it pissed Pruitt off—especially since Spoor was clearly more provocateur than prankster.

Not yet looking away from the river, Pruitt said, "George Holtwater's dozer was ruined over the weekend." Between the house and river lay Spoor's vegetable garden. A few pumpkins left unharvested stood out orange against the blackened stalks of dying peppers, a hint of their rankness reaching him. "A textbook copy of the strategies outlined in that pamphlet of yours."

Uttering the words by rote, Spoor said, "The pamphlet is satire."

Pruitt turned his gaze back on Spoor. "Somebody poured dry sand in the oil reservoir, then made sure to wash it down the neck with WD-40. Jonathan Swift wrote satire, David; you wrote an eco-terrorist how-to manual your people treat like a bible."

"They are not *my* people, Sheriff."

"Save it for the lawyers," Pruitt said. "You and I both know that the moment you start distancing yourself from the actions people take who believe in the movement you lead, you're no different than the corporate Pontius Pilates you claim to despise."

Spoor smiled to himself, the burgundy-colored frames of his glasses giving him a raccoonish quality. "I got to admit, Gavin, it's a hoot knowing a cop who actually once believed in giving the power back to the people. But what you haven't done one thing about is those cowards out in the middle of the night shooting our dogs."

"C'mon, David, don't you think I'm outraged by that? Don't you think everybody in this county is outraged by that?"

"It's being tolerated."

"No, it's not. You tell me how I'm suppose to patrol for drive-by shootings. It's impossible. Until this blows over, bring your dogs in at night. In the meantime, give my investigator some time. I promise to keep you up to date. Give me your fax, I'll post you every hour."

Now it was Spoor's turn to gaze out over his property. Though he'd quit his position with a national conservationist group because he'd found the compromises necessary to working in Washington DC unacceptable, Pruitt had found him wholly ready to compromise if he was offered something significant in return.

"I'll consider it," he said.

Pruitt nodded. "I'll take that as an indication of good faith."

Returning to his cruiser, he hoped that it had been.

CHAPTER THREE

The duplex that John Carpenter had called home for the past eighteen months sat on the grassy shoulder of a hill overlooking Elkhorn, the county seat and, at 5,000 inhabitants, Willapa County's largest town. Although the building itself was nothing more than a characterless box, drab in color and dreary for lack of landscaping, the view was commanding: Elkhorn abutting the south bank of the gray-green Willapa River, tributaries as fine as capillaries probing the vast mudflats to the west. On the other side of the river a fertile valley sprawled verdantly to the hills. A few hundred yards away from the north bank and wetlands sat the Camenzind dairy farm—red barn, green pastures, two-story white house surrounded by a picket fence. An apple tree in front to boot.

Deputy Ing Yen was waiting by Carpenter's dark blue Isuzu Trooper, a vehicle that always looked dangerously top-heavy to Pruitt. With an efficiency typical of him, Yen had cordoned off the area by stringing crime site tape as meticulously as the Camenzinds had laid out their fences.

It was sometimes hard for Pruitt not to hold Yen in special regard. He was small for a cop, five-four on tiptoes, and Laotian, two factors that might have combined to make police work outside of his own community of recent immigrants impossible. Yet Yen had something that for Pruitt constituted the difference between a police reservist like Glen Hampton and a professional cop, and that was *The Look*. Yen could size a trouble-maker up, internalize what it would take to subdue him, then share that knowledge wordlessly: you will lose, I will win; you will hurt, I will walk. It took Yen less than two months and a half dozen encounters to convince the local bullies he wasn't worth the trouble.

Pruitt parked his cruiser next to Yen's, got out and strode towards him. From their plant near the river, Westcoast Oyster Company was cooking and canning oyster stew and the milk-and-brine smell of it rose up on the wind blowing eastward off the mudflats. It made Pruitt's stomach pang.

Pruitt watched Yen watching him approach, his usual half-smile fixed in place.

Smiling back, Pruitt said, "Got the apartment keys?"

Yen made them appear like a magic trick, dangling from his fingers. "Not a problem," he said, "but we should do vehicle first."

Once they were gloved up, Yen used a Slim Jim to open a door. A thorough search netted a handful of interesting trinkets hanging off the rearview mirror stem, but little else, so it was on to the apartment, darkened by blackout drapes and smelling like burnt joss sticks.

"Police!" Yen shouted. "Anybody here?"

They received no reply, heard no rustle of movement. Yen flicked a switch near the jamb, but the anemic light cast by a spindly-armed chandelier in the dining alcove helped little. It wasn't until the drapes were thrown open that the meager extent of John Carpenter's holdings were revealed: a futon rolled up underneath the front room window, three Japanese prints tacked up along one wall and a small ceremonial table placed under them, upon which sat a brass incense burner, a fragile cone of ash inside.

After a quick sweep to make sure they were truly alone, Pruitt and Yen began their search. The bedroom door was padlocked from the outside—Carpenter hiding something, obviously, which they would get to soon enough.

Yen led the way to the dining alcove. "He was having a meal," he said, passing through to the kitchen.

The meal consisted of a bowl of noodles—cold now and with a sprinkling of congealed fat floating atop the broth—a half-eaten tuna sandwich, and a bottle of mineral water. Pruitt touched the top slice of bread with the tip of his finger. A hint of freshness remained, which narrowed the time frame of the murder, sometime late Sunday night or early Monday morning—assuming this was Carpenter's food. Near the sandwich was an opened hard-back book. With his thumb marking the place Carpenter had been reading, Pruitt looked at the cover. A manual on Brazilian rainforest fauna. On the inside, a lot of Latin.

"This was taped to the fridge." Yen handed Pruitt a greeting card.

Pruitt received it as it was handed to him, by the edges. A birthday card. On the cover was a dog standing perilously close to a cliff. "I laugh at birthdays," he was saying, arms crossed defiantly. Inside it said, "Especially yours. Ha! Ha! Ha!" Written underneath was: "We'll laugh through each one together, John," and signed "Love, your little possum."

"Woman's hand-writing, you ask me," Yen said.

Pruitt said, "Somebody we're definitely going to have to track down."

"Bedroom next?" asked Yen.

After dispatching the padlock and hasp mechanism with a crowbar, Yen and Pruitt stepped into the bedroom and stood transfixed by what they saw, so stark in contrast was it to the bare front half of the apartment. An enormous roll-top desk piled high with books, manuscripts, and journals dominated the room. Makeshift shelves of cinder blocks and planking fanned out along the walls, sagging with their load of boxes and files. On a folding table arranged parallel to the desk sat a personal computer, a printer, and a fax machine. To the left was a stereo system housed in a tall oak cabinet with plastic, smoke-colored doors.

Pruitt said, "His data on Black Bear Ridge could be in here. We're going to have to move it back to the station. Every bit of it."

After a moment of silence, Yen said, "Who's going to sort it?"

Pruitt made a move to rub his face, but had forgotten he was wearing latex gloves and startled himself with his slickened fingers. He dropped his hand back to his side and regarded the mountain of paperwork.

"I'm going to request a forensic accountant from the Investigative Assistance Section."

"State Patrol," Yen said. "They get something hot, governor knows in an hour. Hour after that, newspapers have it. Whole investigation shot to shit."

Pruitt had to agree. Secrets didn't seem to stay secret long in Olympia.

"What we can do," he said, "is have Joyce draw up a security contract. If they balk at signing it, we ask for someone else."

This pleased his deputy and for a moment longer the two of them regarded the incredible pile of clutter silently, Yen finally observing: "Neat out front, pack rat in back. Complicated fellow, this John Carpenter."

Pruitt left Yen in charge, then drove down into Elkhorn from Carpenter's apartment, catching one last glimpse of the dead man's view: the river, the mudflats, the distant farms and fields, and, as ubiquitous to the county as blackberry vines, the clear-cut hills. Pruitt wondered what Carpenter had thought of this tree farming. Time and again, newspaper articles quoted him claiming to be nothing more than an impartial scientist. But regarding Black Bear Ridge, how truthful was he being? Maybe the paperwork would reveal his mind—not a comforting thought considering how much of it there was. As the Grateful Dead had noted in *Easy Answers*, there weren't any.

Yet before pursuing the case even one scrap of paper further, Pruitt dropped by his house to change from the sweater and slacks he'd worn since early that morning—damp still from the deluge at the crime site and beginning to itch—into a proper uniform. He then had to ask himself where the time had gone. His grumbling stomach told him he'd forgotten lunch and, sure enough, it was nearly two.

After lunch at the Torchlight—a vegetarian stir-fry—Pruitt drove four blocks to the Elkhorn Civic Building. Stucco-sided and undistinguished, it was built on a raised foundation to account for the semi-regular downtown flooding, and included an office for the mayor, a meeting room for the town council, and a modest suite for the police department—which always smelled faintly of violets; in other words, like Wilma Gillespie, the receptionist. Wilma was in her early forties, though she passed for late twenties. She was tall and statuesque and had the best legs Pruitt had ever seen, which she emphasized with skirts that rode just over her shapely knees. Every time he saw her the melody from *Scarlet Begonias* popped into his head and the lyrics about there being nothing wrong with the way she moved. Nothing whatsoever. She was on the phone when he entered and used an elegant arc of glossy fingertips to wave him into Dan Louderback's office.

The Chief of Police was also on the phone, pacing behind his desk as far as the cord would allow him. Louderback stood about six-two and had finely chiseled cheekbones, rich brown eyes, and the chin of a matinee idol. Had he and Wilma not been married to others, they would have made a drop-dead handsome couple. The prevailing sentiment was they'd been having an affair since the day Louderback took over the position and inherited Wilma from his predecessor. Whether it was true or not Pruitt had no idea, though he had to admit that physically the two seemed made for each other.

As Wilma had, Louderback waved to Pruitt, indicating an empty chair.

To whomever he had on the line, Louderback said, "Look, I can only tell you that the situation's under control."

He listened a moment as he paced, then winked at Pruitt and said, "There've been no complaints to this office about log trucks being shot at. You want to know about the county roads, you're going to have to talk to the sheriff."

When he made a gesture to pass the phone over to him, Pruitt held his hands up in defense. Yes, a truck had been shot at—but only one as far as Pruitt knew, and nobody had been hurt. Could have been accidental, kids target practicing too close to the road. He'd covered the incident at a press conference three days ago.

Louderback, in the meantime, was listening to another question. The police chief, unlike Pruitt, seemed to enjoy bantering with the media. Of course Dan Louderback just plain loved to BS; it didn't matter much with whom. "No," he said, "there hasn't been a bear sighted on Black Bear Ridge in fifty years…

"Ironic?" Arching his eyebrows to Pruitt, he said, "Well, if you say so. But I'll tell you something, out here in the boonies, people haven't got much time for irony."

Pruitt could no longer stand having to watch as well as listen to an administrator's version of trash talk. He rose to examine the photos hung on the wall opposite Louderback's desk. Dan hunting, Dan fishing, Dan receiving a commendation. Behind him, Louderback said, "Sure, I knew Bernard Henry Hickson…He didn't want it touched was all…No, he was no community benefactor. His daddy made a fortune in the early part of the century—at one point he owned half the county—then left it all to his only child, Bernard Henry, who sold everything but Black Bear Ridge. Never gave a reason why. But now he's dead and his kids want to sell it...

"Hey, if you say it's the most valuable stand of timber in the entire northwest, I believe you. We just don't want people getting hurt fighting over it...

"You're entirely welcome. Hope I was of some help. You got the name spelled right? That's L-O-U-D-E-R-Back."

"Dan," Pruitt said as he turned from Dan's photos, "you really think anybody buys that 'We're just little ol' town cops' routine of yours?"

The police chief grinned at him. "Local color sells, Gavin. If it's an act, it's one everybody loves."

Pruitt sighed.

Sitting, Louderback said, "What about Carpenter? All I've gotten is what's been on the scanner."

Pruitt placed a flat hand knuckle-side up under his chin. "Up to here," he said, then shared what he knew.

When he'd finished, Louderback said, "You think you're gonna feel some heat out of Olympia? High profile victim and all?"

"We shouldn't. It's clearly our jurisdiction."

The police chief grinned at him.

"C'mon, Dan, turf wars are a thing of the past. We'll coordinate and cooperate with all the appropriate law enforcement agencies."

Louderback laughed. "Now who's sounding like a little ol' town cop?"

CHAPTER FOUR

At Prospect, Pruitt turned left, then parked in the vacant Texaco gas station parking lot, a spot where one could keep an eye on the union hall, Ugly Bob's Tavern, the Spar Tavern, and two of the six motels in town, the Mountcastle and the McKibbin. A perfect stakeout position if things came to that.

Pruitt parked, crossed the street, and pushed through the plate glass door of the International Woodworkers of America Hall—known to everyone as the IWA—redolent with old fashioned urn-brewed coffee and bakery-fresh doughnuts. He could hear the postering party before he encountered it—staple guns echoing like distant small arms fire from the main meeting room, twenty or thirty men and women fashioning pickets. Dale Slater, the union president, was presiding, and while the activity in the room didn't exactly come to a screeching halt when Pruitt entered, the intensity of the work slackened noticeably, a few nods and acknowledgments cast his direction.

Slater, however, a large, florid man, greeted him loudly. "Sheriff, we just heard John Carpenter's dead."

"He is."

"Good God. So are you here with the paddy wagon?"

"Yes, Dale. I've got a box of handcuffs, too. Gotta watch the budget, though, so I bought those plastic ones Judy has over at the dime store. And I'm kind of short-handed today, so you think you could get everybody to cuff themselves up for me?"

Which got guffaws from most of the postering crew, though not Slater, who handed his felt pen to the union member standing nearest him. "People," he said, "the sheriff appears to want to have a chat. I'll have a full report later."

The bluster Pruitt accepted as part of Dale's public persona, and the crack about the report he knew was only half true. Slater would tell his people what he felt they needed to know and nothing more. For twenty years he'd manipulated his reputation as a straight-shooter unmercifully, crowing aloud information he decided was safe, obfuscating anything he considered was not. Union members knew Dale's methods, but never questioned how he ran the local, knowing he was loyalty incarnate. Indeed, he was to his union as Jerry Garcia was to Deadheads: trusted, forgiven, and loved.

Slater left the picket-making in the able hands of Evie Demaris, the IWA secretary, and led Pruitt to his office, located between the kitchen and the main office. Pruitt shut the door behind him as Slater rolled his chair up to a computer screen. "Got time for a game?"

"One, Dale."

"I don't know about you," he said as he raced the mouse arrow around the screen, "but I'm rusty as hell."

"To say the least." Pruitt rolled up a chair of his own and sat at Slater's shoulder. The game came up, a variation of mah-jong. Using the mouse to manipulate the elements of various games was the extent of Pruitt's computer skills. The county had yet to buy a system for the police department, and he had no need for one at home. When he and Dale had first begun their biweekly lunch-time tournaments he'd suspected that the union president's superior knowledge of computers also gave him an edge to the games. But as the months had passed and the crib sheets had shown a balance of wins and losses, that bit of myth died in Pruitt's mind.

"Up and ready," Slater said as he slid out of Pruitt's way.

The set-up wasn't a great one, but Pruitt got to work. After half-a-dozen matches, he said, "What're you up to out there?"

From his shirt pocket, Slater produced a pack of gum. "Little demonstration we got planned." Extracting two sticks, he offered one to Pruitt, who declined, the nebulous fruit flavor not appealing to him. Slater unwrapped both sticks anyway, bending them against his tongue as he stuck them in his mouth.

Pruitt said, "For when?"

"Big rally on Wednesday in Olympia, so you don't have to worry."

"I wasn't worried."

"Yeah, you were."

"A little," he admitted.

"You've got matching seasons," he said, pointing. "Just begging to get blasted."

Pruitt clicked them into oblivion.

"Tell me you weren't worried, the way you missed those."

"Especially with this Carpenter deal," Pruitt said, "I just hope to avoid any more incidents like we had last week."

Suddenly ferocious with his gum, Slater said, "Damnit, Gavin, our driver had every right. That was MacClinton's operation, second-growth, nothing to do with Black Bear Ridge. What were those crazy greenbacks doing trying to block us that way?"

Pruitt was down to sixty-two tiles, but could see that he wasn't going to go much lower. "The guy was almost killed," he said. "Your driver should have waited for us to disperse the demonstrators."

Slater said, "These men are under quotas. Not to mention afraid of losing their jobs. They got wives biting their nails to the quick, kids with nose rings telling them to kiss their asses. How do you expect them to react?"

From behind the computer screen came a beep, then the prompt indicating no more available matches. He'd gotten it down to fifty-four tiles.

Slater said, "Could have been worse considering how long it's been."

Pruitt wheeled away as Slater swooped in to reload.

"If somebody gets hurt out there, Dale, how's that going to help the guy who's still got his truck driving job? I'd have to take him in, book him. He'll make no quotas that way."

Slater moved the gum from one corner of his mouth to the other. "The trouble is these guys are seeing Black Bear Ridge as some sort of salvation. Those retraining programs?" he said. "Right down the tubes. I mean, yeah, there'd be jobs for while, but if we get to cut Black Bear Ridge down to the last scraggly hemlock it's maybe three or four year's worth. Then it's right back to square one. Automation's the real problem, not owls or bugs. But you didn't hear me say that. The only thing you hear me talk about is sustainability, a concept most timber companies only gave lip-service to until the greenies, of all people, called their shit."

"But I didn't hear *you* say that."

"Not a word, by God. We hate greenies—especially if they're right."

"The problem I've got with you, Dale, is you're one of the few rational people around, but only I know it."

Slater laughed. "What I'm telling my people is get their kids off to college, and maybe get off to college themselves while they're at it. Figure out some way to make a living other than going out and killing trees every day."

"Jeez, nice layout," Pruitt said after the reload.

Slater said, "For a change," and began darting the mouse arrow around the screen. He may have been plodding in real life, but in cyber-space Dale Slater was nimble as a ballerina.

⊕

Staff meetings for the Willapa County Sheriff's Department were held in the conference room of their administrative offices, housed below the jail section of the court house complex. Washington State and county maps hung on the long wall. At the far end from the door was a kitchenette. Opposite the map wall, a long window afforded a view of The Swamp—where the administrative assistants and Joyce Cody, Pruitt's personal secretary, had their desks. Usually the conference room reeked of coffee, but somebody had just microwaved a burrito, the smell thick enough to taste.

Tonight's was a full staff meeting, with only a deputy officer assigned to the Long Beach office missing. Pruitt had just shown the video Lee Wilson had shot earlier in the day at the murder site, and the room was buzzing with conversation. After a sip of coffee from his Grateful Dead *Skull & Bones* cup, he spoke over din. "Anything, people?"

Calling out over the ruckus, Raphe Jones said, "It seems personal."

Pruitt called again for silence, said, "What do you mean?"

Finally in the silence, Jones said, "If it was some disgruntled logger, they'd want it over fast. This is personal. They wanted him to suffer."

"Could be a logger and still be personal," Lee Wilson said. "A logger personally pissed off he was out of a job."

"Here's something possibly relevant." It was Bobby Charneski, at twenty-six the youngest of his deputies. "There may be some sort of death squad formed—supposedly made up of some of our vets. Word has it they're sick of the whole show: the greenies, the media—us, too. It's probably just a wild rumor, but it might give us something to look into."

"Why don't you," Pruitt said. "At this point I wouldn't write anything off as too wild a rumor." He checked his clipboard. "E.L., you got a list of people we should talk to?"

Ethan Laymont was undersheriff, Pruitt's second in command and head of the Long Beach office, brought up to help during the Black Bear Ridge crisis, activity at the beach slow in the winter anyway. He was a large man in his late fifties who had just shed some thirty pounds, which if you hadn't known him before would have hardly been noticed. Even thirty pounds lighter, E.L. was imposing. Yet those who knew him marveled at the difference, how his cheek bones had begun showing through, for instance.

E.L. said, "I made a list, but it's short."

Pruitt accepted it from him and scanned. It was short indeed and probably next to useless—just a few neighbors.

Lee Wilson said, "Where's all the crap from the apartment supposed to go?" He thumbed to the stack of boxes and equipment along the map wall that had forced everybody to one side of the conference table.

Pruitt handed the list back to E.L. "I have bad news. Jones and Charneski are going to have to vacate their office."

Jones, after a moment of silence, said, "What is this, you're handing out pinks?"

After the good round of laughter died down, Pruitt said, "I guess I didn't phrase that right. You two are going to room with me. We need a place for the Technical Support Unit's man."

The deputies in question groaned, almost in unison.

"Hey, I'm not thrilled about it either."

Wilson said, "You going to say something to that pack of wild dogs out front?"

Pruitt shot back his sleeve. It was after six. "Damn. I told them five-thirty."

Charneski said, "They're gonna *love* you, boss."

⊕

Charneski's assessment hadn't touched the surface of it. Not only had the ranks of reporters swollen, they now included stringers for *The New York Times* and *Washington Post*, which had sparked the killer instinct in the lot of them.

"Carpenter might be the most respected environmentalist in the country," one of big guns barked at him. "With your limited resources, how do you expect to solve a crime like this?"

"Old fashioned gum-shoe police work," Pruitt replied.

"There gonna be any LSD in that gum?"

Once the press corps had their laugh, Pruitt said, "You keep going in that direction and these press conferences are over." Then to emphasize his point, Pruitt ended the proceedings and retreated to the inner sanctum of his office.

There he tried to catch up on some paperwork before he went home. But he hadn't been at it long before he remembered that he was supposed to have called his daughter, Olivia, and—ah, jeez—met Molly at his house. An hour ago, easy.

☮

Yet late as he was, Molly's car was not in its accustomed spot. Probably she'd come and gone—but why hadn't she called the office for him? Maybe she had and in the hubbub her message hadn't reached him. He parked his cruiser in front of what would have been the left door of a two-car garage, remodeled now to accommodate two of Pruitt's passions: a float tank room—modified from a sauna kit—and a percussion studio. He would have loved to jump into either right now, let those Epson salts—all 800-pounds worth—suck the ache right out of him, or maybe just lose himself in a long 7/4 rhythm exercise. Leave his cellular in the car, close the world out, have a little peace and quiet...

Unfortunately, he knew it wasn't going to happen tonight. Time for floats and drumming had been about as scarce as time for living a regular life—visiting friends, keeping in touch with his sisters and brothers, a round of golf with his father. He stood from his car and took a last, longing glance at his sanctuary. Then Cleo, his tortoise-shell tabby, streaked by, squeezed through the two slats in the yard fence she unerringly chose every time, slowed at the back steps, and finally dove cleanly through the cat door.

His was a modest two-bedroom house in the Riverdale district of Elkhorn, eight hundred and fifty square feet. He'd bought it when he'd first joined the sheriff's office and had kept it exactly the way it had come: white clapboard siding with gray-green window trim, a white picket fence, flower beds surrounding the cement foundation and a rose trellis on the garage wall facing the house—yellow roses that came back like gangbusters regardless of how far back they were pruned.

He was letting himself in through the back gate when, from the night shadows, a voice called. "Sheriff Pruitt?"

Startled, Pruitt whirled and saw Richard Emmett, a stringer for the *Seattle Tribune* who had been covering Black Bear Ridge since the beginning.

"C'mon, Richard," Pruitt said. "I've always been happy to have a cup of coffee with you, but this is my *home*. You're not going to start up that paparazzi bit, are you?"

"It's going to get crazy fast now, Gavin. Carpenter was like the Ralph Nader of the environment. And now a Deadhead is in charge of the investigation? You saw it tonight, man, reporters coming in from all over the country."

"So what do you want that can't wait 'til tomorrow?"

"A scoop. You know, the ol' up-close-and-personal?"

"You know me already. Just write what you know."

Apologetically, Emmett shook his head. "The angle's new. Before it wasn't about you, it was about a stand of timber— an important stand, of course, but just trees. Now it's about you and Carpenter. Once you've got strong personalities, it all changes. And sure, we've talked a lot, but I didn't write anything down, wasn't making it formal."

Pruitt mulled it over. Emmett had always been pleasant, not to mention thoughtful, his articles a voice of reason among the screeds of hardliners. He was about Pruitt's age and, though they'd never spoken of it out loud, Pruitt sensed of a similar 60's background. He had the kind of wide-set eyes that gave him a trustworthy appearance—had a slight overbite to boot. He stood patiently, letting himself be taken stock of. "If you haven't eaten…" he began, leaving the rest unsaid.

"This is your lucky night." Pruitt opened the gate. "But we'll stay here. If what you say is true, there'll be no place in town we could talk without getting bushwhacked by your colleagues."

❀

Pruitt led the way across the narrow back yard to an enclosed porch—washer, dryer, and a wooden clothes rack on his left—and then to the inner door that led to the kitchen. He flipped on the light and directed Emmett to the breakfast nook, which consisted of a built-in table and matching benches—geese amidst small white flowers painted on the side panels. The color motif of the nook, indeed the whole kitchen, was sky blue and white. White lace cafe curtains adorned the kitchen window; next to a series of canisters marked sugar, flour and coffee was a dish rack, tidily holding this morning's coffee cup, cereal bowl, and spoon.

Emmett said, "Can I record this, or would you prefer I took notes?"

"Suit yourself."

While the reporter fussed with a micro cassette, Pruitt searched the refrigerator for dinner items. He found bricks of cheese wrapped in cling plastic, jars of condiments, and the soup he'd made two days ago—tomato minestrone with basil.

He poured the soup into a pan, lit a burner, and placed the pan over the flame. "This is a basic lunch-for-dinner deal." He pulled bread from a drawer. "Soup and three-cheese sandwiches, which I like with sweet pickles. That work for you, Richard?"

Emmett said, "Fine, just fine." He let a moment pass. "It might be a little awkward, because we do know each other a little already, but if I'm going to do this right, I'm going to pretend I don't know you at all."

"All right, then."

"So some basics. You're divorced, for instance?"

"Yep."

"With a teenage daughter. How old, exactly, and where is she?"

Pruitt said, "Eighteen. A freshmen at the University of Puget Sound."

"And you've got a college degree in what, again?"

"In music education. University of Washington. I'm going to grill these," he said, "unless you want yours as is." Having slathered the bread with brown mustard, Pruitt began slicing the cheeses: Swiss, cheddar and pepper jack.

Emmett said, "Grilled sounds good to me. Music education? See, that I didn't know. Do you play something?"

"Percussion."

"Drums? You're a drummer?"

"I don't play traps too often; I think of myself as a percussionist."

"Bongos? That sort of thing?"

"All of it: claves, congas, guiros…"

"And you're a huge Grateful Dead fan. I mean, these posters here in the alcove kind of say it all."

"Yes, now everybody seems to know I'm a Deadhead."

"Why the Dead? Why not Pink Floyd or the Beatles? What's so special about the Dead?"

"The Dead are different."

"I'm a casual music fan," Emmett told him. "The radio, whatever someone else has on their stereo? I've heard a couple of Dead songs." He shrugged. "I don't see how they're different."

"A while back," Pruitt noted, "Bill Graham said the Grateful Dead aren't just the best at what they do, they're the *only* ones that do what they do. For instance," he said, anticipating Emmett's next question, "they never play the same set list twice. Other bands play the same songs, same order, year in and year out. The Dead could play a week, never repeat themselves."

"Okay. Lots of different songs."

"And lots of different styles, and a co-mingling of styles, folk and Appalachian, rock, R&B. And also music from all over the world: reggae, African rhythms. Very diverse. And also completely willing to take chances. They will fall flat on their faces in front of thousands, trying something different, some new way to reach people's souls. And we let them. Me, all their fans, are okay with it—more than okay, really. It's why we're there—because the Dead are not trying to put on a show, they're trying to connect with the cosmos through music, and by the fact of our being there, connect us to something higher, too. But more than anything else," Pruitt said, raising a finger, "they have poetry in their lyrics. Robert Hunter, their main lyricist, started off a poet, and he's never lost his poet's sensibilities. I just love their lyrics."

Emmett was nodding. "You know, I may have to go back and take a closer listen." In spite of the tape recorder he jotted something down in his notebook. "But with your degree, why not teach?"

"Right out of college I was going to, but things happened and I took a break."

"After your divorce, or something like that?"

"Right. My ex-wife was heading home, so I decided to go home, too. It seemed appropriate at the time, both of us going off in opposite directions to lick our wounds in familiar surroundings."

Emmett said, "Yeah, been there, too, unfortunately. A couple of times. But about who you are now, you didn't just waltz into the sheriff's office."

"Not hardly. My first job back was in a shake mill."

"So this is what people are going to be interested in: how'd you get from the shake mill to the sheriff's office?"

The sandwiches were assembled, so Pruitt lit another burner and placed a black iron frying pan over it. "I started seeing a woman I'd known in high school, Jacki Hujack, whose father was Arthur Hujack, the County Sheriff. Jacki had recently moved home, too—literally moved back with her dad—so he and I ran into each other a lot."

"I remember Hujack. From when I covered that strike in '83. He was an institution down here. How'd you get along with an old-timer like that?"

Pruitt chuckled. "You're right. This tough old Switzer and a Deadhead? But the thing was Arthur had a great mind. He just loved the idea of a dialectic, you know? He didn't call it that, of course. It was always, 'Just let me play devil's advocate here.' And I was, like, 'Doesn't that make you a friend of the devil?'"

Emmett laughed. "I've heard *that* Dead song. Did *he* get that?"

Pruitt, too, chuckled; it brought back fond memories of Hujack, his mentor and friend. "He got the play on words, but I had to explain the song reference. Anyway, we'd go down to the Chesterfield and *discourse* until they threw us out. Drink beer and eat clam strips."

Pruitt held his hand a couple of inches over the skillet, which was getting hot, but not quite ready for the oil.

"So he hired you?"

"It wasn't quite like that. For a couple of years I'd see him off and on. I'd make some money, you see, then follow the Dead around until it ran out, come back, pack shakes, head out again. And then there was an opening on the force. I'd stayed in touch with Arthur and he asked me if I was ready to put my money where my mouth was and work within the system to make it better, or was I going to be one of those who complained about everything but never did anything about it."

"He back your run for sheriff, too?"

"He did. When he decided to retire." The pan was ready, so he dolloped in a little oil, rolled the pan to coat the bottom. "I'd been a deputy about ten years by then."

"We've never talked about your military background."

"I don't have one. During Vietnam I was a CO."

"Conscientious Objector?" said Emmett. "And now you're a cop? How do you explain *that* to the average person on the street?"

Pruitt painted a light coat of extra-virgin olive oil on the top of the sandwiches with a basting brush. "Cops protect and serve," he said, "soldiers are trained for combat. There's a helluva difference."

"You know what people are going to want to know: you were a conscientious objector, but you'd shoot somebody?"

"If I had to I would. Not that that has anything to do with my CO status. Being a soldier is *only* about killing; police work is not at *all* about killing. Besides, it's been twenty-five years since we had a police shooting around here."

"But a Deadhead peacenik out busting heads?"

Pruitt looked up from his cooking to give Emmett a smile. "C'mon, Richard, you know we don't bust heads in Willapa County. We establish positive neighborhood relationships and foster proactive community networking."

Emmett smiled back. "Oh, man, that's maybe the best bureaucratese I've ever heard." He was back at this notebook again, jotting it down.

While he did, Pruitt placed the sandwiches alongside each other in the pan, where they sizzled hotly a moment, then settled down to browning.

"You still go see the Dead in concert?"

Pruitt said, "Absolutely, though not as often. But at least once a year. My friend, Biscuit, usually gets the tickets and I hook up with him wherever it is. He's talking about maybe Chicago next summer."

"Biscuit?"

"Nickname from college. It was his usual contribution to the community meals."

"Good," Emmett said. "That's where I wanted to go next. So, in college, you lived an alternative lifestyle?"

"I lived communally in a big old house, yeah. Everybody did in those days. It was fashionable. Community meals. Community involvement. In a way, it's where I first got the notion of community service. Which is what real police work is, plain and simple."

"You smoke pot in those days?"

Pruitt said, "Yes, I smoked pot."

"Acid? You try that?"

"Nobody's business if I did or didn't," Pruitt said.

The pause in Emmett's questioning was palpable with feeling. "But, Gavin, it's what everybody wants to know. It's maybe the most important part of the story, man. Think about it: the first public official to admit he took LSD. Start an honest discussion of the issues surrounding drug use, not all this 'Just Say No' crap. Blow the lid off it. Cop took acid, doing just fine. Get *over* it, people."

Pruitt stirred the soup. "Look, Richard, I'm not unsympathetic to where you're trying to take this. But it's not me. Okay?"

In a much harder voice than Pruitt had ever heard from him, Emmett said, "I'm not going to be the only one, Gavin, pursuing this line of thought. I mean, you admit you're a Deadhead, so of course you took acid. That's what everybody's going to think."

Pruitt turned his attention from the soup back to Emmett again. "People can assume what they want. I don't have to answer questions like that. I uphold the drug laws of our county and our state. What I may have done in the past is irrelevant. I am who I am, and I'm good at my job. End of discussion."

"What about some ol' Dead buddy coming forward, saying they saw you leading a drum circle in a parking lot at a concert?"

"I've done that. But if they said I was *leading* it, they'd obviously be lying, 'cause *leading* is not what a drum circle is about."

"How about twisty dancing in front of the ol' Wall of Sound? What if somebody said they saw you doing that?"

"I've space danced. So what? I'm not ashamed of it."

The sizzling sound of melting cheese touching the bottom of the hot pan drew Pruitt's attention back to the sandwiches, which he could see were a golden brown now, ready to come out. "Cocaine or mescaline?" Emmett said. "What if someone said they saw you doing something like that?"

Pruitt turned and caught him in full eye contact. "What do you think might happen, Richard?"

Emmett sighed. An expression played across his lips that Pruitt couldn't decipher. Disappointed? Elated? "Be a helluva shit storm," he said finally. "Wouldn't you think?"

CHAPTER FIVE

The fact was Pruitt's constituents didn't give a fig about his status as a Deadhead. You couldn't hide much in a small town, so he never had. He got ribbed about it sometimes, and his detractors had tried to make it an issue during the election, but clearly most voters shined it on. Maybe it shouldn't have, but Emmett's contention that Pruitt's past was going to be a big story honestly caught him off guard. It made him angry that the press would focus on something Pruitt considered irrelevant. This wasn't about the Dead, it was about a dead man, an individual named John Carpenter. But he let it go. Emmett was simply doing what came naturally to him, pursuing the story angle he felt would most interest his readers. Instead of arguing, Pruitt served the food he'd prepared, removing the sandwiches from the fry pan and halving them on his cutting board, then shoveling them onto plates and placing them, along with bowls of steaming soup, on the table.

Emmett uttered a sound of approval and began to eat. If he was the sort of man who took pleasure in making other people uncomfortable, it had not affected his appetite.

Pruitt sat across from him and began to eat, too, thinking how weird it was sharing a meal with a man who he now realized wouldn't hesitate to ruin his life for a by-line. One dire wolf among many, as the Dead pointed out, running around the woods of Fennario, waiting for some sucker like himself to let them into his home for a game of cards he could never win.

Outside a car pulled up. Emmett craned to look out the window. A moment later hard soles were clicking up the cement walkway leading to the back door.

Pruitt rose, muttering, "Where's my mind?"

The porch door opened, then the kitchen door.

Molly Burkhalter started when she found Pruitt standing practically on top of her. She was holding a steaming pizza carton. "Gavin," she said, "didn't you get my note that I was bringing dinner over?"

Pruitt glanced at the message board. There it was. 'Gone for pizza' it read, initialed. "Sorry," he said.

"I waited, called the office, but they said you were swamped, so I thought I'd go out and get something for us—" She saw Richard Emmett. "Oh," she said.

Pruitt said, "This is a reporter. From the Tribune."

Emmett stood, unable to hide his delight. "I was curious about this. A single man in a small community and all."

"Lookit," said Pruitt, "our conversation is over."

Any problems Pruitt might have with the press and his past were just that, his problems, not Molly Burkhalter's. Richard Emmett had no right to pry into her life, nor, for that matter, into their life together. He agreed to meet with Emmett again, remained cordial, but turned him out the door quickly, his sandwich wrapped in a sheet of cling plastic.

As Emmett drove away, Pruitt turned to Molly, who started to speak then stopped when he took her in his arms and pressed her against the kitchen door jamb. His need for her was sudden and enveloping, a maelstrom she, too, got caught in, tugging at his shirt. His lips on Molly's throat, Pruitt tasted the day's tension on her. As he ran his tongue along her collar bone, the fine gold chain she always wore ended up his mouth—another taste he'd grown fond of.

Half-dressed, they managed to stumble to the bedroom.

⊕

Afterwards, Pruitt got to thinking about their life together, the absurdity of the logistics they maintained to serve the hypocrisy demanded of them. If Molly stayed the night, for instance, she had to rise by six and drive home, park her car in the garage and quietly close the door, loudly reopening it after putting on her make-up and eating some breakfast, remembering to wave 'good morning' to Mrs. Guglomo, the vigilant neighbor, posted at her kitchen window, 7:30 sharp, coffee in hand, waiting to see if Molly was following protocol.

If anybody was tactless enough to ask, Gavin and Molly could steadfastly claim they did not live together. Molly's car might have been parked in the sheriff's driveway into the wee hours of the morning, yet as long as it was gone before most of Pruitt's neighbors woke, it was as if it had never been there. Generally, their affair was tolerated—even appreciated. A Deadhead they could deal with, but not a playboy, nor—heaven forbid—even the remote fleeting thought that he might be gay.

Pruitt's arm was falling asleep and he had to move it, though he hated to, loved his nose at the nape of Molly's neck where he could drink in the smell of her perfume, White Shoulders, which had, as usual, rubbed off on him. On more than one occasion he'd forgone showering just to catch whiffs of it during the day. But the arm was tingling now and he had to pull it out from under her, which rustled Molly from her post-coital reverie. She turned to her side to look at him, wide-eyed and a little disoriented. "Wowsers trousers. Where did *that* come from?"

Pruitt laughed. Molly smiled, but only for a moment before her mouth drew into a taut line.

"What?"

"It's..." But she hesitated. "No, it's nothing."

"No way," Pruitt joked. "Now you have to say it. I won't sleep until I know what it is."

"The thing is..." she began, then touched a hand to her mouth. "No. This can wait. Really."

Pruitt grinned at her. "C'mon, it's can't be *that* bad."

Molly inhaled a quick breath. "Gavin, I just...I just don 't want to."

"Just what? Jeez, when did we start keeping secrets?"

She sighed, then, and said, "I want to have a baby."

Pruitt could only keep gazing into her walnut-brown eyes, the color he always imagined when the Dead played *Brown-eyed Women*—not only because of the obvious reference, but also because when the lyrics got to the part about thunder and rain pouring down it recalled for him the night he and Molly made love the first time, at a borrowed beach house in Tokeland, a winter storm lashing the roof and window panes.

"Dang it," she said, rolling to her back. "I did *not* want to talk about this yet. I really didn't."

"A baby," he said. "Jeez, Molly...I mean, I just got Olivia off to college."

"I know, I know. I've been so reluctant to bring this up. I was going to wait until this Black Bear Ridge stuff blew over. But...Jeez, the way you swept me up tonight." A tear escaped the corner of her eye and she wiped it away. "I'm thirty-two, sweetie. Tick-tock, you know? I've lived nearly six years in this limbo, grieving over Mom and Dad and Steve, floating along with you. Which has been great, Gavin. Really. Just what I needed: space to think, to truly come to grips with how strange life can be, how one morning you forget to say good-bye to your husband and then that afternoon everybody you've loved so dearly is taken from you. After the worst thing that ever happened to me, meeting you was the best thing." She reached to touch him. "But the last few months I've felt a change."

Pruitt said, "Having another baby is, like...You know... The work involved, marriage and diapers and..."

"I'm not talking about getting married, Gavin."

"We couldn't have a baby and not get married," he said. "Not in this town, not with the job I've got."

"At this point, Gavin, those sorts of things have to take a backseat to what I know I want. I'm asking you to be a part of my life in this new way. I want you to be with me, be my live-in lover, my friend, a father to our baby, my husband if need be."

Molly rolled to her side again, to look him in the eye. "I love you, Gavin. So much. But I want this, too. Equally as much."

"I'm forty-five," he said. "I'd be, like, into my sixties by the time I saw this one off to college. Is that fair to a kid, having a father that old?"

Molly said, "C'mon, Gavin, it's not about that. Older men make great fathers. And you're in excellent shape."

A flush of panic ran through his body. "You're not pregnant, are you?"

A quick tug pulled at her lips, as if an amused thought had passed through. "No, no. I would never do that. Sorry," she added, hiding her lips with her fingers, "but the idea makes me so happy."

"So you're still—"

"On the pill, yes. Please, this is just meant to get it out here in the open. So we can talk."

"But it's kind of an ultimatum, too."

She touched him again. "I hate the idea of it being that. I hope it's not. But it's not tonight's worry, or even next month's. This murder investigation has to pass before you can really think about it—I know that. But now that it's out, I have to be honest: it is important to me. And I hope to you, too."

⊕

Hundreds of autopsies had been performed at McKenna's Mortuary—the county had been performing them there since Dr. Trammel closed his clinic in the mid-1970's—though nobody could remember ever having to wade through a crowd of reporters to get to one before. As he untangled himself from his cruiser Pruitt was beset from all sides, the same expectant faces he'd been seeing for weeks, plus a lot of new ones. Richard Emmett was there, looking both apologetic and smug. An ace up his sleeve, or did he just want Pruitt to think so?

One of them, not Emmett, yelled, "We hear the FBI's coming in."

Yesterday, with Dan Louderback, Pruitt wondered aloud how long before the heat would get turned up. Not long, apparently.

"There's been no interstate crime committed," he said, "which leaves the FBI out of it completely."

"We've heard the governor's taking it away," another voice knifed.

The smart thing Pruitt did was take a deep breath before opening his mouth. "Law enforcement doesn't work that way. We get along fine. Everybody's doing their jobs. Yes, we've made a request to the State Patrol for a forensics bookkeeper. And they're going to send someone. So you see, we're all working together to solve the case. Now look," he added firmly. "I'll maintain regular press conferences and issue regular press releases, but not if you're going to veer off into rumor mongering and stupid questions. And you know what I'm talking about." He let his words settle a moment. "I'll see you at six."

☮

John Carpenter's autopsy had been scheduled for ten AM, but the attending pathologist, Dr. William Creedy, was running late. Formerly the lead pathologist for the State of Oregon,

"Wild Bill" was now a private hire, working small counties from Northern California to the Canadian border. Actually, he wasn't that late, just finishing his scrubbing up. When he walked into the embalming room, he acknowledged all present: Pruitt, Seamus "Shamie" McKenna, the owner of the mortuary who would also serve as assistant to Dr. Creedy, and Lee Wilson, who never missed a chance to add to his store of forensics knowledge. Unusually, Carl Pulkkinen was also present, drawn by the notoriety of the deceased. By law, he was the coroner. By procedure, he rarely showed up for the cuttings, only signed off on the paper work once the pathologist was finished writing the reports. Pruitt was remembering the tiff Pulkkinen and Wilson had gotten into at the crime scene about the blow to the back of Carpenter's head and worried that they might be there to settle the argument.

"Sheriff," Creedy said by way of a greeting. "I see you've got yourself a world-class stiff. Let's see if he'll tell us a world-class story."

☮

Especially depending on body decomposition, the stench of an autopsy could be unimaginably rank, an unholy mix of an open body cavity and the bleach and solvents used to keep the embalming room germ and bacteria free. Yet it was the sounds more than the smell that tied Pruitt's stomach in knots. The saw through bone, the sucking and smacking of the viscera as Creedy searched and probed the internal organs. It was all so indelicate regardless of how professionally it was done.

And Creedy was always thorough. Like any dedicated professional, first and foremost he loved his work for what was separate from politics, business, or remuneration. But this was also a marquee event in an already distinguished career, and he seemed to be more exacting than ever.

Unfortunately, all he was able to do was confirm everything Lee Wilson had summed up so succinctly at the crime site. Carpenter had gone up alive, and had probably suffered a slow and horrible death. The blow to his head had come post-mortem—the mention of which caused Wilson to grin malevolently at Carl Pulkkinen.

"Wipe that wise-ass smile off your face, Lee," Pulkkinen said, "or I'll wipe it off for you."

Pulkkinen rarely swore or got angry, but if he did it was usually because of something said or done by Lee Wilson, who was that good at getting under a person's skin. Even Wilson realized he might have pushed one button too many and kept any rejoinders to himself. After some uncomfortable moments, Pulkkinen said to Creedy, "I'll expect the report this afternoon," then left.

Pruitt, too, bade farewell to Creedy, leaving Wilson to see that the various tissue samples got directed to the appropriate labs. Most likely, the findings would have minor value, but with nothing else yet to go on, Pruitt was willing to take any shot in the dark available to him, and he instructed Wilson to request more than just the routine screenings, but everything in the book. He would also put in a call to the governor's law enforcement liaison and ask that the lab work receive top priority. In routine cases the results of such tests could take weeks, even months. But this case was far from routine—everyone wanted it solved as quickly as possible. Equally so, everyone further up the law enforcement food chain understood that if they expected results from Pruitt, he expected results from them. He didn't think he would be disappointed.

⊕

When Pruitt got to his office he indicated to Joyce Cody, his personal secretary, that he didn't want to be interrupted. He had some files to update, and a call to make to his friend Marion Jones, the doctor with whom he worked on child abuse inquests. Her receptionist rang him through. Marion said, "Hi, Gavin. What's up?"

"Thought we'd follow-up on yesterday's interview."

Which didn't take them long, not because there wasn't plenty to talk about, but because of the short-hand they had developed over the years working these horrible cases together. When it came to child abuse, both were emotional, but knew the eventual outcomes depended on their ability to stay detached. Pruitt always felt their work was akin to astral projection: they were both fully aware of the child and family, of the heinous nature of the circumstances, but they also floated above all of it, which allowed them to find importance in details they might have missed when emotions were in charge.

Once they'd finished their business, Marion asked about John Carpenter's murder, Pruitt supplying her a summary.

Marion said, "You must be ready to scream. When's the last time you were in the tank?"

"Weeks it seems. I've lost track."

"Gavin, regardless of what is going on, you need to take care of yourself. Have a float. What's that Dead quote you always say to me: the world might be going to hell in a bucket but at least you're enjoying the ride?"

Pruitt laughed. "You're my good friend for saying that."

Marion said, "I'm your good friend regardless. Hey, are we still on for clam digging on Friday, or has that gone to hell in a bucket, too?"

"We're on as far as I know," he said. "Barring a damn bomb going off between now and then."

CHAPTER SIX

After ringing off with Marion, Pruitt shuffled paperwork until almost three. In spite of how mad they'd made him outside McKenna's Mortuary, he had decided to accommodate the media's request for earlier briefings—starting tomorrow. Today he needed to visit a tavern down on First Street, Ugly Bob's, and have a chat with its proprietor, Bob Porter, who in spite of his nickname was in no sense of the word ugly. He may have had a paunch, and thinning salt-and-pepper hair, and glasses that seemed to get thicker with each year, but at worst he was an average-looking man in his early sixties. It wasn't Bob Porter but rather the building in which Bob's business was housed that was ugly. Bob's Ugly Tavern would have been a better name, and it wasn't just the sagging clapboards and flaking paint. Most of the north end of Elkhorn had been built on reclaimed wetlands, but only in front of Bob's had the sidewalk separated from the threshold exposing the gluey mud and creosote pilings that served as the building's foundation. To those who complained he should do something about it, Bob iterated that he wasn't about to sink a dime into a place that a high tide might just up and float away, his investment down the hole, so to speak.

Ugly Bob's on the inside wasn't as much ugly as bizarre, a cross between a drinking establishment and a supermarket for discontinued television gimmicks, most from the seventies: VegoMatics, Ginzu knives, Kitchen Magicians—all collecting dust on shelves over the bar. Ugly Bob also sold black velvet paintings, Elvis license plate frames, car fresheners, plastic barf, eight-track tapes—everything from the Cowsills to Count Basie—and a vast array of key chains, pocket knives, and nail clippers.

Though he wasn't in there often, Pruitt always got a kick out of the place. As the door swung closed behind him, Bob looked up from his crossword puzzle. "Sheriff Gavin Pruitt."

"Innkeeper Bob Porter."

He smiled. "Pull you a draft, Sheriff?"

"Sure thing, Bob. Think I'll just sit down here in my uniform and get shit-faced in the middle of the afternoon. If I fall down walking out and happen to roll into the mud, make sure to snap a photo. Sell it to the *New York Times* and retire to Florida. "

A gaggle of regulars spread along the bar chuckled. Ugly Bob, too. "God, I'd love to see that."

Pruitt spotted Duane Wildhaber, his friend since grade school, in confabulation with Monte James. He raised an eyebrow in acknowledgment. Duane raised an eyebrow back. They were the same age, though it would be hard for a stranger to imagine, not since Duane's return from Vietnam, when his hair had changed from ink black to smoke white, his eyes still friendly but also ineffably sad.

To Bob, Pruitt said, "Tell you what you can get me is a glass of your redeye."

From a pitcher in the cooler Bob poured a full measure of his notoriously hot tomato juice. Just a sip made Pruitt wince. "Whew, that's good. Better gimme a napkin."

Bob snapped one out of a dispenser and handed it over, smiling, proud of his concoction. Pruitt blew his nose. "To get to the point," he said, "I wanted to know if you'd seen Ron Talbot, Skeeter MacDonough, or Conrad Denny in the last while."

"Three of our young vets." He scratched under his eye. "Well, you got Skeeter in the back throwing down Heinies like he thinks Denmark's going to get eighty-sixed from the UN."

Pruitt laughed. "Been a good boy, our Skeeter?"

"I've been pasting gold stars to his forehead every night as he leaves."

"Denny? Talbot?"

"Denny's been in, just to blow through. Talbot I haven't seen much of."

"Heard anything in regards to what he's up to, Talbot?"

Ugly Bob looked puzzled. "I think he's still clearing small timber stands on private property. I don't think he's been breaking any environmental laws, though."

"It's nothing like that." Pruitt finished off the aptly fire-colored juice. "Thanks for taking my questions, Mr. Innkeeper, sir."

Still looking puzzled, Bob said, "Well, any time, Sheriff. Is this somehow related to John Carpenter's murder?"

Pruitt said, "Probably nothing at all," and was raising his hand in farewell when a flurry of elbows and knees—all connected to the bone-skinny frame of Skip Ekrem—careened out of the pool table alcove. Ekrem tripped on something, began falling, then all but flew into Pruitt's arms. Both men were momentarily at a loss what to do, until Pruitt did the most logical thing and hoisted Ekrem back onto his feet.

Not so much as thanking him, Ekrem spun around and said, "Goddang it, Duane, watch'er feet, will ya?"

"Watch your own feet, Skip," Duane Wildhaber replied without malice. "I was just sitting here."

"Goddang take up half the aisle, why doncha."

Ignoring Ekrem, Wildhaber gave Pruitt a look—what can you do?—then returned to his conversation with Monte James.

Ekrem spoke to Pruitt. "Frickin' Duane, Sheriff. Him and his goddang feet." Not exactly an apology for falling into him, but as close as Ekrem would ever be likely to get.

Pruitt said, "No problem." Ekrem reeked of beer and something rank—likely fertilizer, since he worked as a hand on a farm in the valley. "You're not getting behind a wheel of a car are you, Skip?"

"Nosirre, sheriff, my chauffeur's waitin'."

Pruitt regarded him. "You got a friend could run you home?"

Ekrem grinned. "What about you, Sheriff?"

Pruitt scowled, not pleased with the amused glimmer behind Ekrem's alcohol-sheened eyes. "I'm a little busy right now, partner, but I'm sure Bob would be happy to call a cab for you."

"You still got that daughter comes down in the summer, Sheriff?"

Pruitt's scowl deepened. "How's that any of your business, Skip?"

"Maybe you could bring'er down to old Ugly Bob's next time she's around," Ekrem said, ignoring the fact that Olivia was three years too young to enter a tavern. "Introduce her to everybody."

The juke box had gone silent, but nobody was rushing over to shove more quarters in.

"What a cutie, that gal of yours." Ekrem gestured vaguely to all that was around him. "I can tell ya straight up there ain't enough *cuties* in this goddang bar! Especially not enough with them cute teen-age *titties!*"

As Ekrem threw his head back and roared with laughter, Pruitt felt that snap inside him, his anger unleashed like lightning—the gift of instantaneous rage handed down to him from his alcoholic father. But then two things happened at once: the fist Pruitt was bringing up from his side with which to hit Skip Ekrem's face ran into some sort of barrier, and Duane Wildhaber leapt in front him, taking Ekrem down, the farmhand finding himself on the floor, Wildhaber's knee in his chest, his hand at his throat.

"Shut-up and get out," Wildhaber told him. "Nobody needs your crap in here."

"Skip, you got the social graces of a baboon." Standing behind Pruitt was Ugly Bob himself, the barrier that had come between his fist and Ekrem's face. "And it's starting to piss people off."

Eyes furious, Ekrem struggled against Wildhaber's sure grip. Looking down at him, Pruitt was in awe of the demons that could take possession of the common decency, not to mention the common sense, of the Skip Ekrems of the world and shuck it like so much corn husk.

Finally the pilot light to Ekrem's sense of reason got lit; he stopped struggling and in a garbled voice promised he would leave.

Wildhaber lifted him off the floor as if he were no more than a rag doll. At five-foot-six, Wildhaber now had to crane his neck to glare at the six-foot-three Ekrem. "Learn some self-restraint," he told him.

Ekrem said, "Screw you," then jerked his arm from Wildhaber's hold, turned and stalked out the door.

"Been in here since noon," Ugly Bob said. "Can hardly watch his mouth sober."

Wildhaber had turned from watching Ekrem leave and was now grinning at Pruitt. "This the start of your re-election campaign, Gavin?" he asked. "Clobber all the dipsticks? If it is, brother, I like it."

Pruitt laughed, as much from relief as Wildhaber's joke. Yes, Ekrem had crossed the line talking about his daughter, but what the hell was he thinking, ready to take a swing at the village idiot? He was about to thank Wildhaber when a voice at the bar called, "Hey, Sheriff. Look at this."

"Look at what?"

"The big story, man."

"On CNN, for chrissakes!"

The television was perched up over the entrance to Ugly Bob's small kitchen.

"Turn it up!"

"...John Carpenter, beloved in some circles, despised in others, murdered in the tiny village of Elkhorn, Washington State."

The voice-over spoke behind a still photo of Carpenter as a much younger man, a head shot with him smiling confidently at the camera, his dark hair not yet peppered by the gray Pruitt had seen in it earlier in the day at the morgue.

"...investigations being lead by this man, Gavin Pruitt, local sheriff..."

And suddenly there was Pruitt himself, also a still photo in head shot, although not the departmentally-approved one his secretary had made available to the press.

Somebody whooped. "Check out the hair, man!"

" ...once a symbol of peace-and-love, Willapa County's most well-known Deadhead is now their symbol of law-and-order."

Pruitt hadn't seen the picture in twenty years and it was rather shocking. His hair had been its longest, thick and wavy to his collarbone. He'd been wearing a plaid shirt when the photo was taken, and a paisley vest. January, 1970, at a Dead concert at Oregon State University that he and a friend had driven from Seattle for—one of the most transcendent he'd ever experienced.

"Look at that hippie freak!"

"Like, wow, man!" somebody yelled. "Far out!"

The newscast cut back to the announcer. Pruitt and Carpenter's faces inset behind her, each turned slightly to the other as if sharing a confidence. In bold red-colored font, the caption read *Murder on Black Bear Ridge*.

" ...Local authorities apparently have yet to develop any clues or leads in the case."

"Too busy gazin' at his belly button!" someone teased.

⊕

Because of the murder, there were now entirely too many reporters for briefings to be held in the waiting room of the Sheriff's offices, so Pruitt moved everything to the foyer of the courthouse building, where he thought the dark wood and smooth marble might also give the proceedings an air of dignity. Unfortunately, the photos on CNN had put the kibosh on anything like that. Half the press thought the situation humorous, the other half a scandal.

"You throw the I Ching yet?" One of the ones thinking it funny quipped. "Develop some leads that way?"

"What drugs did you take when you were following the Grateful Dead around?" asked another. "LSD? Cocaine? Can you give us a list?"

Humorous, scandalous—either way Pruitt was taking a broadside. "I'm only answering questions germane to the investigation."

Yet they veered off track immediately.

"What if you had a flashback during a crisis?"

"That's not germane."

"You carry a gun, don't you? What if you started hallucinating during the middle of an arrest?"

However they were interpreting CNN's little picture array, the reporters had settled on a basic assumption: Pruitt would not be able to solve John Carpenter's murder. His office was provincial, his past had undermined his competence. With no suspects or leads, the story had become Pruitt personally.

Pruitt stuck it out ten more minutes, though it was a waste. He ended the proceedings and fled to his office. He tried to catch up on his paperwork, but his concentration was shot. His good friend Marion Jones was right, he needed a float. He drove home, determined to go straight to his tank, so determined, in fact, that he nearly missed May Ia Yen, his deputy's daughter, sitting on his back steps, a forlorn look on her face.

"May Ia," he said as he stepped out of his cruiser. "What's up?"

"I'm having paradiddle problems," she said. "I can't get them right…Darn it!"

It was then Pruitt noted she had a snare drum case with her. This was another activity he'd been shirking lately, keeping up with the free percussion lessons he gave Elkhorn kids—especially those in the high school marching band, May Ia included.

"C'mon, then," he said. "Let's lick'em."

"Are you sure? My dad said you're busy."

"Never too busy for paradiddles, sweetheart. Grab your snare."

⊕

May Ia was actually quite an adept young percussionist—she had a strong attack and a clean approach, especially considering she was only a freshman—and it took only twenty minutes for her to smooth out the paradiddle rudiment.

"You're rockin' again, May Ia."

"Just in time. I'm trying out for the concert band."

"I'll give you a ride home," he said. The Yens lived only a half mile away, but it had begun to rain.

Her dad came out to greet them when Pruitt pulled into their driveway. Ing signaled with his hand and Pruitt rolled down his window.

"I told her not to bother you."

Smiling, Pruitt said, "She's going to make that concert band, Ing."

Ing smiled back. "Thanks, boss."

When he got home again, he locked the world out behind the cedar door of his float tank room.

⊕

Before he began undressing, he turned up the baseboard heater. The water in the tank was kept at a constant temperature, but the room took a few minutes to get comfortable, so he took the pieces of his uniform off slowly. He unpinned his badge and set it on the bench, loosened his tie and stripped it through his collar, removed the shirt and hung it on a hook. On another hook, he draped his gun belt. He stepped out of his pants, folded them neatly, and set them on the bench over the badge. He gave his stomach a slap, proud that at 185 he weighed only 10 pounds more than he did in high school.

Once completely undressed, he pushed open the revolving shelf set into the wall of his tank room so seamlessly that even he had to look twice on occasion to find it. He kept his supply of wax earplugs there and, some years ago, marijuana in a plastic film canister. The pot was gone now, but some days he wished it wasn't. Though a float and yoga were good together, so was a float and a toke. No, it wasn't for personal reasons that Pruitt had stopped smoking pot. It was just too risky to his career, which may have begun in response to an older man's challenge but which had quickly become an essential part of who he was. Pruitt wanted nothing to do with the whole *Just Say No* jive—at best a glib, cynical response to a complicated problem—but he also loved his job and wasn't about to jeopardize it by appearing "soft" on drugs. It may have been true that at law enforcement conferences, in private, his colleagues were as aware as he was how inane and unenforceable pot laws were, but no sheriff yet had been elected running a *Legalize Marijuana* campaign.

After setting the timer to seventy minutes, he ducked under the hatchback door and into the foot-deep water. He knelt and reached to pull the door closed after him; the buoyancy created by the nearly half-ton of Epson salts made him feel like he was sprawled across a slab of warm glass. Once he was stretched out on the water, it was different. With his weight spread he felt liberated—as close to a free floating state as a person could get without the benefit of space flight.

Foremost he savored the effect of the salts on his body, which not only kept him buoyant but also leached the fatigue from his muscles like a sponge. He stretched languidly. He twisted and flexed. He arched his back and rolled his neck from side-to-side. Aches heightened, then dissolved.

His routine was to take ten or fifteen minutes to get his body relaxed before tackling the hardest work: relaxing his mind. Even with his body at rest, his brain remained in high gear, cogitating, planning, analyzing—anything but shut up. To gain control over it, Pruitt regulated, then followed his every breath. He thought of still water. Distraught at the idea of losing control, his mind fought him, unleashing a torrent of thoughts and images, more fractured as Pruitt paid less attention to them, and then finally, isolated from all forms of stimulation, he found that peaceful spot where he just let himself be, not be the sheriff, a lover, or father. For a few precious minutes he did not allow himself to feel responsible or duty-bound, but to feel instead his physical being at work, the miracle of his heart pumping oxygen and nutrients through his veins steadily and without emotion. Rather than cacophony he began hearing instead a sort of mantra, not words but those sinewy, weaving guitar lines that Jerry Garcia played: playful, enticing, transforming the sounds created by fingertips on steel strings into something so much more— guide posts, maybe, to a world beyond the mortal coil.

CHAPTER SEVEN

The float had been good for his body, excellent for his psyche, and the next day, in spite of the stress-generating hoopla brought on by John Carpenter's murder, Pruitt arrived at the office more ready to enjoy his job than he had in a month. He walked in light on his feet, a Dead melody playing in his mind—*Help on the Way* appropriately enough. *Paradise waits*, the lyrics noted, *on the crest of a wave.* Deputy Charneski and Madeline Box, the office assistant, had gathered at the heart of The Swamp, Joyce Cody's desk. Seeing Pruitt, Charneski put the spin to the story he'd been sharing with the women, then nodded his head to his boss. Joyce and Madeline added greetings, then the three of them waited expectantly as Pruitt stood there grinning…just grinning, waiting for the lugubrious morning energy of his staff to focus, eyes glancing up from desks, faces craning around doorwells. Then, without warning or presentiment, he threw his head back and crowed, "Cock-a-doodle-doo!!"

Charneski was so badly startled he sputtered coffee over himself. The women began laughing—at himself or Charneski, Pruitt wasn't sure. The rest of the office, too, laughing their heads off.

Pruitt placed a hand on Charneski's shoulder. "I'm sorry, Bobby. Really." Though he couldn't wipe the grin off his face.

"You scared the shit out of me!"

"I know. I get a little crazy sometimes."

Joyce Cody said, "Got a float in, did we?"

"Dang right," said Pruitt, giving Bobby one last pat. He gave a glance around the office, faces glowing. Sometimes you just had to shake things up to make people feel better. "And you suckers are gonna pay for it," he said. Then he strode to his office, buk-buk-buking and flapping his arms.

⊕

By noon, Pruitt would shudder to think what things might have been like had he not had the float. His first challenge came in the form of Mr. Andy Messerit, the forensic bookkeeper sent by the Washington State Patrol to pore through John Carpenter's paperwork. He appeared at the side of Pruitt's desk before there'd been time to blow a cool breath across his hot coffee. Without as much as a greeting, this thin, intense man that Pruitt knew from Adam began yapping at him like a hyper little dog. "Why the hell this has to happen Thanksgiving week is the story of my life," he said, "and I'm driving back tonight for turkey dinner with my family, I don't care who this son-of-a-bitching stiff is." Then he stormed off.

Pruitt rose to follow after him, only to reach The Swamp in time to watch the door to the office that had been vacated by his deputies to make room for Mr. Messerit slammed in the collective face of all present.

After a moment of communal stupefaction, Joyce Cody said, "They said he was the best, but also a little temperamental."

⊕

Next at Pruitt's heels was E.L. Lamont, his undersheriff. After tapping the door jamb for Pruitt's attention, he entered with file folder in hand. "Gavin," he said, "another dog got shot last night."

Pruitt rocked back in his chair and ran his hand over his forehead. "Ah, crap."

"This one got sprayed with some sort of automatic. Lee thinks it may have been a 9-millimeter machine pistol."

"You gotta be kidding." He rocked his chair upright again. "Whose dog?"

"George Bridgewater's. And he's fit to be tied. After what the greenies did to his dozer?"

"E.L.," Pruitt said, "we don't know who ruined George's equipment. Not with certainty."

"We know, Gavin. C'mon. To me, this looks like payback. The greenies have had, what, three of their dogs killed?"

Pruitt looked at him.

"I'm just saying it's a place to start."

"Fine, but let's tread easy."

Then, at a quarter to twelve time and space twisted Pruitt's past and present into knots. His *Dark Star* crashed, *pouring its light into ashes.*

"Sheriff Pruitt?" It was Joyce, standing in his doorway. Somebody she did not know must have been waiting within earshot because that was the only time Joyce addressed him formally. "A woman here to see you." She flourished her eyebrows. Somebody interesting.

Pruitt rose. "By all means."

Joyce stepped back and his visitor entered, smiling broadly. "Bet I'm the *last* person on earth you expected."

His visitor's flair for understatement had always been well crafted. Pruitt could only mutter, "Angela."

Her gaze danced over him before she said, "Wish I could say I'd maintained my figure as well as you have, Gavin."

Pruitt experienced a flush of desire for Angela Caracitto wholly out of synch with the moment—as if he were a horny, pot-stoned college student again, not the pillar of local society he had become. Yes, her waist had thickened, and, yes, her hair had begun to gray, but if anything age had made the sum of her even more alluring, her cocoa-brown eyes more full of sexual mischief than ever.

"A hug at a moment like this wouldn't be inappropriate," she said, opening her arms to him.

Still more stunned than sensible, Pruitt said, "Jeez," and stepped into her embrace.

Angela ran her hands up his back. "My god, Gavin, this just turns...me...on."

⊕

Even if at that moment Pruitt could have made Angela Caracitto disappear, she would have been the talk of the town within hours. Though a horde of outsiders was already roaming Elkhorn, none of them looked like Angela, clad in black hose, body stocking, skirt and shoes, and a leather jacket with a red AIDS loop on the lapel. Yet it was as much her walk as her clothes people noticed, how the bounce in her step not so much jiggled as rolled the magnificent parts of her body, riveting every gaze in the office as Pruitt led her out to the side parking lot.

As they crossed towards his cruiser, she said, "Are we riding in the pig-mobile?"

"If you've got a rental we could take that."

"No way, man," she said. "This is much cooler. It'll be my first time in a pig-mobile I'm not getting carted off to a holding pen."

He opened the door for her. "You're not still up to that, are you?"

"Sure. You can still find me out on the streets." She settled in her seat and looked up at him. "Gimme a cause, man, I'm *there*."

Pruitt closed her door, the smell of her lingering— sandalwood essential oil. A smell he had feasted on when making love to her in the sixties. On his way around the car he shuddered, but not from the cold. He'd no sooner managed the key into the ignition when Angela's hand was riding up his thigh, her black-painted fingernails digging into him.

"Take me up one of your lonely county roads, Sheriff, and do me in the back of this pig-mobile."

Pruitt removed her hand from his leg. "No way."

Yet still she was grinning. "Remember when you balled me at the Dead concert at Portland State? Right behind the band?"

"I have no idea how you got us back there."

"It was great. I think Kreutzmann was watching. He dropped a beat," she said, "but you didn't."

"I was scared shitless."

"You were a tiger in heat. And that's all I'm asking for now. Zipless. In the pig-mobile. You must know a million places to hide."

He started the engine.

She placed her hand back on his thigh. "C'mon, Gavin, we used to do some damn good balling."

He removed it again, taking note that she hadn't even bothered to ask if he was married or otherwise attached. But why would she? This was Angela. He backed out of his parking slip. "This isn't then, this is now."

"Jesus, your hair." She touched it gently. "It's like the fifties. I love it short."

"C'mon, rein it in."

Obligingly, she settled her body back in her seat. "The look on your face when I walked in to your office."

Pruitt eased onto the sweeping one-way curve leading out of the courthouse parking lot to Memorial Drive and down the hill. "It's really not funny," he said.

"Of course it is. Funny, outrageous—all of it, man. Maybe your life has gotten predictable, but mine hasn't. Everyday I wake up and it's an adventure, my life. Two days ago I was hanging out in a blues club on the south side of Chicago, today I'm riding in a pig-mobile with an old lover. I'd say that was funny, wouldn't you?"

Pruitt said, "You live in Chicago now?"

"Most of the time."

At the corner of Memorial Drive and Yew Street they caught the red light. "There's a place up the street with good clam fritters."

"Ribs in Chicago, clam fritters in...What's the name of this place again?"

"Elkhorn."

"Elkhorn," she repeated. "That's great. Lead me, Sheriff Pruitt. I'll buy lunch."

⊕

Clam fritters, steamed babyneck clams, fresh shucked oysters, cold cracked Dungeness crab, smoked salmon—these items Pruitt ate. Thus in the strictest sense, he was not a vegetarian. He avoided beef, pork, and fowl completely—with the exception of a little white meat turkey at Thanksgiving—but would dig for razor clams in season, buy live crabs off the boats in Bay Center, and smoke the salmon he caught in the creeks and rivers of the county. He was too much a local boy to live without them.

"Those fritters would sell like hotcakes back east." Angela mopped up the vinaigrette dressing from her salad with a hunk of bread. "Not as backwater a place as I expected." A drop of oil had clung to her finger. She made sure Pruitt was watching, then mouthed it off deftly.

"Cut it out, Angela."

"What?"

"You know what."

She winked. "You think I knew my way around a cock in the sixties?"

The restaurant was buzzing with noontime business, and nobody—as Pruitt expected—could stop taking glances at Angela. She'd let her jacket fall open, the lacy edging of her red bra drawing Pruitt's attention to her cleavage like a matador's cape. Yet no one would be able to say Pruitt was hiding anything—hiding something in plain sight, maybe. "Why are you here, Angela?" he said. "I'm not buying that crock about you seeing my picture on TV, either."

She snapped open the dessert menu. "I'm here to take John home."

"John? You mean John Carpenter?"

"Of course. His mother's dead and he's the only child of an only child. We made these arrangements years ago."

"You kept seeing him?"

"Of course. After the University of Washington, we ended up in grad school in Chicago. Last ten years I've edited a newsletter he sponsors."

"You must be closer than that. If you're the one here collecting his remains."

"Close enough. Not lovers anymore, if that's what you're thinking." She smiled at him. "Not since we were all together."

Pruitt scowled. "We were not *all together*. You were with me, you were with him. I met him once, that time you brought him to the grape boycott rally—we didn't even shake hands. He was in my office a couple of months ago and didn't even get that look people do when they see somebody they *think* they might remember."

Angela cut him a look. "Are you saying nobody knows you met John before?"

Pruitt held her gaze a moment. "I haven't mentioned it."

Angela stared back at him. "You go to college with the most influential environmentalist in America, who gets himself killed in your hometown twenty-five years later, and nobody knows the connection but me?"

"What connection? You could lose six Elkhorns in the U-Dub alone, not to mention Seattle. I was in music, he was in science. We may as well have been living in different countries."

"Please, Gavin, don't be so naive." She signaled for the waitress and ordered plain cheesecake. After the waitress left, she said, "If you guys sat in Husky Stadium at opposite end zones, the media's going to concoct a conspiracy out of it."

Pruitt sighed and looked out the window. Charley Zerba's crabber, the *Mona Belle*, was chugging up river for the bay,

Charley standing in a wheelhouse not much bigger than a phone booth.

He looked back at Angela, across the table observing him.

She gave him a half-smile and said, "So you've got the hair picture all over the news, everybody interested in what drugs you took, and now I show up, a witness to your moral degeneracy." She winked. "No wonder you won't do me."

Angela's dessert arrived. After the waitress left them again, she said, "Look, Gavin, I didn't come here to cause you trouble. I'm here for John's body. Besides, it looks like you've created plenty of trouble on your own. Lying about your pot-smoking days."

Pruitt held his coffee cup chin high, looking over it at his ex-lover. "I've never lied about them, I've only refused to talk about them."

Forking up a bite of cheesecake, Angela said, "What I say is screw'em if they can't take a joke."

"Fine for you," he said, "a radical, nothing to lose. But the rest of us feel we have a right to our privacy." He took a sip of coffee, which was now tepid. He sat the cup back down.

Angela pushed her cheesecake plate aside, wiped her fingers on the napkin in her lap, then reached across the table to take Pruitt's hand. "More than anything I'd like to make love to you again. Sweet nostalgic love. You and me for a couple of hours, then a clean getaway."

Her fingers were beautifully proportioned, the nails manicured to perfection. It didn't take much for Pruitt to imagine the rest of her body as equally well tended. She'd been an amazing sexual partner. "I'm involved with someone," he told her. "It wouldn't be right."

She searched his eyes. "You haven't gone *that* straight, have you?"

"When it comes to things like that, yes, I have."

She rubbed his hand fondly. "Oh, well. It doesn't hurt to ask." She kept looking at him, her eyes getting a little misty.

"Wow, Gav, I'm going to think about what we're not going to do for the rest of my life."

Her sudden tenderness moved Pruitt. "Hey," he said, "me, too. You look fabulous."

Without warning she was pinching his hand, nothing sensuous about it anymore. "From the body, could you tell if John suffered?"

The outrageous, fun-loving Angela had disappeared, replaced by the angry, outraged Angela he also knew her as, the woman he'd been relieved to breakup with, despite the great lovemaking.

Not about to let her see the pain her grip was causing him, Pruitt answered her in the flat tone his years as a cop breaking bad news had perfected. "I'm afraid he did. I wish I could tell you otherwise."

She let go of him and dabbed at her eyes with her napkin. She blew her nose on it. "Somebody's paying for this," she said.

CHAPTER EIGHT

Back at the courthouse complex, Pruitt pulled into his parking slip and switched off the engine. When he turned to say something to her, Angela leaned across the seat, put a hand at the nape of his neck and kissed him passionately on the mouth, her lips lemony from the cheesecake. Before he could pull away, a muffled pop sounded; almost instantly the cruiser began tilting slightly to aft on the driver's side.

Angela lurched away. "Was that—"

"A gunshot, for chrissakes!" Pruitt pushed Angela's head down and covered her with his body.

"Jesus, Gavin!" she cried. "What the—!"

He reached across her and pushed open the passenger door. "Scoot out," he said. "Cover with the car. The shot came from my side."

Angela rolled out as instructed, Pruitt right behind her, drawing his service revolver. The two of them with backs pressed against the side of the cruiser.

"What's up there?" she asked.

"The hospital, of all damn things."

"Is he going to shoot again?" she asked, sounding surprisingly calm.

"Stay down." He twisted to his knees, raised to kneeling and aimed his revolver over the top of the cruiser, barrel tracking left to right. The sun was behind him and visibility was clear, but he could see nothing unusual.

Then in his peripheral vision he spied Joyce Cody exiting through the Sheriff's Office rear doors, on her way to her regular late lunch.

"Back! Back!" he screamed at her, Joyce looking at him perplexed.

"Somebody shot at me!" he yelled. "Get back in the office!"

Joyce spun and struggled with the door, her handbag in the way, finally getting the doorknob in hand and taking cover.

A moment later, the door cracked open again, just enough to allow a rifle barrel to poke through near the bottom, followed by about a third of Lee Wilson's face. He was lying on his stomach and aiming up at the hill, where Pruitt still saw nothing unusual.

"One shot, boss?" Wilson yelled to him.

"Only one. Yeah." Pruitt continued to scan the hillside.

"I sent Charneski out the front. He's going to circumnavigate."

"You put him in a goddamn vest first!"

"He's *in* it, boss...He's in it."

Probably less than five minutes passed before Charneski yelled down to them, "I'm coming out! Okay? It's just me! There's nobody up here!"

Pruitt acknowledged, then Charneski showed himself, head and shoulders appearing at the crest of the flat-topped hill where the Willapa Harbor Hospital had been built. "There's a cartridge up here," he yelled. "Right beside the road."

⊕

"One shot," Lee Wilson said. "30-06. Driving by along the exit road. Just pulled to a stop, took a shot—probably right out the window—and split."

An hour had passed since the shooting, and final analyses were being summed up in Pruitt's office, attended besides himself by Wilson, Charneski, and Ethan Laymont. Angela waited with Joyce in The Swamp. Through the crack in the door Pruitt could see his ex-lover regaling his secretary with some story—something outrageous, no doubt.

To Lee Wilson, Pruitt said, "Was he was gunning for me, or just anybody in the lot?"

"Had to be you," Wilson said. "Monitored the backside of the office from the hospital parking lot. Saw you drive in, took a pop."

"Nobody saw anything?" he said, addressing Charneski, who'd supervised the canvass.

"The sun bright like it was this afternoon? Most of the curtains were drawn on that side of the building. And the front desk? They can only see about a quarter of the lot. I mean, who would have even been thinking about something like that?"

"Do we escalate?" Pruitt asked. "We could probably get some help from the State Patrol. The Drug Assistance Unit does undercover."

"This isn't about drugs," Charneski pointed out.

"The DAU does more than just drug undercover. And they're good."

"He shot your tire out," Wilson said, exasperated. "To scare you."

"Regardless."

"We'd look like pansies."

"He shot at a police officer. It's serious."

"He shot a police officer's *car*. It's happened before. Last year? We didn't call anybody then."

"That was a couple of drunk teenagers thinking they were being big men, shooting E.L.'s cruiser parked in front of his house."

"So we caught those little pricks then; let's catch this prick now."

☮

Back out in the lot, Pruitt was finally able to say good-bye to Angela. "I'm sorry about all this," he said. "It started with your basic civil disobedience, a little vandalism. Then somebody starting shooting dogs. Now a murder and what you saw today." He shook his head. "I don't know what to think."

Angela said, "I think it's kind of like old times, Gav. Really setting those fireworks off." She waggled her eyebrows. "In more ways than one."

Her flippant attitude angered him. "You had no right to take that kind of liberty with me."

"It's a kiss I'll never forget, lover."

"I'm not—" But he stopped. He'd never win this verbal tussle. "The main thing is now you can get back to Chicago."

"Oh, I don't know, I think I might have gotten here just in time."

Pruitt scowled. "In time for what?"

She said, "The action, baby," then began walking away.

Not liking this turn of events one single bit, Pruitt yelled, "Have you started the paperwork?"

Angela twirled to look back at him, as light on her feet as a dancer, in spite of the bulky Doc Marten shoes she wore. She waited for an explanation.

"For John's body," he said.

"I'm due for a vacation," she said. "And this Garden of Eden you're the sheriff of looks like as a good place as any." Then she spun on her heel and strode away, that incredible backside mocking Pruitt, the glory it could have provided.

☮

"Where do you know Angela from?" Joyce asked him when he returned.

"An old college friend."

Joyce was looking pale; not exactly drained of color, but definitely like the plug had been pulled. "She's...Well, quite something."

He shuffled the fan of pink memo slips on his desk into a stack. "Joyce, before you go, who amongst all these fine citizens sounded like they needed to talk to me the most?"

"Before I go where?" she asked.

"Home," he said. "You're taking the rest of the day off. And I don't want to see any vacation leave on your time card either."

Placing her hand to her throat, Joyce said, "Thanks, Gavin. I guess I am still feeling a little shaken up." She offered him a brave smile. "My lunch all shot to hell, so to speak."

⊕

Before she left, Joyce advised him to call Sheriff Jack Coogan of Mason County, who had agreed to interview the Black Bear Ridge heirs, the Hicksons, who lived in his jurisdiction. Pruitt asked him how things had gone.

Coogan said, "It doesn't appear they could gain from his death. The way the old man left it, an environmental impact statement has to be completed before any sales can be arranged."

Pruitt said, "True, but to make the most money from the deal they'd want to log all or most of it. Maybe they'd seen a preliminary report and didn't like what they saw. Maybe they would have preferred somebody else on the job."

"You think they'd commit murder for that?"

"I suppose that would depend on how badly they needed the money."

Coogan said, "There's a notion all right. Okay, send me whatever you've got."

When he hung up, E.L. was at his door, tapping on the jamb, as was his way, to adhere to the courtesy of knocking even if he was already standing in your office.

Pruitt said, "By all means," and indicated his undivided attention.

E.L. sat down and thumbed through a few pages on his ever-present clipboard. "Last summer John Carpenter was in here. You remember?"

"Sure do. Earl Ruddell was harassing him. Following him around with binoculars, taking notes, yelling at him. The Jews and the media and Carpenter out to ruin his way of life."

"And you put Raphe on him, and in one of her reports I found this: 'Mr. Ruddell said Dr. Carpenter goes out past Nemah, somewhere out by Little Noisy Creek.'" E.L. looked up.

Pruitt said, "We should canvass that end of the county."

"As of this moment, you've got everybody assigned."

Pruitt grinned. "Not everybody."

After E.L.'s briefing, Pruitt was given some cause to anticipate that his afternoon wouldn't be quite the mad hornet's nest his morning had been. ANGER's David Spoor called to inform him that as a gesture of mourning and respect for the passing of their champion, demonstrations were suspended through the Thanksgiving holidays. Pro-logging activities, too, were winding down, though not without a flourish. Union president Dale Slater had organized a protest that would include dragging a wooden cross to the state capital doorsteps, where an effigy of a logger would be crucified. "Give the governor something to think about over her giblets and gravy," he'd told reporters, most of whom would cover the crucifixion, then head home, too. Everybody looking forward to a break— Pruitt no exception. His daughter, Olivia, would be on her way from Tacoma later in the afternoon. He hadn't seen her since the beginning of the school term and was allowing his heart to feel a little more of the ache it always carried for her, knowing that part of it would be assuaged when he saw her that evening.

What he didn't want to do was worry about Angela, what she might be saying about him in some downtown watering hole. He'd been telling himself for years that the day might come when he'd be forced to admit to some of his youthful indiscretions, among them some film out there somewhere of him and a number of other naked hippies at that nude beach outside of Bellingham—a bunch of chowderheads unable to think of anything better to do with a 16-millimeter camera— and, yes, there were other things from his past that wouldn't weather well if brought to current light…Yet here he was doing exactly what he said he wouldn't do: worry. There was better use of his time. He radioed E.L. that he'd be joining him on the canvass of East Willapa. "Take everything north of Highway 6," he told him, "and I'll get everything south."

To the untrained eye, the southeast corner of Willapa County could appear all but deserted. There didn't seem to be a dozen houses, nor population enough for a one-room school. Yet it was a false first impression. The hills were dotted with farms, double-wides, and modest wood-framed homes. The grade school had six rooms, a gymnasium, and nearly seventy-five students. There were plenty of people here. They just guarded their privacy. Why else would a person choose to live in so remote a place?

But it wasn't just remoteness that made investigation difficult in East Willapa, it was people's ways. Refreshments had to be offered, and polite talk made before getting down to a proper police interview. With the press and the governor breathing down his neck, Pruitt had to fight the urge to hurry folks along, quelling it by remembering his float and finding a calm spot within himself, sound-tracked by Garcia's sweet guitar lines and the lyrics from *Uncle John's Band: like the morning sun you come, and like the wind you go.* So armed, he managed to enjoy not just the juice and cookies, but the opportunity to touch base one-to-one with the people to whom he owed his job.

His efforts got him as far as Squally Jim Junior Road, where he started pulling into every turnout and path he could find. From the proprietor of The Spartan Store he learned that John Carpenter had a woman friend, Olwen Friday, a jeweler and crafts person Pruitt had never heard of, but who he assumed had sent Carpenter the birthday card he and Ing Yen had found in his apartment. East county people knew Olwen Friday, but not where she lived—it was unanimous that she had a hermit-like nature—though Mel Koltz thought he'd seen her truck making a turn along Huckleberry Hill, the last rise before Black Bear Ridge. Squally Jim Junior Road ran along the hill's base and was the logical point to look for such a turnoff, yet all Pruitt could find were decrepit logging roads, left to ruin after Huckleberry Hill had been clear cut fifty years ago.

He was about to give up. It was after four, and if he hurried he might be able to get back to Elkhorn before his daughter arrived from Tacoma. It would be nice, he admonished himself, to meet her at the door. If his bladder hadn't been bursting from all the hospitality, he might have turned around then and there, but he'd finally decided to just pull over and do his business—he hadn't seen another vehicle in fifteen minutes and it would only take a moment to relieve himself. Then he saw it, not even a road but more like a pathway, hidden by wilting grass that drooped over the tire ruts. Even as carefully as he'd been looking, it would have been easy to miss.

He was surprised at how deep into the forest the path took him, the feeling exaggerated by the unnatural denseness of the stand surrounding it—the saplings placed too close together when replanted, a common occurrence during the early days of tree farming. Left alone for a couple of centuries, disaster and natural selection might create a forest of usable timber out of these underdeveloped trees—otherwise it was pulp wood. In the meantime, scrawny, sun-starved limbs scraped the sides of his cruiser as Pruitt pressed forward, reaching finally a clearing of scrabble and hardpan, abused ground that had probably served as a staging arena for the original clearcutting.

He was glad for the privacy in which to relieve himself, but disappointed at finding only another dead-end. Nonetheless, in a be-here-now moment, he looked up to admire the high mackerel sky beginning to color orange from the sunset. It reminded him of *From the Heart of Me*, Donna Godchaux's contribution to the Grateful Dead canon, the lyrics about the glow in the twilight at the dawn of hope. And when he brought his gaze down, he saw at a short distance what looked like icons, but upon closer inspection turned out to be elaborate gate posts, fashioned from mortar and the oblong stones common to local creeks. Oddly, there was no gate, nor any gate hardware attached to the posts. Rather they appeared to serve as bases for the finials atop them, sculptures of leaping salmon whose grace belied the mundane nature of their medium: small parts salvaged from electronic devices, household appliances, and discarded toys. Pruitt recognized the style from the jewelry he'd been shown at The Spartan Store, the work of John Carpenter's woman friend, Olwen Friday.

Nearby he noticed a bower hacked out of a copse of foliage, mostly alder and wild shrubs, but also edged with Oregon grape, sword fern and bracken. Parked inside was a khaki green Ford pickup truck, early-seventies, a little rust creeping up the rear quarter panels.

From the gateless gateposts, Pruitt followed a path of smooth flat stones pressed into the ground and now grown over with moss wound back through a forest of mixed hardwood and evergreen trees that had apparently missed the clear-cutting done so many years before.

Around a bend appeared a small, rustic house, built from the same creek stones as the gateposts, mortared in concrete, the cross-beams rough-hewn and painted a rusty shade of red. At the north end of the house rose a pagoda-roofed garret, on whose topmost point sat a sculpture of a frog, gazing down on Pruitt with chillingly life-like doll's eyes. At the south end, a waterwheel soughed lazily into a broad fish pond. Overlooking the pond was an oval-shaped window, curtainless, though with the sun already set behind the tree line, the glass appeared as opaque as the eye of a beast.

Pruitt paused a moment, cowed by the extraordinary vision. The home and landscaping would have been incongruous in any other part of the county, yet fitted the surrounding environment as seamlessly as fresh sprung mushrooms—magical and dreamlike. The lyrics from *Box of Rain* came back to him again: was this, too, a dream dreamed long ago?

He finished the walk to the door and knocked. When the door opened a woman was revealed who, like the house, would have stood out away from this place, but was perfect within it.

"Olwen Friday?" Sheriff Pruitt asked.

"Yes?"

She had ginger-brown hair, long and thick where it cascaded from a scarf tied around her head gypsy style. Her nose was pierced by a thin gold loop; her ears featured rows of earrings: pewter salmon and cones of shimmering beads. Under a Spencer jacket layered with brocade, she wore a blouse patterned in wild batik. Around her waist and over a full skirt of bold floral design she'd wrapped another scarf. Underneath everything else she wore leotards; on her feet, running shoes.

Yet in spite of the extraordinary clothing, it was her eyes that entranced him, unexpectedly the same ginger-brown color as her hair.

Pruitt removed his hat. "I'm afraid I've brought some bad news."

"John's dead." As if Pruitt were some rube coming to her with news six months old.

Pruitt said, "You were expecting this?"

"I never expect anything," she said, "nor do I reject anything."

"Yes, but why would you think...?"

"Why else, Sheriff, would you go to the trouble of finding me? Which couldn't have been easy."

Pruitt had to grant her that.

"Is there something else?" she asked.

"Yes. I'm afraid the death was a homicide."

She regarded him silently a moment before standing back from the door. "Oh, boy," she said.

Pruitt said, "Ms. Friday, I'm not trying to barge in, but maybe we should sit down a moment."

She looked at him, her expression bordering on the dazed. "Yes," she said. "Come in if you like."

When the door closed behind him, Pruitt was enveloped in the warmth radiating from a wood stove situated at the center of the house, steam rising in curlicues from the spout of the kettle sitting atop it. The stove piping rose straight up, exiting at a junction of six points created by the triangular pattern of the exposed roof beams. There were no inside walls, only partitions; the footprint was probably no more than 400 square feet, shack-sized though anything but shack-like, cozy and surprisingly spacious feeling. To his left and slightly behind him, mounted on the wall, Pruitt took note of a Remington twelve-gauge shotgun.

"I saw your jewelry at The Spartan," he said as a way to take the edge off her shock. "Do you work up in the garret, an artist in her tower?"

"No," she said. "It's just for show. I never go up there."

She slipped out of her running shoes and sat on a chair-sized platform upon which rested a futon. It looked like under her expansive skirt she'd taken the lotus position.

The only other piece of furniture was a pillow-strewn futon couch under the octagonal window, so that was where Pruitt sat.

While Pruitt watched, Olwen Friday carried on as if he weren't there, doing yoga, methodically lowering her head until it nearly touched her toes, then raising it again, as slowly as she'd lowered it. In the air he caught a faint scent of joss stick.

In a strong voice, his host said, "Would you mind going to the kitchen and bringing me a glass of wine?"

"Not at all." He stood. "In the back?"

"There's a jug under the counter."

The kitchen cupboards had no doors. Beans and lentils and grains in frosty-blue, quart-sized canning jars lined the shelves. The steel, two-basin sink had no faucet or spigots. The wine was a pale red color, not like anything Pruitt had seen before. He found a wine glass and poured it about half full.

Sensing him at her side, Olwen Friday opened her eyes and took the glass from him. "It's huckleberry," she said.

For a fleeting moment, he honestly couldn't remember if he'd asked about the wine out loud. Of course he had not. "It's a beautiful color," he told her.

She took a sip. Still in the cross-legged position, she rested her elbows on her knees, the wine glass held out in front of her. "Is this going to be the third-degree?"

Her voice had the timbre of honey—an aural compliment to the remarkable coloring of her eyes and hair. She had a beauty and bearing about her Pruitt had never encountered before. "Not at all," he said. "Just simple things, like when was the last time you saw John?"

"John was last here Sunday."

Pruitt took a notebook and pen from his shirt pocket. "What time?"

"Late afternoon. He brought some new CD's with him."

"When did he leave?"

"He didn't stay long. Just checking in, he said. He was going to try and get back for Thanksgiving."

"Did he ever talk to you about his work?"

"No," she said. "Not really. He was investigating the extent of flora and fauna on Black Bear Ridge. I'm sure you know that much."

"We know very little about him, actually. Anything you can tell me would help immensely. Anything at all."

She took another sip of wine. She remained silent, though her eyes thoroughly searched his face. For what? he wondered.

"You're the first person who's been here other than John since... " A shimmer appeared in her eyes. "I knew people hated him, but I didn't think...I thought you were going to tell me there'd been a car accident or something..." A tear streaked down the valley near her nose.

Hastily, she wiped it away.

For no reason he could explain—because he'd experienced the tears of victims before—the gesture moved Pruitt more deeply than he would have expected.

He said, "Did anybody ever show up here, looking for him?"

"Nobody in person."

Which Pruitt gave some thought to before saying, "Can you explain what you mean by that?"

"Their karma. It hung on John like rot for days."

Boy, oh boy, he thought. How many times had he felt the same way, haunted by the psychic stench of child abusers and wife beaters.

Olwen began weeping openly.

Quietly, Pruitt said, "I know this is difficult. I can come back later, let things settle a bit."

From somewhere in her layers of skirts and scarves Olwen pulled a red print handkerchief—the kind a farmer might carry—and blew her nose. "I shouldn't be so bitter. I'll have him always in my heart."

Pruitt remained silent.

"There are paradoxes," she said, "we can do nothing more than assimilate and live with."

Pruitt said, "I agree. But I also want you to know that it's important to me that I bring John's killer to justice."

"How did he die?" she asked.

Pruitt sighed. "Maybe this isn't the best time."

"Please," she said, her voice getting back to normal.

While he explained, Olwen kept her head down, rapt. When he was through, she said, "Okay."

Pruitt knew, of course, that it wasn't. He said, "I'll be honest with you, up to this point this whole thing has been administrative, a pain in my side as much as anything else. But now that I'm seeing how badly he's going to be missed…"

He found himself choking up and had to stop. He let a few moments pass before saying, "You know the Grateful Dead?"

"Yeah, sure," she said. "Of course."

"Do you know what the name refers to? Specifically, I mean."

"Well, I always thought it meant whatever you wanted it to mean."

"It's a motif, actually, from various folk tales. A hero happens upon some people who refuse to bury a man because he had no money when he died. The hero pays the debts and the man is given a proper burial. A little while later the hero gets in trouble and out of no where a fellow traveler, a stranger, saves him."

"And the stranger who saves the hero is the man he helped bury. He's the grateful dead man."

"Exactly."

"And…?"

"And this is how I feel now about this case. John is dead, but his spirit needs my help. And I'm not going to let him down."

CHAPTER NINE

Although it was dark by the time he'd driven back from East Willapa, Pruitt's daughter, Olivia, had not yet arrived from Tacoma. He thought about a quick float, then dismissed the idea. Quick was not the point of a float. He put on his kettle for tea, then filled his largest pot with water and sat it, too, over a gas flame. In his bedroom, he changed into jeans and a sweatshirt. His answering machine had a half-dozen messages on it. Among them, unusually, were calls from both his father and mother. Divorced going on fifteen years now, they had developed an uncanny sense for when to call when the other hadn't. Maybe the holidays had broken down their radar.

The kettle started whistling, calling him back to the kitchen. He made his tea, turned down the flame heating the pasta water, then returned to his bedroom fortified and ready to make some calls, his mother first. She was just checking in, disappointed he couldn't make it up for Thanksgiving, but understood his circumstances. She'd seen the picture on CNN, of course, and told him not to worry about it, everybody had longer hair back then.

After his mother, he called his friend Marion Jones to see if she wanted to go clam digging with Olivia and him on Friday morning. She wasn't in, so he left a message on her machine.

His father Pruitt would call in the morning. Communication with his old man in the evening was a tightrope walk. Jack Pruitt was what AA called a functioning alcoholic, relatively harmless to the outside world, but a havoc wrecker within his family, both unreasonably critical and given to bouts of soul-numbing sentimentality. Rather than his father, Pruitt called Molly. "What time do you want us over tomorrow?"

"Anytime," she said. "Olivia in yet?"

"Not yet," Pruitt said. "So about one?"

"That's fine."

He held the line, meaning to add something but feeling his mouth go dry.

"Gavin?" Molly said "I'm so sorry the baby issue slipped out. I had every intention of waiting until things had settled down. I'm just not good at secrets, I guess."

"It's alright," he told her. "I understand why it's important to you. I'd never seen Susan more joyful than when Olivia was born. For that matter, it almost kept us together. Except for the fact we were just so wrong for each other. But this wouldn't be like that, would it? We already know we're right for each other. So I'm thinking about it. At little bit at a time, you know? I'm just going to need a little space."

Molly was silent a moment. "One o'clock *and* hungry as horses, okay?"

☮

He rose from the bed and walked back to the kitchen, baby thoughts trailing him like a cloud of talcum powder—he could almost smell it again, and mineral oil, and petroleum jelly. Oh, my god, he thought. All that again? Then to hold the thoughts at bay he plunged into a favorite refuge: cooking dinner.

From the crisper in the fridge he pulled out carrots, onions, and red and green bell peppers. From the garland draped on a hook by the kitchen window he twisted off three fat garlic cloves, shucked the papery skin, and minced them. Once he'd finished chopping up the vegetables, he retrieved his best fry pan and placed it over a flame next to the pasta pot, where the water was at a rolling boil.

The sizzling vegetables were filling the kitchen with a homey mélange of aromas when a familiar-sounding car drove up: the clattering Rabbit diesel Pruitt had bought Olivia as a high school graduation present—which set his heart to racing. The engine coughed before dying. A door opened and closed, than another. A second door?

By the time Pruitt had given the veggies a good swirl, the back door was opening and there was Olivia.

"Daddy!"

"Ollie." He bent to hug her, just as he used to for her mother, though her height and figure were the extent of her mother's genetic gifts. Olivia's hazel eyes, pale Scots-Irish skin and dark brown hair were pure Pruitt.

It wasn't until she'd patted his arm that he noticed what she was wearing: a worn cardigan over a granny dress of thin cotton, a necklace of ceramic beads strung on a leather thong, thick wool socks and Birkenstock sandals.

"New clothes," he said. "Where you'd get the dress? It looks familiar."

"From Mom. When she came down last month."

"What happened to your other clothes?"

"Kid's stuff, Daddy. You know what it's like."

"You're not wearing make-up anymore?"

She dismissed the notion with a wave of her hand. "Who needs it?"

"When you were thirteen," he said, "you fought like a tom cat to wear make-up."

"Grew up, Daddy." She smiled. "What you were waiting for, right?"

"No," he said in an admission that startled him. "I can't say I've ever really waited for that at all."

Then there was a young man standing in the kitchen threshold, rangy and hesitant, some sort of wool cap over blond dreadlocks, the outer edge of his eyebrow pierced by a gold hoop. He wore a blue sweater with cream-colored zigzag patterns over a plaid shirt, loose cotton trousers, and, like Olivia, thick wool socks and Birkenstocks.

"You guys look out of the sixties," he said.

"It's the style, Daddy. Kind of fun, huh? Does it make you nostalgic? Daddy, this is Christopher."

Christopher offered a hand. "Glad to meet you, sir."

Pruitt was pleased with the grip. "Right, same here." Then to Olivia he said, "I didn't know you were bringing a friend. But no problem. There's always enough pasta to go around."

☮

This Christopher…He was a junior, a computer science major. An unlikely looking one, Pruitt thought. He would have expected a nebbish. So how old were juniors? Twenty-one? Older? One thing for sure, he wasn't a boy. He wasn't really a man, either, but something else—what Pruitt didn't know, but it was making him uncomfortable. During the summers when he lived with him Olivia had, on occasion, dated local boys, but they had all seemed like…Well, boys.

"Great food," Christopher said. "Olivia said you were vegetarian."

"I've got a few weaknesses." He explained the clams and salmon.

"And you're a Deadhead." Christopher smiled again, charming. "Me, too."

Pruitt took that in a moment, then said, "Olivia hates them."

"No, I don't."

"You say they can't sing."

"On that one album they sing well. With *Ripple* on it?"

"*American Beauty*," Christopher said. "One of their best."

"It is," Pruitt said, yet found he was thinking mostly about whether Olivia and Christopher were having sex, worrying that he hadn't covered everything. Love and waiting? Being responsible if waiting wouldn't work?

"When did you first see them?"

Pruitt, lagging the conversation, almost said *who?* "1968," he said. "At the Eagles in Seattle. The Quick and the Dead tour."

"Quick?"

"Quicksilver Messenger Service. Another San Francisco band. Popular at the time. I was a freshmen in college," he said. "Same age as you, honey."

Olivia, reaching for her glass of milk, smiled at him. Without makeup, the freckles lacing her nose stood out again, yet her girlishness was waning fast.

"Pigpen was still alive then," Christopher said. "Must have been amazing."

"Actually, it was one of the concerts that ended up on *Anthem of the Sun.*"

Christopher said, "No, kidding. Wow."

Pruitt said, *"Wavin' to the memories in my heart."*

Olivia said, "Is that a Dead quote, Daddy?"

"From *Wave to the Wind*," he said. "Heard it in 1992, in Oakland. First show where I hung out with the clean and sober Deadheads."

Christopher said, "The Wharf Rats? Guys with the *One Show at a Time* stickers?"

"They might be clean and sober," Pruitt said, "but they're dancing fools."

Interjecting, Olivia said, "What's the clam tide like on Friday?"

Pruitt wagged his hand. "So, so. Why? Did you have something else you'd rather do?"

"Christopher's never seen an old-growth forest. We were thinking of a hike to Black Bear Ridge?"

Pruitt said, "Hiking there might actually take all day. But Marion's got canoes. Why don't we take a trip down Little Noisy Creek? It meanders practically through the heart of that old growth."

⊕

On Thanksgiving Day mountainous black-bottomed clouds passed slowly through a sky patched with brilliant blue—a contrast not lost on Pruitt. As rain showers and sun shared the sky, he would share this day with Olivia, the love of his life, and Molly Burkhalter, the lover his life was suddenly in turmoil over.

Molly lived in the Riverview district, on the opposite side of town, and although the distance wasn't so great the feeling of polarity was. On the drive over, he tried to come to grips with his feelings. God, he loved Molly. But especially catching glimpses of Olivia's face in the rearview mirror and thinking of all it took to bring her to this wonderful place in her life, he wondered did he have the energy and focus for it again.

He decided, however, as they pulled into the driveway of Molly's home, a modest three-bedroom rambler, that today it was time to gut up and put on a happy face. Indeed, they were just in time for the afternoon football game. If he could make a clean sweep into the living room and get the television on, there might be enough distraction to set the right tone for the day—light, shallow, a holiday in every sense of the word.

But seeing Olivia got Molly's emotions up. "I love your *look*," she said. "You ought to see if your dad kept any of his clothes from his college days."

"A few tie-dyes," Olivia said, cutting her eyes at him playfully. "But no treasure trove."

When introduced to Christopher, Molly took his hand, then gave him a nervous little hug. They were all crammed into the narrow hallway, creating a stifling energy. Pruitt's mask of good humor felt made of wax. But as if on his same wavelength, Molly whisked up to him all smiles and sympathy. He kissed her, snuggled her neck, which smelled of sage and raspberries and, underneath, her White Shoulders. She told the kids to go on into the living room, then turned back to kiss him once more on the lips. Then she squeezed his hand and said, "Go get settled, dinner's almost on."

If she had seen his agony she also knew this was neither the time nor place to talk about it. Rather she was doing her best to put him at ease. Just one more demonstration of her remarkable character. Wending his way to his favorite spot on the couch, he hoped the rest of the day would go as smoothly. A game was in progress, Pruitt ready to take refuge wherever he could find it: televised football, roasting turkey. Christopher surprised him with his enthusiasm for the game.

"Made second team all-conference in high school," he confessed.

Olivia sat for only a few minutes before she stood and said, "If you *men* don't think you'll miss me, I'm going to go help Molly."

It didn't take long for Pruitt to realize Christopher had an excellent eye for football. "How'd you get from football to computers?"

"Always loved math, too. Computers are all about math."

"Well, then, I've got a computer question for you. What's with this Internet thing I've been reading about? You've heard of it, right?"

"Yeah, we've got access at school. One thing is, you've got to have a pretty fast computer to make much use of it. A 486 with at least 8 mgs of RAM."

Pruitt chuckled. "Tech talk. I wish we could have some of it around the office. There's been no money in the budget for even a slow computer."

☮

By the time he and Christopher were called to the table, he was famished, a little flushed from the glass of red wine Olivia had brought him. The table was sumptuous: candles and a centerpiece, two beautiful women and a spread of fine food.

A line from *Crazy Fingers* flashed through his mind: *Life may be sweeter for this, I don't know*—though this was one moment where Pruitt felt no ambivalence whatsoever: it *was* sweeter for this.

As they ate, he smiled secretly at Olivia. Yes, she was a woman now, no longer his little girl. That part of her was just a treasured past. She caught him looking and blushed. They averted each other's eyes. Pruitt felt his own blush. How did fathers tell daughters they were wonderful, beautiful, yes, even desirable women? Cutting a bite of turkey, he realized maybe he just had.

Christopher was in the process of polishing off his third plateful of food when Molly began to rise from her chair—which Pruitt put a stop to. "I'm washing up," he said. "Don't anybody move."

When he came back for a second load of dishes, he stood for a moment regarding his family tableaux: Molly, his woman, endowed richly in both mind and body; Olivia, his fine daughter, intelligent and thoughtful. Yes, even Christopher, blond dreadlocks and all, looked in place here. He had to retreat to the kitchen so they wouldn't see the tears they'd put in his eyes. Sweeter, indeed.

Molly had loaded the coffee maker with fresh ground beans. As the brewing aroma filled the kitchen, Pruitt rinsed plates and whistled the lilting melody from *Stella Blue*, so romantic. When the coffee was ready, he served, then joined the others. After walnut pie, Molly sent Christopher and Olivia out for a walk.

No sooner had the door closed than she was sitting on Pruitt's lap, kissing him, rubbing him provocatively. "I want you," she said, pulling him up. "Now." She led him to the bedroom where she kicked off her shoes and shucked her panties. Pruitt unbuckled his belt, thinking they were going to undress, but his pants and underwear had only gotten as far as his knees when she began pulling him onto the bed, unable to wait even a second longer for him, a replay of the wave of desire they'd experienced just the other night, twice in one week the two of them like randy teenagers in the back seat of a car.

Yet through this lust panic drove a powerful and unexpected wedge. "You haven't stopped taking..."

Molly's body reacted as if he'd touched with a bolt of static electricity. "Oh, god, no, Gavin. I just *want* you."

But the damage was done. "I'm sorry," he said. "I don't know why I said that."

She drew him down next to her, gently. "I'm sorry, too," she said. "For bringing this whole thing up now. God, I am so sorry."

"I do love you, Molly." He stretched out more comfortably, brought her head to the nook of his shoulder. "I was just thinking earlier about the lyrics to *I Will Take You Home*."

"Oh, I do love that song. Where the father is talking to his daughter?"

"That line *long is the road we must travel; short are the legs struggling behind* just got to me today. How he promises to take his little girl home? That she'll never be left behind?"

"That's a beautiful song."

"It says a lot about being a dad, what I went through with Olivia. How wonderful it all was. But just then," he said, waving weakly to where he'd been standing, pants down and randy as a goat, just moments ago, "I panicked that I was over-romanticizing all of it."

"You're ambivalent, Gavin. Of course you'd be. You've got legitimate reasons not to become a father again. I understand that. I do."

Pruitt felt a pit in his throat, tears forming in his eyes. "This is awful. I wish you didn't want what you want."

She turned, the top of her head under his chin. She was crying. "I wish I didn't either. But I don't know how to stop myself."

CHAPTER TEN

Pruitt and Olivia were close, rarely fought, and even when they had, it never got heated. But because of the divorce and the time apart they necessarily had to spend, there was nevertheless an adjustment period when they were together again. And Christopher, for all his charm, was simply making things a little harder. Walking into the kitchen and finding some tall young man making a turkey sandwich for himself just felt weird. The dreadlocks making it even weirder, like hairy worms growing out of his head. Pruitt fought his feelings, knew they were emotional, but he just flat out felt invaded.

Pruitt said, "Molly send that turkey along?"

Christopher grinned. "A little lapse in my vegetarianism, too."

Pruitt said, "I understand completely."

"Hey, guys." It was Olivia, poking her head in. "I'm off to bed." She gave Pruitt a peck, then Christopher. "We're up early tomorrow, right? For our big canoe trip?"

"Crack of dawn," Pruitt said. "Black Bear Ridge, here we come."

"I wish Molly could have made it."

"She's actually got to work." Which was only partially true. She could have taken some vacation time, but she'd begged off. "You need some time apart from me," she'd told him.

"I changed your sheets yesterday," he told Olivia.

"Busy as you've been and you still found time to do that." Then it was one last peck and off to her room at the back of the house.

Then to Christopher, he said, "You figure out that hideabed? I've hardly ever used it."

"Comfy." Christopher raised his sandwich in salute. "Thanks."

Pruitt used the bathroom, then trundled off to bed.

The message light on his answering machine was blinking. He figured it was his father, whom he'd forgotten to call. He was surprised when it turned out to be Carl Pulkkinen, who said he was sorry to call on Thanksgiving but needed to talk to Pruitt regardless of the hour. He left his number.

Pruitt wonder what the heck could be so important that Willapa County's Prosecutor/Coroner would call like this.

"Gavin," Pulkkinen said. "How was your turkey day?"

The chattiness irritated him. "Carl, whatever this is, couldn't it have waited until tomorrow?"

"I didn't want to talk at the office. I took a call from the Governor's office. This morning, for chrissakes. Guy got all over me, Gavin. They don't think the investigation is moving fast enough."

"It's moving as fast as we can move it, Carl."

"They're willing to send some undercover officers down."

"Okay. I'm not against that. But I don't like the pressure."

"*You* don't like the pressure? They're not calling you on Thanksgiving!"

"No, but you are, Carl. And you're supposed to a colleague."

"This hippie-cop issue doesn't play well outside the county, Gavin. You've got to understand that."

"Goddamn it, Carl, how long my hair was twenty years ago is irrelevant to who I am now and my ability to solve this case."

"*I* know that. C'mon, I'm on your side."

"You're not *acting* like you're on my side. You don't *sound* like you're on my side."

"Look, Gavin, an undercover guy might get next to the pissed off logger we all know did this. So you need get them down here and get'em on the job, and get the bastard behind bars."

Pruitt held the handset away from his ear a moment. When he brought it back to reply he was barely able to control his anger. "Carl, are you telling me how to do my job?"

"I'm telling you to get Olympia off my back. I don't want to hear from them again—and that's on you." Then he hung up.

For a moment, Pruitt thought he might be able to crush the handset just by squeezing it in his hands. Up until this moment the only person who'd been able to get him this angry this quickly was his father. Sure, Pulkkinen could be dismissive, but Pruitt hadn't understood until now what a prick he could be. No wonder Lee Wilson took such pleasure in showing him up every chance he could. Get the *logger* that killed Carpenter? As if nobody else had motive? Pruitt knew, of course, that Pulkkinen had a bulldog reputation, and maybe that singularity of focus worked in a courtroom, with the investigation completed and the evidence lined up. But proper investigating itself was not built on preconceived notions and prejudices. An investigation had to go where the facts and evidence lead it.

What really stuck in Pruitt's throat was the point about getting a couple of undercover agents. It was actually a good one—Pruitt himself had considered it just the other day. But to get *ordered* to do it by a colleague? As the Coroner of Willapa County Pulkkinen may have been the only person with the legal authority to arrest the County Sheriff, but that didn't give him the right to talk to him like an underling. For that matter, nobody did. The heat was up all right—but from a totally unexpected source.

⊕

Pruitt slept in fits, which normally would have made him grumpy in the morning, but not with Olivia home. She greeted him in the kitchen with another peck on the cheek, bright-eyed and chipper, and he put yesterday's baby issues behind him, however temporarily. Time to get on with a new day. With a little adventure thrown in besides: canoeing down Little Noisy Creek. Get away from it all for a few hours.

And what a better way to kick a new day off than breakfast at the Torchlight, which, surprisingly, was brimming with business when they arrived at seven-thirty. What with the horde of press, environmentalists, and the curious gone for the weekend, Pruitt had expected the place half-empty. Yet more than just the numbers, it was the change in ambiance he noticed—no longer an invasion of strangers but rather a gathering of clans. Deservedly, the Torchlight had always been the Elkhorn's favorite restaurant. With the advent of the Black Bear Ridge controversy, it had become so, too, for the outsiders who, not knowing any better, had usurped the booths and seats regulars had taken for granted. Even knowing that the owners, Chuen and Loy Hsia, could do little about it, local people felt slighted. This morning, however, the turf lost to the besieging hordes was being reclaimed, an omen that once the issues were resolved things might get back to normal.

Fortunately, Marion Jones had already found a table, sparing them a wait. After waving the Pruitt entourage over, she and Olivia hugged. Christopher was introduced and he and Marion shook hands. Pruitt thought Marion was looking particularly great this morning. The gray that stood in contrast to the raven color of her hair was a little more pronounced— and sexy as hell as far as he was concerned. She was his friend, probably his best friend, and for the most part he'd put his sexual fantasies about her in the furthest reaches of his mind, yet especially when he hadn't seen her in a while her beauty amazed him. With her high cheekbones, hazel eyes, and straight, strong nose, it was a beauty age could never undermine but only complement.

Pruitt snapped open a menu, a smile tugging at his mouth. "Since we're not clamming," he said, "we can settle for second best, Torchlight clam fritters."

"If the oysters are fresh, I'll have this hangtown fry," Christopher said.

"The motto here," Pruitt said, "is that the oysters on your plate today slept in Willapa Bay last night."

Christopher flashed a grin at Olivia. "Let's hope they got the sand out their eyes."

His daughter laughed and touched Christopher's arm. As they exchanged meaningful looks, Marion cast a glance at Pruitt, raising her eyebrows—a gesture he ignored.

Breakfast, as usual, was excellent. Chuen and Loy served local seafoods, of course, but didn't stop there. They also used local eggs and dairy products, and recently had joined the coffee craze by switching from an institutional to a gourmet brand—of which Pruitt had three cups. Marion and Olivia chattered away, catching up on each other's lives. Like Molly, Marion was enchanted with Olivia's 60's retro look. "You've got to come over. We'll haul *all* my boxes out."

Olivia said, "You kept stuff?"

"Did I ever. You're looking at a *major* pack rat. Fringe leather, tie-dye, you name it." She winked at Pruitt. "I've got a Pigpen t-shirt from the 60's your dad's been hounding me about for years. How I ought to have it framed."

When the bill arrived, Pruitt swooped it up. "We'd better shake a tail feather. Before they saw down every Doug fir on Black Bear Ridge."

As they approached the cash register, Pat Crowley caught Pruitt's eye. They hadn't seen each other since Monday, when Carpenter's body had been found at Saginaw's logging show. Crowley was grinning, motioning him over to his table. Pruitt didn't like the looks of it.

He asked Olivia to take care of the bill, handing her the cash he'd taken from his wallet, then strode over to Crowley's table. "Pat?"

"Loved those pictures, Gavin. Can't wait to see what develops next."

Pruitt glared into the malevolent grin of the Saginaw manager for a moment before saying, "Screw you, Pat."

He walked away.

"Just what we needed, my friend," Pat called after him.

Olivia was getting the change back when Pruitt caught up to her. When they turned from the register Skip Ekrem was just bursting into the restaurant, all gangly legs and arms, like some wind-up toy designed to bounce off walls. He came to attention in front of Olivia, recognized who she was, whereupon a leer began to form on his lips, which wiped off quickly when he saw Pruitt standing behind her. He reached for what would have been the brim of his baseball cap had he not been wearing it backwards. "Nice to see you folks out and about."

He stumbled over to a counter stool, leaving a faint smell like fertilizer in his wake.

Out on the street, Olivia said, "Who was the bizzaro?"

"Local character," Pruitt said, though he was actually pleased with Skip, for having at least made an attempt to act civil. Maybe there was hope for him yet.

A horn blared and Pruitt looked over to see Tom MacKee flashing him the peace sign from inside his cherry red 1965 Mustang. He was grinning like an idiot and Pruitt ignored him. Everybody in town a dang comedian.

Addressing Christopher and Marion, Olivia said, "So typical. People judging you by your appearance. If you look a certain way, or in Daddy's case if you looked a certain way a long time ago, everybody assumes they know all about you. It's so unfair."

Immediately, Pruitt realize what he'd been wanting to say to Olivia and Christopher since they had showed up looking like 60's throwbacks: that even though issues might change, who you were inside would not, but don't feel sad about the passing of youthful idealism, because somehow or other—in ways Pruitt had yet to completely understand himself—as things changed they also remained the same. But before he could even clear his throat, Olivia had taken Christopher's arm and the two of them were walking off toward the car, oblivious to the grand moment before them, the wheel of life revealing its inner workings right here on an unremarkable street, only needing someone to point out that this now was also an echo of their past and a glimpse into their future. *Wake up to find out that you are the eyes of the world* is how the Dead said it.

Yet even as it had been flung open, Pruitt saw the window of their epiphany slam shut. Rather than the poignancy of a cosmic moment, Pruitt felt like stakes were being driven through his heart by the smile Olivia directed at Christopher, love in her eyes for the young man. Thank god for Marion, at his side taking his arm and smiling that inner-secret smile of her own, because surely he would have collapsed from the pangs of letting his daughter go.

When John Carpenter had moved to Willapa County to begin his work, conservative logging-rights activist Earl Ruddell immediately began hounding him, staking out his apartment, following him, writing everything down on a yellow note pad. Carpenter had visited the Sheriff's Department looking for a restraining order and been told he'd have to make a formal complaint. And that was it. Pruitt never heard from him again.

The canoe trip down Little Noisy Creek to show Christopher the Black Bear Ridge old growth offered a plausible explanation why. The Little Noisy ran alongside and sometimes onto the low-lying parts of the forest, and was the most logical way to get equipment in. Coming to it from any other direction would have meant an arduous hike. And feeding into the Little Noisy was a narrow rill that flowed very near to Olwen Friday's property. Pruitt surmised that Carpenter had eluded Ruddell's pursuit by ducking onto the property, using Olwen's secreted home as a staging area for his work. That Carpenter had colluded with his lover to avoid a right-wing whacko like Earl Ruddell was hardly suspicious;

that she'd said nothing to Pruitt about it may have been. Another talk with her was in order, but in the meantime it was always satisfying to tidy up loose ends.

The excursion also allowed Pruitt to get to know Christopher a little better, seeing him in an environment new to them both. He was a bright kid, thoughtful, and treated Olivia well—which was making it easier for Pruitt to let down his protective instincts, to allow Christopher into the pack.

Pruitt wanted to celebrate his burgeoning sense of comfort, and treated everyone to one of his favorite restaurants, The Dunes. Grandfathered around various shoreline protection acts, it sat magically on a North Beach berm line with the attendant view of the roiling breakers, hard sandy beach, and flocks of darting seabirds. After dinner, they picked up a bottle of champagne to take home. Pruitt felt some toasting was in order.

"Toast what?" Olivia asked.

Pruitt said, "General good vibes, I guess."

Olivia wrinkled her nose. "Good *vibes*, Daddy?"

Marion laughed. "Just goes to show that you can cut the hair off a Deadhead, but you can't cut the Deadhead out of Gavin."

Pruitt grinned. "Far out, man. That's just so…heavy."

About nine, Marion rose to say good-bye, she and Olivia hugging and making promises to write and have Marion come up to Tacoma. Shortly afterwards, Pruitt, too, gave Olivia a hug, then shambled off to bed, leaving her and Christopher on the hideabed sofa watching MTV.

As he removed his clothes, he considered calling his father, whom he'd forgotten to call now two days in a row— an oversight with potentially damaging repercussions. But it was entirely too late. If he wasn't already in the sack, Jack Pruitt would surely be in the bag. The morning was the best time to call. At nine AM a civil, even enjoyable conversation was possible.

Pruitt himself was so tired he didn't even pretend that he had energy left for his book and uncharacteristically left his reading lamp off. The last two days had exhausted him. Yet it was a good tired, and no sooner had he gotten his pillow punched up the way he liked it than he was fast asleep. Some time later, two or three in the morning he assumed, he heard what he thought was the sound of glass breaking. Was it part of a dream or was it Cleo, his cat, knocking something off the kitchen counter? If it had been Cleo, he'd sweep up the mess in the morning…Too damn tired to fuss about it now…The dream had been nice, maybe he could recover it…

The concussion that followed dispelled all dreams. It rocked the house to its foundation and propelled Pruitt from his bed like a springboard. He landed heavily on his left shoulder, grunted, and remained stunned there. For a moment he thought he might be on the verge of death. Then he felt his extremities moving as if on their own, his fingers wiggling, his legs folding up so he could turn over, willing himself up to his hands and knees. His holster and revolver had been shaken from the chest of drawers. He found his gun when he crawled right over it. He released the safety as he stood, pushed open his bedroom door. The short hallway between his and Olivia's bedrooms had already filled with a thick, acrid-smelling smoke. "Olivia!" he yelled at her door. "Are you alright!"

"Yes! Alright!" she yelled back. "What's happened!"

"Keep your door closed!"

In the living room. Pruitt couldn't see two feet through the haze, so got back on his hands and knees and crawled, blindly waving his free hand in front to find his way. He bumped into the hideabed sofa, whose mid section had been folded upward, the framework twisted and bent.

Ominously, Christopher was missing. Had he been thrown to the other side? Dread of the bloody mess that would greet him tightened Pruitt's chest as he made his away around. He found nothing but debris—glass and splinters of sash from the window through which the bomb had been thrown.

He yelled Christopher's name, but got no response. Had he stumbled out the back?

Still on the floor, Pruitt groped until he touched the front door knob. He undid the deadbolt and flung the door open. When the smoke began billowing out, he used it as a screen and tumbled across the porch, bumped down the three steps and sprawled prone onto the front lawn with his gun raised.

There was only a dark, empty street, and the indistinct sounds of a neighborhood waking.

"I called emergency!" It was Bill Logan, his next-door neighbor.

"You see anything?" Pruitt shouted.

"Nothin', Gavin. Just that godawful explosion. Those kids okay in there?"

"I can't find Christopher!"

Then he had an idea where Christopher might be.

He scrambled to his feet, scanned his pistol up and down the street one last time, then loped back into the smoke and stench. He was still in his pajama bottoms, and barefoot, and not a step or two back in his house he felt a stab of pain in his arch. He cursed loudly, and had to hop over to a chair, whose back he used to support himself while he pulled a shard of glass out of his foot, all the while choking on the noxious fumes that were thinning but not yet cleared. His foot bleeding like a stuck pig, Pruitt limped back to Olivia's room and opened the door. There they were, crouched under the window, which had been thrown open, Christopher covering her protectively. Olivia was wearing an old-fashioned fleece nightgown; Christopher wore only print boxers.

"Can we get up?" It was Christopher.

"They're gone, whoever they were," Pruitt said.

Olivia stood and rushed to him. He hugged her, patted her back. He looked back at Christopher. "You okay? You weren't out—"

At the same time, Christopher was saying, "We...I mean..."

"It's okay," Pruitt said. "I understand. Thank god."

"Daddy! You're bleeding. Christopher," she said, "grab a towel."

The fire trucks arrived shortly, and although there was no fire to put out, as a precaution and an exercise the volunteers hooked up the hoses anyway.

The ambulance arrived moments later, and the paramedic, Charlotte Vande Mark, went to work on the cut on Pruitt's insole, which wasn't nearly as bad as it looked. "Just a couple of stitches," she said. "Keep this bandaging on for a couple of days, it'll be as good as new."

Raphe Jones and Lee Wilson pulled up, their cruisers lurching to stops. They looked in on Pruitt, sitting now on the edge of the ambulance. He was beginning to feel distant and displaced—the aftermath of the shock and the post reaction to the adrenal dump that had bounced him out of his bed like a trampoline. Yet he did not lose sight of procedure. "Seal it off. See what's in there."

Once she was done with Pruitt, Vande Mark looked Christopher and Olivia over and pronounced them fine. They objected when Pruitt asked them to go to Marion's, but he insisted. This was police business now, he told them, please don't argue. Reluctantly, they drove off in a cloud of blue diesel smoke and the rattling sound of the Rabbit's engine.

The paramedics were through with him, so he moved to Raphe Jones' cruiser, sitting in the back with one leg hanging out the open door. Bill Logan brought over a wool blanket and wrapped it around Pruitt's shoulders, then came back a few moments later with a steaming cup of coffee. "Anything else, Gavin, I can do?"

"Bill, hey. This is greatly appreciated."

Logan gave Pruitt a pat on the shoulder, then had the good sense to fade away.

Deputies Wilson and Jones were back at the cruiser sooner than Pruitt would have expected—although he realized his sense of time had probably been skewed pretty badly.

"Got enough of this to know what it is," Wilson said. He held out a plastic evidence bag with what looked at first glance to be a length of bright orange-colored wire.

"I'm a little fuzzy, Lee. Can you give me a blow-by-blow?"

"Length of fuse. Judging from what I saw in there, I'd say somebody threw a half-stick of TNT through your window."

Pruitt rubbed his forehead. "Good lord."

"They fastened it to this with electrician's tape." He handed Pruitt another plastic evidence bag, this one containing a long nail. "It's a bridge-timber spike, the kind those eco-freaks use on trees. My first impression is the package rolled under that hideabed. This spike came right up from underneath."

Pruitt groaned. "They couldn't have been trying to kill Christopher."

"Not likely." Lee spat. "This late? Your lights out? Half a stick of shot? I'd say what they really meant to do was put a bad scare in you."

Lee looked back at the house. "Actually, because the bed and mattress took the brunt of it, the damage isn't so bad. You may find some odd damage in different parts of the house 'cause of the way a blast works—like water, looking for the path of least resistance—but your walls aren't buckled or anything. Hell, your TV tube didn't even blow out."

The deputies shifted their weights from one foot to the other, drill-like.

Pruitt said, "All right, it's time to call in some help."

Lee grimaced.

"We're not being weak, Lee, we're being practical."

Lee looked unconvinced.

"ATF needs to get called anyway," he said. "An explosive?"

"Not by the book they don't. This wasn't a big enough blast. Technically, this falls in the area of a prank."

"C'mon, Lee. A prank?"

Lee held up his hand. "Technically."

"You must know somebody at ATF, Lee. Anybody you feel comfortable with? Plus they've got their own labs. I could put in for a travel voucher and you could take your evidence to Portland."

Lee gazed off across the street. "Yeah, actually, I do know somebody I could work with."

"All right, good. Get hold of him tomorrow." Pruitt looked back at his house. "So a message was being sent."

"But by whom?" said Raphe Jones.

Lee held up the bag of evidence. "Any asshole with a rudimentary knowledge of shot could make a bomb like this. The trouble we got is there'll be no latent fingerprints, so we're stuck with having to suspect every asshole in the county."

CHAPTER ELEVEN

His house stank, so for what was left of the night, Pruitt took up Bill Logan's offer and slept fitfully on his neighbor's couch, covered in an afghan that smelled of mothballs.

Logan, a retired longshoreman, rose at dawn and padded through the living room on his way to the kitchen. At the doorwell, he paused. "Coffee, Gavin?" His bathrobe was threadbare and the vamps of his leather slippers had cracked into untold wrinkles.

Pruitt stripped off the afghan and sat up. "Whatever you're having, Bill."

"You're a young man," he said. "Probably don't need what I need to get your ticker goin' in the morning."

"After last night," he said, "I could use anything you've got."

Logan said, "You betcha," and went to make the coffee.

Pruitt rubbed his forehead, his cheekbones, his temples. He tugged the grit out of the corners of his eyes with a finger. He rolled his head slowly a couple of times to try and loosen his neck. His wrist was sore and he tried to twist the ache from that, too, without much luck. When he looked into the kitchen again Logan was at the sink filling up a glass carafe at the tap, his nearly hairless, yet substantial calves sticking out from under the worn bathrobe as sturdy as tree trunks. Carafe filled, he carried it to the coffee maker and disappeared from sight.

Pruitt pulled his jeans on and slipped into the pair of old basketball shoes he now used at home. The shoe going on the foot with the cut had to be tied loosely, and walking on it caused him a slight limp, though the pain wasn't as bad as the amount of blood he'd seen pouring from it the night before might have indicated. He folded the afghan in half and draped it over the back of the couch, then went to use the bathroom.

By the time he'd joined his host in the kitchen, an espresso machine was steaming away under a row of cupboard eaves.

"Whatcha makin' there, Bill?"

Logan said, "Something I call a Morning Thunderclap."

Pruitt leaned against a counter and watched as Logan took the fresh-brewed espresso and parceled it out into two mugs, then added a leveled teaspoon of instant coffee to one of them.

"Sure you can handle this, Sheriff?" Logan asked, a flash of devilry crossing his face.

Logan didn't smile much, and Pruitt was charmed. "By all means," he said.

Logan said, "You betcha'," then added instant coffee to the other mug. He stirred each vigorously, then turned to heft the carafe of drip-brewed coffee from the burner and fill each mug.

"You want some cream and sugar with that?" Bill asked.

Pruitt said, "How do you usually take yours?"

Logan grinned. "Usually with a shot of Irish Cream and two aspirin."

Pruitt chuckled. "Well, okay, my friend."

"The whole shee-bang?"

"Yes, sir."

Logan said, "You betcha'," and retrieved the bottle of Irish Cream from a lower cupboard, adding healthy splashes to each mug. Then he took a large plastic bottle from an upper cupboard and shook out two caplets of generic aspirin each.

Standing at the kitchen window, the men downed their pills with sips of coffee, which was strong but not bitter, the Irish Cream adding a nice body and sweetness. Pruitt couldn't remember having a drink this early in his life.

As if reading his mind, Bill Logan said, "I don't know how it is for you, but for me morning pain's the hardest to get rid of. The booze seems to loosen up my joints, kind of paves the way for the aspirin. After that, it's kind of worthless."

"You mean the booze?"

Logan nodded. "I don't want you gettin' the wrong impression, Gavin. I ain't no alky. This is my drink for the day."

"I watch it pretty closely, myself," said Pruitt. "You got alcohol in the family, you gotta. My dad, as I'm sure you know, can be a handful when he's been drinking."

Logan took a sip from his mug. "My dad never let a drop pass his lips," he said, "and he'd whip us kids something awful. I learned to fear him, but never liked him. He might have made me a good citizen, but I swore I'd never do to my kids what he did to me."

Pruitt had just learned more about his neighbor in about ten seconds than he had in the ten years he'd lived next to him. "You must've kept your promise, Bill. Your kids are over here all the time. And they seem to genuinely like you. From what I've seen."

"Never even raised my voice to them, Gavin. I just figured out other ways to teach'em what was right."

"I gave Olivia a whack on the butt once," Pruitt said. "Because she ran out into the street. It was the only time."

Bill took another sip.

"I've never had the opportunity to voice it before, Bill," Pruitt said, "but you've been a good neighbor."

"Feeling's mutual, Gavin," Bill said. "I've taken a lot of pleasure watching Olivia grow up into the fine young woman she's become."

Pruitt thanked him. "I suppose it's about time to consider going over there and seeing what's to be done."

Bill, of course, offered to help assess the damage and lend a hand however he could. "It's only this bum knee and bad back might preclude any heavy lifting I can do," he said. "It's not like my body's falling apart or anything."

⊕

By eight-thirty Marion, Olivia, and Christopher arrived. They formed into a loose knot at the front of the house and were taking stock of the outside damage when the first of what would become a cavalcade of vehicles happened by, slowing to parade speed, waving to Pruitt, who would wave back perfunctorily if they didn't flash him the peace sign. A smattering of press showed up, notably Michelle Parnell of the Elkhorn Echo and a stringer from nearby Riverton.

"You guys get a scoop," he told them, and delineated what little he knew. He was relieved not to have to deal immediately with the rest of the press corps, still at home enjoying football and their families, he hoped.

A few minutes later Molly Burkhalter drove up and parked in her usual spot.

Pruitt walked over to her as she got out of her Escort, hugged her and gave her a kiss.

She said, "If this isn't comfortable, I'm out of here, okay?" She had come dressed for work in an old sweatshirt and worn jeans, a pair of paint-spattered black high-top tennis shoes.

Pruitt said, "Why would I be uncomfortable with you here?"

She stood hip-shot, mock angry with him. "Because we said we needed some time apart to think things over, and it hasn't even been two days and here we are again."

Pruitt shrugged. "Well, it can't be helped. And, besides, you're going to want to keep using the float tank, regardless of what we decide to do."

Then Bill Logan was calling. There was work to be done, a lot of work. Pruitt would allow the bomber no public display of satisfaction, no slab of plywood thrown up over the broken window. The work would not stop until all signs of the bombing were gone. There would be nothing left to gloat over, nothing whatsoever.

While Bill gathered tools, and Olivia, Molly, and Christopher began cleaning, Pruitt and Marion drove to Hardware Sales for glass and sash and glazing. The store had been open only half-an-hour when they arrived, yet word of the bombing had already reached deep into the community. The shared sense of outrage was palpable. "Anything I can do," everyone said—staff, the smattering of customers. Pruitt knew that if he were to ask he could have had the whole town over at his house by noon—though he wouldn't. He didn't want an event created out of this, an importance that would make the bomber feel like his or her goal had been accomplished.

As he and Marion were walking out with the supplies, Pruitt saw somebody waving frantically at him from across the park whose south end Hardware Sales abutted. In the last of the morning's lingering ground fog he couldn't quite make out who it was and assumed it to be another well-wisher—until he recognized Angela. Apparently she'd been sitting on a bench near the logger's statue, which depicted three eras: turn-of-the-century, World War II and present day. As she moseyed toward them, she was smiling, waving in good cheer.

Marion said, "Who's this? The woman with the waterwheel?"

"College friend," he said. "From our alma mater."

"I'm flabbergasted I don't remember her," Marion said.

"She was gone before you arrived."

"Is this the wild one you've mentioned a few times?"

"The one and only."

"Gavin!" Angela called, maintaining her even, leisurely pace. "Good to see you!"

As she pulled up alongside him, Pruitt said, "Hey, Angela, how was your Thanksgiving?"

"You should have called me, you rat." She was again decked out in black: Danskin and tights, an outrageous leather jacket with metal studs and embroidery, and another pair of Doc Marten boots, studded to match the jacket.

"Angela, this is Marion Jones. Marion, this is Angela Caracitto."

When they shook hands, Angela said, "Charmed."

"Caracitto?" Marion said. "Editor of *The Earth Today*?"

"Not anymore," Angela said, "but it was a good run while it lasted."

"And you know Gavin? I wish he'd told me. I liked the work you did."

Angela said, "Thanks. Gav and me are old buds from the acid-dropping days." She winced nearly at the same moment as completing her sentence. "Geez. Gavin. Sorry. I'm not shitting you, I haven't been saying that stuff around town. "

"It's okay, Angela," he said, giving her a look that only almost forgave her. "I have no secrets from Marion."

Marion said, "Gavin said you went to the University of Washington, too?"

"Only for a couple of years," Angela said, "though I think I left my mark."

Pruitt snorted. "I would think. Meet Miss Hair Trigger, 1969. One word out of a police bullhorn, Angela's pulling a brick out of her purse."

"I'd do it again tomorrow, too," Angela said, "if I could get anybody who used to give a damn interested in something other than their house payments or how much tires for their Beemers cost."

Pruitt shot back his sleeve and glanced at his watch. "I'd love to stay and chat, but somebody threw a bomb in my house last night, and we've got some cleaning up to do."

Angela gaped. "Somebody frickin' bombed you, man? On top of getting shot at? Whoa, and I thought Chicago was rough."

Marion said, "You're welcome to join the work party, if you'd like."

⊕

Predictably, while Olivia and Christopher were smitten with Angela, Molly was guarded. In the kitchen, while Pruitt put some coffee on, she said, "I thought you said you'd lost touch with her?"

"I had. Completely. She just showed up in my office a few days ago."

"Saw you on CNN?"

"That plus she's somehow connected to John Carpenter's estate."

Molly said, "Weird."

"Yes, very." And then it was time to get back to the tasks at hand. While Pruitt and Marion set to work on the window, Angela went to rummage around in the storage shed attached to the garage for paints. Pruitt thought he had surpluses of both the siding and trim colors. When she rejoined them she was wearing a pair of Pruitt's bib overalls, but little else, her arms bare, her smooth white back criss-crossed with the overall straps. Though snug through the hips, even the slightest bend forward exposed a scandalous amount of breast.

Pruitt said, "I've got an old sweatshirt you could wear if you're cold."

Angela said, "Oh, don't bother. It's warm out today."

Pruitt knew if he were to press the issue he risked triggering a protracted argument on feminism—if a man can work bare-chested in bib overalls, so can a woman, by god—so he returned to chipping away the remaining glass shards and sash putty. As far as he was concerned, Angela could do her work buck naked; it was constituents, passers-by, and neighbors who would be scandalized. Bill Logan, for instance, who walked up with a snack of triangular-shaped deviled-ham sandwiches on white bread with yellow mustard and caught the sights availed him as Angela leaned forward off a step ladder to take a swipe at some smoke stains with her paint brush. Pruitt thought Bill might have a second coronary and drop the plate on the ground to boot.

When she saw Bill and the sandwiches, Angela said, "Out-a-sight, man!" She hopped down off the ladder. "I haven't had something like this since I was a kid." She helped herself. "So who are you, Gavin's dad?"

Bill Logan gripped the plate as if it was the only thing left holding him up. His mouth began forming words as if to explain who he was when Angela tried to get at an itch under one of the straps of the overalls and flashed a nipple.

She said, "Oops," and gave Bill a friendly wink as she tucked the little mouse nose back in again, fondly, like a pet in its nest, which left Logan speechless and his mouth agape— what they called in the sixties mind blown.

"What do you have there, Bill?"

It was Molly, standing behind him on the front steps. "Are those for everybody?"

Bill turned to the voice, dazed.

"C'mon in," Molly said, her voice smiling while her eyes cast daggers at Angela as if to say, *How could you do that to poor Bill?* Out loud, she said, "That's so thoughtful, Bill. The kids would love something to eat."

She held her hands out, encouraging him to take a step in her direction. Bill finally found his legs and headed shakily towards the front porch stairs.

"I've made some hot chocolate," she said to him. "Let me get you some."

Once Bill had been ferried inside, Angela said, "His color's kind of bad. Has he been sick?"

Pruitt said, "Any chance of reconsidering that sweatshirt?"

Angela plucked at the edge of the overalls where the nipple had made its break for freedom. "This freaked him out? Unbelievable," she said, "to think there's a place in this country where the sight these old pods can still stir things up." She winked at Pruitt. "But I'm not here to make trouble, Gav. Where do you keep that sweatshirt?"

CHAPTER TWELVE

Pruitt had purchased the original hideabed at Elkhorn Furniture five years earlier, and they had another like it on the display floor that Saturday. He charged it on his card. Adamant about getting everything back to normal, he asked for immediate delivery. The salesman, Randy Jacobson, told Pruitt they could load it into the van right that minute and haul it over to the house. The least he could do, he said.

By the time they arrived home, Angela was adding the finishing touches to the window frame. Bill Logan, watching from the front lawn, said, "Jeez, Angie, you did a great job there."

Angela grinned broadly, first at Bill, then at Pruitt. She flashed a grin at Molly, too, who had just come out to the porch. Molly did not smile back.

Randy Jacobson said, "You sure something happened here last night? That new paint's feathered in like you can't even tell where the old is."

Angela said, "Thanks. I don't know how many times I've started art school and dropped out."

In spite of the turmoil her presence had already caused and was apparently going to continue to cause in his life, Pruitt was especially pleased with Angela's work. The fourth estate would be sorely pressed to make much of the event now. Pretty wimpy bomb if everything got back to normal in less than half a day.

✪

About the time they got the hide-a-bed set up, Marion, Olivia and Christopher returned from Riverton, where they'd taken a truck load of debris to the refuse receiving station.

Pruitt sat on his new couch. "I'm right back, goddamnit."

Angela said, "This seems like a good time for pizza. Bill, you like pizza?"

He patted his stomach. "No pepperoni. But other than that, you betcha."

"Why don't I go with you?" Angela said. "You got wheels, right?"

Bill Logan smiled and said, "You betcha," and trundled off to fire up his Pinto.

Molly crossed her arms over her chest. "He seems to have taken to you," she said.

"Older men like him," said Angela, "working class and basically with sweet dispositions, aren't afraid of a woman with a few crazy ideas."

After searching her face for signs of sarcasm and finding none, Molly spoke in return with a kinder voice. "Tell Bill we'll meet at the Pizza Palace."

✪

Determination—to get the work done, to feel that control had been restored—had served everyone well that day. That night was a different matter. With no activities on which to focus their attention, determination turned into anxiety. After tossing in bed for a couple of hours, Pruitt got up to make some herbal tea only to find Olivia and Christopher already making a pot. Three o'clock found the three of them playing Scrabble at the kitchen alcove table.

During the course of the game, Olivia said, "I don't want to go back to school, Daddy. I should just take the rest of this semester off."

"For what it's costing me, hon, I'd rather you were up there knockin'em dead in those classes."

Yet Olivia would not be swayed. Even with the car packed and Christopher in the driver's seat, she talked of staying.

"It would make me feel better if you weren't around here right now," Pruitt told her. "You know?"

"But that's why I'm worried. It's getting crazy."

"Honey, if you're not around, nobody can do anything to you to try and hurt me. You see?"

She thought about that, but then said, "What about your foot? Maybe you should get a tetanus shot."

Pruitt assured her he would have Marion tend to it. "Really," he said, "this is nothing. Remember swimming out on the South Fork when you were in junior high school? You stepped on that broken bottle while you were wading? I'll bet there's still a little scar on your sole."

Olivia sighed. "A scar on my sole. Right. Is that another quote from a Dead song?" She kissed him. "Okay, Daddy." Then she joined Christopher in the Rabbit.

No sooner had they turned the corner and were out of sight than Pruitt breathed a sigh of relief. He sorely wanted his daughter out of Elkhorn right now, safe and sound in some anonymous dorm in Tacoma.

He loped gingerly to his garage. He'd earned a float. Lord knew he needed one. The tricky part was keeping the salts off his wound. He accomplished it by wrapping his foot in a produce bag and securing it with tape just above his ankle. A plastic-encased foot felt odd, but once he was on his back and buoyant, he forgot about it.

What he remembered after his float was the call he owed his father. It was nearly five o'clock, an edgy time of day as far as communicating effectively with his old man, who'd assuredly had a few beers during the football games. Yet it was also early enough he might not have pulled the Stoli from the freezer. It could go either way, but Pruitt chanced it and phoned him—if he put it off any longer it wouldn't have made any difference if his father had been drinking or not, he'd read Pruitt the riot act for ignoring him.

"Gavin," his father said, "why didn't you call back?"

Jack Pruitt's tone was one that usually got his son's dander up—which would get them nowhere fast. Pruitt said, "You can't believe what's come down around here." Then he began delineating his woes and disasters, quickly so his father couldn't get a word in edgewise.

His father had always been his best with his children in times of crises and he was solicitous, telling Pruitt that his call had been no big deal, he'd only wanted to touch base with him before heading off to Pruitt's stepmother's side of the family for turkey day.

"I've misplaced Olivia's new address, too. You got that handy?"

Pruitt kept his book near the phone and they exchanged the information, then groused about the Seahawks' continuing offensive woes—even in their recent upset of Denver, it had been the defense that had scored the two touchdowns.

When it was time to ring-off, Pruitt said, "Love you, Dad."

"We love you, too," his father said, who always referenced love in the third person, even during that period of time between the divorce and remarrying when he had nobody else in the house to refer to.

Yet Pruitt let that quirk go. As he placed the receiver in the cradle, he was thinking only of how proud he was of them both for doing so well by each other this time around.

⊕

At his desk Monday morning he found a stack of requests to look at John Carpenter's files. They'd come from a variety of parties: environmental groups, private timber companies, the

Washington State Department of Natural Resources, the U.S. Forest Service, the Japanese lumber industry coalition.

Pruitt had a problem. Carpenter's data held more than just the potential key to a murder investigation, it possibly held sway over the sale of the timber on Black Bear Ridge, how much timber could be cut, how much would remain in its natural state. Many millions of dollars were at stake.

No way was he going to get mixed up in those politics; the politics dogging him already were politics enough—just the thought of the Prosecutor's Thanksgiving call roiled his stomach. Yes, he was going to make that call to the State Patrol for the undercover agents but, no, he wasn't calling for the cavalry. Instead he asked his secretary in.

"Joyce, let's do up a memo, send it to all these parties interested in John Carpenter's data. Have it say, in so many words, that even if I find the Black Bear Ridge files, I don't have to share homicide information with anybody other than who I'm told I have to share it with. If they want to see what Carpenter's got, go fight it out in court."

Joyce smiled. "You're going to disappoint a lot of high-rollers."

"Better them," he said, "than the people who vote for me."

⊕

After Joyce left, Pruitt uncharacteristically shut his door. He needed a few moments of solitude. His temporary office mates were out in the field and he had the office to himself. He was absent-mindedly gazing at his Grateful Dead skull and lightning bolt coffee cup. Affectionately known as *Steal Your Face*, it was a brilliant little logo originally designed as a stencil to mark the band's equipment cases. Then he looked out his window. His was the only office in this section of the courthouse complex with a legitimate view—albeit a narrow one, framed to the north by the south wall of the main building and to the south by a copse of beech and red alder. He watched gray clouds pass over the river and tideflats, splattering Elkhorn with a cold stinging rain. The day was approaching its apex, yet the light was dim as dusk.

Some son-of-a-bitch had shot at him.

Some son-of-a-bitch had thrown a bomb into his house.

Some son-of-a-bitch might have hurt his *daughter*!

His outrage was so immediate, and so profound, Pruitt started shaking. He put his coffee cup down, and placed his head in his hands and rubbed his forehead, his eyes.

He stood and grabbed his hat from the rack, and on his way out announced to Joyce that, no, he hadn't gotten to the paperwork but he'd do so later in the afternoon—promise—and in the meantime just take messages…Oh, and if anybody gave her any flak about not getting the reports they were asking for, to be as nice as she felt like being to them or, if she didn't feel like being nice, be nasty, he'd back her up either way.

So far, the John Carpenter case appeared outwardly simple—motive, for instance, having to do with logging or not logging Black Bear Ridge. The most inexplicable part of the case was Olwen Friday. Through all the holiday's craziness he'd thought about her quite a bit, yet he'd been unable to get a fix on her. She was elusive, mysterious—which of course drew him to her like solder to flux.

As he drove out the east end of the county, he caught himself checking his rearview mirror far more often than he usually did. Was the shooter and bomber the same person? How much surveillance could one person do? Could this whole thing be the work of a crew or gang? Yet whether they wanted Black Bear Ridge cut or saved, how would harassing the sheriff make a difference? Maybe this had nothing to do with timber. Could it be a personal vendetta? Some recidivist with a Pruitt grudge?

Back out in East Willapa he recanvassed the neighbors, pushing more strongly through the pleasantries—the cookies, the coffee—and got through in half the time with twice the information. Among other things, Olwen Friday bartered both her construction skills and garden crops—her herbs, one woman said, were the best around. Besides her jewelry sales at The Spartan, she also packed cedar shakes at tiny operations set up in barns and performed a variety of odd jobs.

The mounting details provided Pruitt a sturdy assessment of Olwen Friday's life: vibrant, organic, bohemian. Olwen herself competent, independent, strong-willed. Summed, Olwen presence in the here and now was powerful and eccentric. Yet he was also struck by what he could not find out, and that was anything about her past, anything about her family or education. Not only had she hidden her physical self from people, she had hidden her history. Hidden herself very well indeed. Even on his second time back, he missed the turn that led to her home and had to reconnoiter.

Trudging up her path, he felt the cold blue eyes of the frog atop the garret tracking his every step. When she came to the door, Olwen looked much as she had the first time Pruitt had met her, a collision of hippie, health faddist, and gypsy. The medley of scarves, blouses and shirts had changed, but the overall effect remained.

"You're going to beat that path down," she said. "Then Amway's going to be pounding on my door."

It spite of himself, Pruitt chuckled. She had a great understated smile. And eyes you could practically dive into.

He had to glance away, remind himself what he was doing out here. "That bit of a rill running across your property," he said, "was that where John portaged his equipment onto Black Bear Ridge?"

"Some kook was following him. John was concerned."

"We've collected everything from his apartment. Did he leave anything with you?"

"Some clothes," she said. "Do you want them?"

"I probably should," he said. "Run some forensics on them."

"Give me a minute." She closed the door, gently. When she came back out again she was wearing an overcoat of gray and black weave—drab in contrast to the radiant attire she wore beneath it. She handed Pruitt a short stack of men's clothing—jeans, white tee-shirts, a Pendleton shirt, and a pair of socks.

"That's it?"

"Everything," she said.

From the table by the door, she picked up a ceramic bowl with yellow meal in it.

"I need to feed my fish," she said. She strode passed Pruitt, who followed.

As they walked, he said, "I've heard you built all this."

"You did? Who from?"

"Moseley Brainard."

"Mose," she said, "helped me with the cement." She glanced back at him. "Talked to all my friends, did you?"

"I wished I'd found Moseley first. He's the only person who actually knew where you lived."

She led him to the middle of the short, arched wooden bridge spanning the shortest distances of the loosely figure-eight shaped pond. On the other side of the bridge a flagstoned walkway led to the burbling waterwheel.

Olwen dug into the bowl of meal with her fingers. Pruitt noted she had lovely hands, hands that seemed more suited to playing piano than packing shakes. A school of mottled carp—orange, white and black—had already congregated beneath them. As the yellow meal alit softly on the water's surface, her charges began snapping—both at the meal and each other, reestablishing their pecking order.

There was a lull in the rain, although with the water dripping off the surrounding trees the sound of rain continued, as if where they stood was sheltered even as the ominous gray sky towered above them, the subdued light easy on the eyes if not demanding, occasionally, of the soul.

Pruitt leaned against the bridge railing, looking back over her holdings.

"This is really something, Olwen. What you've got here. I've never been in a place more peaceful. It's amazing what you've built. I'm not kidding, I've never seen better quality work, and we've got some talented craftsmen in this county. But it's more than that. It's the sum of the parts." He thought a moment. "*Show me something built to last,*" he said, quoting from the title song of the Dead's last studio album. "*Or something built to try.*"

After another moment passed, Olwen said, "You're not really a hardass, are you? I mean, for a cop."

"I'm a hardass when I have to be," he said, turning to her. "*You're* not going to be a hardass, are you?"

She said, "No," but sounded sad about it. "I'm just thinking I might have to protect myself."

Pruitt said, "Protect yourself from whom?"

"John was killed, wasn't he?"

"Unless you know something that the killer thought was important—something John told you, for instance, that would have an impact on the sale of the Black Bear Ridge timber—I don't see why they'd want to come after you."

"In other words, I don't know if I should be concerned about protecting myself or not."

Pruitt pushed himself away from the bridge railing. "If you've got a concern, now is the time to share it with me."

"I've just a sense, is all. Nothing concrete."

"Tell me anyway. Don't worry about how crazy it may seem."

She considered it, her brow furrowing. "Can't yet," she said.

He let a beat pass. "Now you *are* being a hardass."

"No, I'm not. I'm protecting myself."

"From whom?"

She turned from him and began walking back to her house. "Have it your way, then. I'm being a hardass."

CHAPTER THIRTEEN

The next morning Pruitt was up before his alarm. Unable to sleep any longer, he decided to go into work early. Sometime during the night a cold snap had descended on the county and his house was freezing—but thank God it was small. The forced-air gas furnace in the half basement heated it up quickly.

Outside, the usual morning fog was freezing as well, and nipped at Pruitt's nose as he closed the back door. He pulled the lapels of his jacket up around the nape of his neck, then noticed that Bill Logan's kitchen light was on, Bill himself standing at the window, probably firing up all his coffee apparatuses. In the cold and gloom of pre-dawn, a mug of Bill's strong coffee—minus the Irish Cream this time— sounded very good, and Pruitt decided to be bold and see if his neighbor would appreciate an early visitor. He vaulted the low picket fence that separated their properties, mindful of the narrow strip of flower beds on either side, then strode up to Bill's back door and knocked.

If Bill was surprised to see Pruitt he didn't show it. "Sheriff," he said, and left the door open for him as he turned back into his kitchen.

Pruitt said, "Saw you were up."

"Glad you did."

"Going in early today," Pruitt said. "Thought one of those Morning Thunderclaps might be just the thing."

"Working one up as we speak."

"Hey, everybody." It was Angela Caracitto, fisting the sleep out of her eyes. "Do you guys *all* get up at the crack of dawn around here?"

She stood under the kitchen door jamb wrapped in a blanket, apparently naked underneath.

Pruitt was not pleased.

"Did you want the whole shee-bang this morning, Gavin?"

It was Bill, trying vainly to suppress that look of devilry Pruitt had seen for the first time two days ago.

"No, I guess just the coffee this time."

"What're you cooking up, lover?" Angela walked over to Bill and ran her hand up and down his back.

Pruitt said, "Look, you've got to start another shot of espresso if you're going to make three. Why don't I just drop by another time."

Bill said, "It's no problem."

Angela said, "We're in no hurry." She smiled at Bill, who smiled back. She smiled at Pruitt, who made a point of frowning.

"My honey's retired," she said. "We can do any damn thing we want today." Her hand that had been perched on his shoulder dropped suddenly to take an Angela-sized handful of Bill Logan's retired longshoreman's buns. "Can't we, sweetie?"

Bill smiled at her. "You betcha, Angie. Any damn thing we want."

Thankfully, before he said something angry, Pruitt's beeper went off. "Gotta get this," he said, and beat a hasty retreat from Bill Logan's kitchen.

⊛

Though he was only fifteen minutes from the office, Pruitt called in on his cellular phone. Maybe there was something in the field he'd need to do before coming in. "What's up, Ed?"

"There's been a break-through, Sheriff. Lee wanted you to know right away."

A few minutes later, Pruitt and Lee Wilson were conferencing in Pruitt's office. "How did you know to look for it in Earl's truck?"

Lee, his feet up on a desk, said, "Got us a phone call while you were out yesterday afternoon."

"You got a judge to go for a search warrant on a phone call?"

"Didn't call a judge. Just went over there and asked Earl if I could take a look around."

"Earl let you do that?" Pruitt was more than a little disbelieving.

"'If it'll make you feel better, Lee,' he said, 'you can look through my dirty laundry as well.'" Wilson cackled. "Should've seen the look on his face when I came back this morning to arrest him."

Pruitt sat down and whistled. "The length of wood used to hit the back of Carpenter's head."

Lee Wilson said, "Ain't it great?"

"We don't have an official blood sample yet."

"We worked it up last night," Lee said. "It's the same."

Though unofficial, Lee and a young doctor at the Willapa Harbor Hospital just as fascinated with forensics had never been wrong in the past.

"The tipster, what did he say exactly?"

"That Earl had been acting odd of late. Sneaking around in the middle of the night."

Pruitt snorted. "Gotta be a neighbor."

"Be good to flush them out," Wilson said.

"It bothers me," Pruitt said, "that he let you go fishing without a warrant."

"Earl's got an ego the size of a whale."

Pruitt agreed. Earl was intelligent, but also full of himself, enough so that he might do something absurdly stupid.

"He have an alibi?"

"Said he was home; his wife says so, too."

"In that case," Pruitt said, "we're going to need corroborative evidence to link him to Carpenter: hair samples on his clothes, blood spots on the seat of his truck. Collect his coats, hunting vests, anything he might not have thought to wash. We need the tire track patterns at the shooting site to match the patterns on the tires of Earl's truck. We need everything we can get our hands on to bust their story."

Lee cracked a grin. "We can do that," he said, "or we just sweat a confession out of him."

Pruitt chuckled. It wasn't often Lee made him laugh. "That, my friend, would save the tax-payers a whole lot of money."

⊕

One of the first things Earl Ruddell said was, "I didn't kill anybody."

Of course not. It was the first rule of investigation: everybody lies, and the nearer you got to the truth, the bigger and more adamantly told the lies became. The gaze more earnest. The ability to stare you down more enhanced.

"How'd that hunk of wood get in your truck, Earl?"

The fluorescent tube lighting reflected off the pale green walls of the windowless interrogation room and cast a sickly glow over everything, but it was particularly unflattering to Earl.

"You think I'm that stupid to leave something like that lying around my truck?" Earl said.

"A lot of things to think about when you're out murdering a man on a logging show, Earl. I mean, why'd you hit him with it anyway? He was already dead. Or didn't you know that?"

"I didn't hit anybody with any piece of wood."

"Yet there it was in your truck, just waiting to be found."

"They're setting me up," he said. "It's as clear as day."

"Okay. That's fair. Who's setting you up?"

"The watermelons," he said, meaning environmentalists—green on the outside and red as commies in the middle. "And, of course, the eastern Jewish media moguls bankrolling their entire operation."

A well-groomed, handsome, and soft-spoken man, Earl looked more like a community college English teacher than an unemployed logger. Part of what made his vituperative rhetoric work so well was that he couched it in proper manners and decorum. "They killed Carpenter," he said, "and now are trying to make it look like I did it."

"Why would the environmentalists kill Carpenter, Earl?" With a pencil, Pruitt was tapping out an irregular beat on the plain, metal desk.

"Reverse espionage. Make the loggers and timber companies look bad. Or maybe they didn't like what he'd found, that there was nothing keeping it from getting logged. They couldn't allow *that*, could they? And they got just the man to do the dirty work, too. David Spoor. Ex-Marine who at one time worked the woods."

Pruitt said, "How would the environmentalists know what Carpenter had?"

"Collusion, of course. They're all in this together."

Pruitt smiled. "Why would they kill him," he said, "if they were already colluding with him?"

If he'd been a fish, Earl would have wriggled on the line. Instead, he forced his face to go blank. "I'll talk no more to you," he said. "The conspiracy reaches right down to the grassroots. I feel sorry for people like you." He scowled. "I'm going to be watching my back better next time, I can tell you that."

"Earl," Pruitt said, "if I don't start hearing some better stories than ones you're cooking up right now, there won't be any next time."

☮

The interview with Earl didn't get any better, and finally Pruitt handed him over to the jailer. They would hold him as long as they could, but until the official word on the blood sample came back, that wouldn't be long.

Later that afternoon, Lee Wilson was back in Pruitt's office with an update. "All frickin' day I been out there," he said, "and I can't find one scrap of corroborative circumstantial evidence."

Pruitt said, "There's got to be something. A perpetrator leaves something, takes something away. Like you always say: it's a forensics law of nature."

"Other than that hunk of wood, there is nothing. Nada. Nil. Earl's saying it was planted, and with his wife supplying an alibi, he's got a case."

Pruitt rubbed his forehead. "I talked to the Prosecutor. Carl said if it came down to the wood versus Laura's alibi, Earl walks."

Wilson scuffed at the floor. "We're going to have to cut bait."

"We'll have to give up some line, that's all. He still looks good for it."

"How're you spinning it for the press?"

"Person of interest. Which should back them off a little."

Wearily, Lee stood. "Gimme a day. There's got to be *something* out there."

Once Lee had left, Pruitt caught up on some paperwork, including some forms related to the child abuse case he'd been investigating before Carpenter's murder had taken precedent over everything else. Child Protective Services had the boy tucked away; the family wanted him back—even though it had been a family member who'd abused him. It might be heading for trial; it could equally have been pretrial posturing. He sighed as he affixed his signature to the affidavits. Regardless of which direction the legalities went, he prayed the poor boy would find a good therapist, that the scarring was not permanent, that it wasn't too late for him to have a good life.

Then he found himself momentarily idle—at which point he thought of Olwen Friday. With the Earl Ruddell situation not panning out the way he had hoped, it was back to square one: Olwen and what she might be hiding. The first thing he thought to do was some basic background checks—utility and telephone bills, for instance. But obviously, he hadn't been thinking too clearly. Olwen Friday had no phone, no electricity, no running water, no lines or pipes or cables of any sort, nothing whatsoever connecting her to the fabric of society in ways most people were. Seriously "off the grid." All she had was her land, a thought that brought Pruitt to his feet.

"Be next door," he told Joyce. "Back in a flash."

A covered breezeway ran between the Sheriff's Department and the courthouse, Pruitt trotting through the ice cold wind. He'd heard that with computers people could sometimes find information without ever leaving their desks. What a convenience *that* would be on a day like this. It was closing in on 1995, for criminey sakes. He wondered how long the county could keep putting off buying a computer.

But it was warm inside the courthouse, so he let go of all that and walked briskly down the corridor leading to the lobby, then bounded the stairs to the second floor and the Assessor's Office. The trouble was the deed only told him Olwen didn't own the land she lived on—which surprised him. J. Michael MacClinton owned the land—which both did and didn't. MacClinton, a private timber company operator and life-long resident of nearby Riverton, owned only slightly less Willapa County land then the monolithic Saginaw Corporation he rivaled. Ironically, over the past thirty years the fiercely independent MacClinton had purchased thousands of acres of timber from Bernard Henry Hickson, the old Black Bear Ridge eccentric, a fierce independent from an earlier time.

What was Olwen Friday doing living on land owned by J. Michael MacClinton? Surely not renting or leasing it. Why would a big-time player like MacClinton bother with a small potatoes deal like that? Buying and selling huge parcels of land was his style, not renting a few dozen to some hippie woman.

The thought that MacClinton was having an affair with Olwen Friday was only fleeting. By local standards, MacClinton was a celebrity, and if he'd been within twenty miles of Olwen the whole of East Willapa would have known about it.

Olwen's house sat amidst an arm of second-growth timber, primed for logging within the decade—what would be the point of building on land you didn't own? He considered that she might have squatted the land originally, then let things get out of hand from there. In the last number of years squatting had become fairly common in the county, a rural response to homelessness. Pull a trailer or RV onto some land, dig an outhouse hole, stay until told to move along, do again somewhere else—though rarely was anything larger than an outhouse built, and never anything like Olwen's house.

Yet it was all speculation until he could nail down some facts, which maybe J. Michael MacClinton could supply. He made a call to Riverton to see if he could arrange a meeting, and maybe his luck was changing. MacClinton was available, which Pruitt took as a good omen, a chance he might move this case along some. There were even a few minutes to go home and have a bite to eat before he dashed off. From his freezer he took a serving of red beans and rice—which he made in large quantities to parcel out for quick meals—and stuck it in the microwave. While lunch was heating, somebody knocked on his back door. Pruitt ducked to looked under the cafe curtains on the kitchen door window and guess who: Angela.

He confronted her on the stoop. "You've got some nerve," he said. "My neighbor, for chrissakes. Don't you know he's got a bad heart?"

"If he's got a bad heart," she said, "it hasn't affected the rest of him."

"Goddamnit, that's just the attitude I'm talking about."

"Back off, Gavin, and let me in, willya." She hugged herself. "It's cold as hell out here."

He made way for her.

In the kitchen, she turned to him. "We're going to Chicago."

"You and Bill? Are you nuts?"

"He wants to go to some blues clubs."

"Bill Logan wants to go to a Chicago blues club? A *blues* club!?"

She crossed her arms, still chilly. "You don't really know the guy very well, do you? He used to play trumpet in a Dixieland band. Did you know that? He's even got a recording of them. He wasn't half bad. And he listens well and has soft hands. By my standards, those are solid credentials in a lover."

Pruitt said, "It's just so...Out of the ordinary. Showing up here after all these years, parading around in wild get-ups, balling my next-door neighbor. You're up to something, and I don't like what I think it is."

Angela grinned. "Would you expect anything less of me?"

"No more crap, Angela. What about John Carpenter? Didn't you come out here to take care of his body, or was that all malarkey?"

"The body's gone, in case you hadn't noticed."

"Of course I noticed. I'm talking about why you're still here. Don't you need to get back and attend to his services?"

"That can wait," she said, "until a few things get resolved." Angela, too, had lost all interest in trying to keep things chatty.

Pruitt said, "If you're dogging me on this murder investigation, the friendship's off."

Angela said, "Someone has to pay for this."

"Somebody will, but that's *my* job, not yours."

"Nothing's happening, man. I'm not leaving until something does."

Here it was again, full blown, the dangerousness in Angela that had ultimately caused him to shy away from her. Physically fearless, sometimes she would do something crazy—throw a brick, yell an obscenity—rather than wait for something to happen. She'd once been Pruitt's lover, and until now he'd always thought of her fondly. But he also knew her as a reckless agent provocateur—not the kind of person he needed in the middle of a murder investigation.

Though he wasn't about to back down. "What's between me and you is one thing, Angela, but dragging Bill into all of this isn't fair."

Angela stood her ground. "Even if I was dragging Bill into something, Gavin—which I am *not*—I don't think he's feeling unrewarded."

CHAPTER FOURTEEN

J. Michael "Mac" MacClinton lived in Riverton, a city of some 45,000 in nearby Gray's River County. When Pruitt called MacClinton Logging headquarters earlier, he'd been told Mac worked at home, but that, yes, he could drop by; as a general rule, Mac accepted visitors. The secretary gave him an address that Pruitt recognized as along the so-called "Miracle Mile," a towering ridge where some of the wealthiest timber barons in the Northwest had built magnificent estates. Pruitt thought it a fittingly feudal location for Riverton's elite, scanning from on high the flat, marshy floodplain between riverbank and cliff where the mill hands, loggers and longshoremen whose toil had provided the loot to build the palaces that oversaw them lived in gritty, blue-collar neighborhoods.

He turned onto the east end of Elm Street, a former logging road that led up to the ridge, nicknamed the Grapevine for its twisting switchbacks, treacherous but exquisitely manicured, the clipped and pampered rhododendrons and azaleas bearing testament to the different sort of life lived on high. Boom and bust may have played the rest of Riverton like Satan's yo-yo, but up on the ridge old money held the devil at bay.

Pruitt had bumped into Riverton's monied class before, and he didn't care for their airs, the jaunts to Europe, the private schools, the way life centered not within the city but at the Gray's River Country Club—which they guarded from outsiders more vigorously than their own homes. They were especially guarded toward upstart flatlanders like J. Michael MacClinton, the son of a green chain puller, a "swamp rat" in local parlance, born into the mill fodder class, expected to work hard when the work was there and take his place in the unemployment queue when it wasn't.

That he wouldn't accept such a fate was the beginning of MacClinton's myth. When he returned to Riverton after a stint in Korea, he sunk every dime he could beg, borrow, or steal into a tumbled-down shake mill operating in the back shadow of the vast Saginaw holdings on the Gray's River waterfront. A shrewd businessman, before long he owned a number of mills, then parlayed the lot into a deal for one of the largest. As one savvy maneuver followed another, Mac became as rich as any "Miler," the sole owner of MacClinton Mills and MacClinton Logging.

Rich, maybe, but still not welcome by the old money, and especially not in the Gray's River Country Club, where the thinking went that once a swamp rat always a swamp rat. Exorbitant fees, it turned out, were but a trifling formality when it came to membership. In arcane language that could be fully appreciated only by scholars of middle English were regulations that said while money was important, a member foremost had to have breeding.

Eventually, though, money did talk—loudly through a number of high-priced lawyers—and Mac got admitted. Yet admittance did not translate into acceptance. He might have won the right to walk into the bar, but his social standing remained a half dozen rungs below that of a bathroom attendant.

Then Mac delivered a startling coup by offering the club a magnificent bronze statue to be sculpted by a popular local artist. Mac also hired a top Seattle advertising firm to present the drawings and mock-ups to the committee in charge of art acquisitions, an afternoon deemed an event in itself. Duly impressed—overwhelmed, even—by Mac's generosity and good sportsmanship, all was forgiven. Like wildfire the scuttlebutt spread that Mac, while of low birth, had been imbued—miraculously—with a mettle of highest repute. On recommendation of the committee, the Gray's River County Club Board of Trustees accepted the prized work of art and, in a show of its *own* generosity and good sportsmanship, decided to feature it prominently between the clubhouse and first tee, elevating the statue to the position of centerpiece in an already lauded demesne.

The statue's unveiling became Gray's River Country Club's cultural event of the season—probably of the decade. No expense was spared: the red carpet rolled out, the finest china laid, a sumptuous banquet prepared. An entire row had been dedicated to seafood alone—shrimp, crab, oysters, the works—all because Mac had mentioned casually that seafood was his favorite. The event was radiant and proceeding without a hitch until a somewhat tipsy art critic, speaking loud enough for all to hear, said, "Hey, that looks like J. Michael himself."

And so it did, Mac having modeled for it. The artist captured splendidly Mac's infamous grin—a marvelous combination of arrogance, cunning, and wicked sense of humor. The acceptance committee, to a man, paled. The drawings and mock-ups had carefully misdirected the eye from the face, emphasizing instead the graceful sweep of arms and perfectly squared hips.

By then, of course, proceedings were too far along to circumvent, and removing the statue at any time after would have set the art media to howling, and so Riverton's elite had to grit down on their silver spoons and live with Mac's sneering visage ever since. As for the afternoon of his exaltation, Mac held court for the press, smoked expensive cigars, put away a quart of the club's best French brandy, and completely ignored the seafood table. "Bunch of (expletive deleted) water roaches," he'd been quoted as referring to the jumbo tiger prawns. It was also the last time he set foot in the Gray's River Country Club.

Similar stories about J. Michael MacClinton seemed to crop up every year, and whether even half of them were true really didn't matter to Pruitt. He was tickled at this opportunity to meet him, approaching his home now, which was, like most on the ridge, hidden from the idly curious by a fence, over the top of which could be seen the shake roofing of a spread as palatial as any. The wrought-iron entrance gate was open.

Pruitt parked on a wide, washed-concrete carport that served a four-car garage. One of the bays was open, a gleaming 1956 Chevy Bel Air visible, baby blue with mag wheels and ornate pinstriping. Seeing it made Pruitt chuckle, envisioning Mac driving it down to the flats where he still turned up occasionally in one of blue-collar taverns to hoist a schooner with the regulars.

The door to MacClinton's house stood at least ten feet tall and was a work of art in itself—hand carved rosettes, fluting. It looked as if it had cost as much as Pruitt's whole house. Yet knocking on it did not produce the booming cannonade Pruitt was expecting. Rather, a rich thump brought the squelching of soft-soled shoes on a hard-surfaced floor. If he'd come to this estate not knowing who lived there, Pruitt might have expected a liveried butler to answer the door, rather than MacClinton himself. Clad in a collarless white cotton shirt, jeans, and penny loafers, the maverick timber baron said, "You're not a local cop, are you? You don't look familiar."

Pruitt removed his hat and introduced himself. "From Willapa County, sir."

"No 'sir' crap around here, Pruitt. Call me Mac."

He extended his hand. As Pruitt expected, the grip was firm. MacClinton stood about five-ten. His dark hair was graying, but he still had most of it, the style blow-dried James Dean. "You've obviously got something on your mind," he said. "Why don't you come on in."

"That's gracious, Mac. I appreciate it."

Pruitt followed his host across a spacious foyer tiled in Italian marble, whorled in shades of green. Overhead was a railed loft where the gleaming edge of a hardwood pool table could be seen, the smell of cue chalk faint in the air. The foyer featured paintings of forest scenes—beautifully rendered. The wainscoting was done in dark woods; the Victorian-styled wallpaper complemented the tile exquisitely.

After the magnificence of the foyer, Pruitt was expecting to be led to a vaulted drawing room, but was surprised and delighted to find himself in the kitchen, which was ample without being ostentatious and where the green and natural wood theme of the foyer carried on in quieter tones, the green subdued, the wood light—possibly maple. A modest living room adjoined the kitchen, sunk one step, the furnishings comfortable, usable. A blaze crackled in the fireplace. The accommodation exuded a warmth that spoke of Mac's heart as clearly as the foyer had spoken of his riches.

MacClinton said, "I was just cracking some crab. You care for some?"

Pruitt caught a glimpse of the ruddy points of boiled Dungeness crab legs peeking over the edge of the sink.

"Crab?" Pruitt said. "But I'd heard—"

"The famous water roaches quote?" MacClinton grinned. "It's one of my favorites. Those country clubbers? Not as smart as they'd like you to think. MBAs be damned, those people rarely see the big picture." He chuckled. "And now every tee-off, I'm on their asses. I've heard they try not to look back at me, but I know they're scared shitless what I might have planned for'em next."

Pruitt smiled back. "I don't want to be any trouble."

"I'm going to crack that crab regardless, and there's plenty. We can crack this crab and you can ask me whatever questions you came up here to ask. C'mon, Sheriff, don't be shy. Got an apron here, too."

They worked on either side of the double stainless steel sink, cracking the crab and shucking the meat into porcelain bowls.

"Throw the shells in here," Mac said, indicating the sink nearest Pruitt. "That garbage disposal can chew up steak bones."

Pruitt contented himself with small talk about the superb quality of the crab, holding back his real business at least until this pleasant chore had been finished. The countertops where they worked abutted the window side of the kitchen, the view magnificent. From the ridge the grimness of Riverton seen close-up became an urban planner's model of utility. Here was industry, here was shopping, here a park, and here a place for people to live. Riverton from on high appeared orderly and safe. Backdropped by the steel-colored waters of Gray's River and the verdant Wishkah Hills, it even looked pleasant. A nice place to bring up your kids, close to schools, picnicking, and baseball.

MacClinton squeezed the points of his nutcracker together and pointed with them to the west. "They know I'm watching them," he said.

Pruitt said, "Who's that?"

He chuckled. "My boys. They run the mills and swear I can see them from here."

"You've got how many sons?"

MacClinton wiped his hands on his apron. "C'mon, I'll show you," he said.

Pruitt, too, set down his crab cracking tools, wiped his hands and followed Mac to the living room and the fireplace mantle. "Three boys," he said, gesturing to framed 8x10 photos. "John, Barry, and Norm. Here they are at high school graduation, then at college. Never got to college myself, but the boys wanted to go."

Pruitt stepped in for closer look. "Great looking kids. You must be proud."

"I don't show these much. Most visitors I get up here don't give a rip about family stuff. Mostly it's accountants and lawyers. But I got a good sense about you, Pruitt. You got kids, don't you?"

"I do. I have a daughter."

Mac pursed his lips. "Cherish her while you got her, 'cause you never know."

Which left Pruitt uneasy, not knowing exactly what he'd meant. And there was something else, the way Mac was allowing a quiet moment to study the pictures, like he had a certain effect in mind, Pruitt realizing the story was not in the photos of the sons, but in the one surrounded by them, a black and white in full stature rather than head shots in color. In it, a woman wearing a suit fashionable in the fifties was holding a baby swaddled in a cashmere blanket. Pruitt knew that MacClinton had been widowed many years ago, his wife killed in an auto accident along the Grapevine, whose switchbacks were still dangerous in spite of the extensive safety engineering done over the years.

Mac said, "I lost both my girls."

It took Pruitt a moment to understand. "The baby was your daughter?"

"Yes, sir."

The woman in the picture was obviously his wife. Pruitt felt his mouth go dry. "I'm sorry for your loss," he said. "There's a song," he added. "*Looks like Rain* it's called. It says after something tragic a person has to brave the storm to come. But I tell you, if something happened to *my* daughter I don't know how I'd do that. "

MacClinton was biting down on his lower lip. In a constricted voice, he said, "That's about right."

Reacting to people's unexpected reactions were part and parcel of a sheriff's duty, but this one had really thrown him. He hoped he hadn't said anything to make things worse.

MacClinton took a deep breath. "Damnit, Pruitt," he said, his voice normalizing, "I'm sorry. I know what you're thinking: old fart up here grieving all day. I'm not, I assure you."

"It would be a hard loss, sir."

"It was. And sometimes it just hits me." He offered Pruitt his famous grin. "Lucky you to be here, eh?"

There was dampness on Pruitt's fingers and he wiped them again on his apron. "I don't mind. I really don't."

Mac said, "Thank you. I sense you understand. Having a daughter of your own. I've got more recent photos, you know, but this is the one I like best. Just back from the hospital."

He turned to Pruitt, eyes dry again, and clasped his upper arm. "So, Sheriff, let's finish up that crab and then you tell me what's on your mind over a big bowl of it."

⊕

J. Michael MacClinton had more than lived up to his reputation, a man unconcerned with the conventions of his ilk, no suits, ties, or business-like formality. He may have had a "miracle miler's" portfolio, but he still had a "swamp rat's" taste. He and Pruitt ate their crab the way Pruitt had grown up with it, dressed with mayonnaise, fresh lemon juice, and dashes of salt and pepper. In some ways, Mac was rather like Pruitt himself, who swam in the same sea as law men and women, but rarely as part of the school. Thankfully, unlike Mac, tragedy had not had a hand in shaping Pruitt's character; indeed, he hoped to be dead long before Olivia passed on. His most sacred wish for all families would be that death remain in sequence, that no children would die before their parents, the cycle of life and death remaining its most natural. He flushed for a moment with anger at the thought of the son-of-a-bitch who had thrown that bomb through his window, endangering Olivia, some cabbagehead toying with nature's patterns.

Anger, sadness, empathy—the afternoon had been a profusion of strong feelings; unfortunately, he had found out nothing that had to do with Olwen Friday. When asked if he knew of any squatters on his Willapa County properties, MacClinton said he did not; furthermore, he didn't care. "Better hiding out in the woods than hounding me for quarters on the street."

Pruitt asked him if he knew anybody named Olwen Friday.

"Olwen Friday?" he said. "No, that name means nothing to me."

Professionally, the afternoon had been, to some degree, as much pleasure as business, for which Pruitt felt a bit guilty. To make up for it, when he got back to the office he shut his door and pored over the reports that had arrived in his absence. Scanning each quickly, he stamped where necessary, signed where needed, then brought them out to Joyce to be shuttled along.

"You got a call from a Jerry Pemberton," she said. "From the State Patrol?"

"Oh, good," Pruitt said. "I'll get to it in just a minute."

In the break room, he poured coffee into his *Steal Your Face* mug. Somebody had been microwaving burritos again, which in Pruitt's experience usually smelled far better than they tasted. Yet the aroma was not at all unpleasant and he took his time at the coffee pot, stalling a bit, because he didn't want Joyce to think the call from Pemberton, the Director of the Drug Assistance Unit, was of great importance. He didn't like "need to know" circumstances, but it occurred to him that undercover work was one that fit that need. Indeed, rather than rush back to office to return the call, he decided to check in with Andy Messerit, the state's forensic bookkeeper.

"Things are looking pretty good in here," he said. "Mind if I check out what you've already got organized?"

Messerit said, "It's your evidence."

"Yes, it is," Pruitt said. He sat down and began examining the stacks of Carpenter's paperwork and boxes of books that had already been labeled. Much of it was technical—research papers and legal documentation—but there was also fiction and books on psychology, anthropology, and nutrition.

Which told Pruitt the man had far-ranging interests and was well read, but not much else.

More to the point were Carpenter's personal papers. Pruitt started with the diaries—which were filled, mostly, with ramblings about nature. Some of it was pretty dark. Musings on death and decay, both of the individual and of society generally. That piqued Pruitt's interest as he recalled Deputy Yen's statement at Carpenter's apartment: neat out front, chaotic in back. Was his personality similarly polarized? Had he been falling prey to demons as easily as exorcising them? Pruitt thought of the lines from *Clementine*—a rare collaboration between Phil Lesh, Dead bassist, and Robert Hunter, Dead lyricist—when the narrator admits that his cup has a hole and is unable to hold things of value any more. Had Carpenter begun seeing his life this way? Empty? Unfulfilling?

The ecologist's checkbook showed the usual payments for rent and utilities, car insurance, a dentist, a doctor. The dentist was local, the doctor from out of town. There were also regular, sizable deposits. His savings account was hefty. He also had a number of term deposits and an IRA that would make a man of Pruitt's means envious.

He wondered where the money was coming from and asked Messerit for the print-outs of Carpenter's banking records, which indicated that many of the deposits had come from a Chicago-based environmental organization called The Rare Earth Foundation. Pruitt looked up the number in Carpenter's phone diary and called them. He got a recording as it was already after business hours in the mid-west.

Back in his office, he finally made his call-back to Jerry Pemberton, the DAU director. Pruitt asked for two or three undercover agents.

"No problem," he said. "Got word from upstairs to help you any way we can. Two or three? You want more?"

"We're too small for more than that. I get an army down here, everybody's suspicious."

"Yeah, good decision. What we'll do is send them in one at a time, and from different locations. I got the map here, and it looks like there's three ways into your jurisdiction: north, south, and east. How about one from each, north through Montesano, south from Long Beach, and east from Chehalis."

"Sounds good. But I don't even want my crew to know who they are."

"Do you want to meet and brief them in person, or through me?"

"I'm thinking through you, mostly." Pruitt then gave him the gist of what he wanted from the undercover officers: to try and get close to the so-called "hit squad," if there was such a thing, and also, if possible, ANGER.

"I don't know if you can do it, but I've got some timber businessmen down here I'd like to know a little more about. You got a guy could pass himself off as a Japanese businessman?"

"Wow, that's specific. But, yeah, actually. There's an officer in Spokane we could pull over for that." He chuckled. "Guy's got a marketing degree from Gonzaga. Cleans up great. He's mixed race, but takes mostly after his Japanese side. If anybody can do it, he can."

"It's worth a shot," Pruitt said, then added, "These guys know each other, right?"

"It's one gal, too. I think she's perfect for getting close to ANGER. And they *will* know each other before they head in. We don't want undercovers following each other around."

"So why don't I meet with one of them, just to establish a rapport. You got your map out, right? There's a little café in Boistfort. It's the only one."

Pemberton chuckled. "Boistfort, huh? Man, that place is further out in the boonies than you are."

"I was only through there once, but I remember the café. They had great coffee. Nobody'll know who the hell we are. So you got a woman, a Japanese man, so I'm assuming the other guy will be white?"

"Right. Still need a few of those for undercover," he joked.

"Okay, tell him to dress like he's going hunting, and I'll do the same. And if you can, have him drive a pickup truck."

⊕

A half-hour later Joyce put a call through from Jack Coogan, Mason County Sheriff, whom Pruitt had asked to investigate the Hicksons, the heirs to Black Bear Ridge.

"Looked into their business dealings, Gav. They're solvent, but appear to be going through the money at a pretty good clip."

Jack explained the gist of what his investigation had uncovered: a lot of selling, very little reinvesting.

"Anything at all you've uncovered to link them with criminal activities? Unsavory known associates? Anything at all?"

"Not yet, but we're keeping our eyes peeled."

Pruitt thanked Coogan and rang off. It was the last call he took for the day.

⊕

The next morning, the first call he made was to The Rare Earth Foundation. A secretary answered and when he identified himself patched him through to the director, a woman named Rosalind Creagh.

"This is the most horrible tragedy," she said. "I was devastated when I heard, just devastated."

Pruitt commiserated a moment, then said, "You were funding John's work on Black Bear Ridge?"

"Actually, no. We helped draw up the contract, and were acting as intermediaries, but the Hickson estate was paying him."

"Did you broker the deal?"

"No, John got it started."

"Apparently, though, he was still receiving checks from you."

"John was always juggling projects. Which we had no problem with whatsoever."

"You were in touch with him?"

"Yes, we were. For all intents and purposes," she said, "we've supported him from the beginning. He may have gotten money from other sources, but never because he needed to."

"Had you been in communication with him recently?"

"He called on the Friday of the weekend he was killed."

"At that time, or in recent weeks, had he mentioned any names that were unfamiliar to you?"

Rosalind Creagh said, "You know, before you called, I didn't realize how much of this was at the back of my mind. John got his share of crank mail, of course, 'dirty rotten environmentalist' stuff, but nothing with any specificity, nothing John or any of us took seriously. Actually, the last time I talked to him his spirits were high. My feeling was he was about to break this whole Black Bear Ridge thing wide open."

CHAPTER FIFTEEN

The meeting with the DAU agent in Boistfort went well. They were a different breed, undercovers, demeanors like actors or artists. Almost too average, if you paid close attention. Which he doubted anybody in Elkhorn would be, locals getting inured to the ever-changing faces of the Black Bear Ridge players. John, as he identified himself—likely an alias—would work the so-called "death squad," while his compatriots worked ANGER and the Japanese businessmen. Pruitt liked the guy, but he especially liked the fact that these few extra hands freed up his own people and allowed him some creativity with their time. He sent two officers to Riverton to run background checks on the flood of new faces that had been pouring into Elkhorn since Carpenter's murder. Via motel records, license plates, and simply asking around, some intelligence had been collected, but without a computer system Pruitt would have to wait far too long to find out who these people were or what their stories might be. He wanted to know who they were now, and had come to an agreement with the Riverton police. They had a very nice system, connected to valuable law enforcement data bases through that up-and-coming technology—what Christopher had talked about at Thanksgiving—called the Internet.

Thursday night Pruitt had a float. Marion had used the tank the day before and cleaned it thoroughly. There was new water, new Epson salts. Afterwards, images from the Dead's *Sunshine Daydream* came to mind: breathing more freely, feeling like he was walking in tall trees.

Friday morning, as he was on his way out to his cruiser, Angela caught his attention, waving to him from Bill Logan's kitchen window. A moment later she was standing on Bill's back porch.

"Yoo hoo!" she called. "Ain't it great being neighbors, Gavin? After all these years? I feel like June Cleaver."

"June Cleaver wouldn't be dressed like a model for Frederick's of Hollywood," Pruitt called back.

Angela looked down at herself. She wore nothing but a halter top that barely covered her breasts, and black bikini panties. She said, "Oops," then waved one last time before returning to Bill's kitchen.

Her behavior was galling. Although she would deny it, Pruitt knew she was dogging him and that her interest in Bill had little to do with him as a man and mostly to do with the fact he lived next door to the sheriff in charge of the Carpenter murder investigation.

Yet he let that go. The previous night's float had worked its small magic, and by the time he got to work he was feeling good again. When Joyce brought in an armload of mail and reports and thumped them on his desk, he cried, "All right, paperwork!" and grinned at her.

Caught between laughter and dismay, Joyce finally laughed. "I'll say this, Gavin, you do keep things interesting."

She'd already opened the routine stuff, which Pruitt put to one side. What caught his eye first were letters from the pathology labs: one would be the Carpenter autopsy reports; the other would the blood analysis report from the sample taken off the wood found in Earl's truck.

Out loud, Pruitt said, "Thanks, Guv."

He opened the blood analysis report first, which told him that the blood on the hunk of wood found in Earl Ruddell's truck did indeed match Carpenter's, for as much good as it would do them without corroborative evidence. For all they knew, Ruddell could very well have been the patsy he claimed to be, a scenario Deputy Raphe Jones had put an interesting twist to—that after Earl Ruddell and some right wing cohorts committed the murder, Earl had disenfranchised the others and got pinned with the deed by his own people. Jones' contention that Earl's megalomania would turn colleagues against him seemed, to Pruitt, completely plausible.

Then he read the autopsy report, couldn't believe what he'd just read, so had to read it again. Twenty minutes later he was in his cruiser driving out to Olwen Friday's.

⊛

"I really would like to stop and talk, if that's all right," he said, speaking to Olwen's back.

He got a grunt for a reply as she continued to trudge ahead of him. A few minutes earlier, when he'd knocked at her door, she welcomed him in and said she was perfectly willing to talk, but needed some fresh air, so if it was all the same, how about taking a walk.

Why not? he figured, and followed her out the back door and across the flagstone patio to a barely discernible opening through the bushes and grasses behind the herb garden. Although dense, the foliage surrounding was no more than a deep fringe of hedge. Once under the canopy of evergreens, the underbrush all but disappeared, and Pruitt found himself scurrying to keep up with Olwen as she marshaled along a worn path that wound through the stand of spare, column-like trunks of second-growth Douglas fir.

Olwen had promised they could talk as they walked, yet was walking so vigorously Pruitt hardly had time for a breath, much less conversation. They climbed a rise, then angled along a rocky ridge where the soil thinned and the trees got spindly. At the crest Olwen came to a stop. Pruitt figured this was his moment to broach the topic he'd driven all the way out here for, but lost his thought when his gaze was drawn a hundred yards down the slope to the demarcation between the Black Bear Ridge stand of old-growth and the tree-farmed second-growth.

Back-to-back the forests were a stark contrast. Both were green, but the second-growth Douglas fir emphasized one hue cloned endlessly, while the old-growth—hemlocks, cedars, and various firs—showcased a myriad of green variation: green tinted with blue or gray, smoky colored or bright as a lawn. In the second growth, crowding had begat short arrowhead-shaped crowns and long, naked trunks. In the old growth, time and natural selection had created elbow room, the crowns growing deep and rounded. Old growth branches, too, had bowed and spread and become festooned with a yellowish-green lichen called old-man's beard. Both forests had their peculiar beauty, but it was a difference between pretty and sublime, between pleasantly green and richly verdant. It was the difference between a child prodigy's first lovely musings on a violin and the passionate rendering of a full-blown concerto by that same child as a great artist.

Then Olwen was marching off again, and Pruitt had missed his moment. A few minutes later, they were deep into the old-growth, the earth under his feet spongy, a sweet rotting smell in the air, which was still as a cathedral—though more inspiring than a mere church, for this was not man's vanity but nature's simplicity allowed to attain profound proportions.

Then he realized he'd gotten to day-dreaming again, as well as lagging further behind Olwen. He called to her to wait for him, his voice small and muted, yet clear in the vast stillness. Olwen stopped and looked back, silently chiding his inability to keep pace.

When he caught up to her, he said, "I'm thinking that John's hanging could have been staged. An elaborate suicide made to look like murder."

She looked at him as if he'd just spat in front of her grandmother. "Why would he do *that?*"

"To become a martyr for his cause. A last ditch attempt to

save Black Bear Ridge."

"That's ridiculous. What would possess you to think such a thing?"

"I just got the lab report," he said. "He had cancer. If he was going to die anyway…" He shrugged.

She said nothing.

"Did you know he had cancer?"

"Of course."

So matter-of-fact. She drove him mad. "Then why didn't you tell me?"

"You didn't ask."

He was furious with her. "Cut this out!" he said. "I'm not one of the bad guys. If you ever want John's killer brought to justice, you've got to start talking to me."

"He wouldn't commit suicide. He wasn't going to die. It wasn't that kind of cancer."

"What are you talking about, *that* kind of cancer?"

"It was rare. Chondrosarcoma. Cancer of the cartilage. Up by his neck. Did you ever meet him?"

Pruitt said, "I did. He came to my office once."

"You ever notice how he held his head? A little cocked to the left?"

"Yes," he said. "Now that you mention it."

"Well, that's why."

"You're saying he wasn't concerned?"

"Of course he was concerned. It was cancer. But he'd been fighting it for twelve years. Every four or five years they'd cut it out again."

Pruitt pulled a face. "That wasn't depressing him?"

"Absolutely not. He was feeling great. We'd started a preventative regimen. Herbs, yoga, sweat baths, hypnotherapy." She lowered her chin. "He'd never felt better. He did not commit suicide."

Maybe not, Pruitt was thinking, but he wondered if Carpenter had told Olwen everything about his illness. Maybe it had finally become inoperable. He'd need to get some information on this cancer. "Look," he said, "maybe this idea of John committing suicide is far-fetched, but there's so little to go on, and you're not helping. Talk to me. Let me decide what's important and what's not."

Instead, Olwen just straightened her shoulders, turned around and plunged further into the massive pedestals that were the trunks of the trees of the ancient forest.

Pruitt cursed under his breath and followed. Olwen Friday might be a tough nut, but so was he—though he was discovering that aerobically she was in far better condition. While he labored to keep up, Olwen strode effortlessly, relentlessly onward, the hem of her skirt swaying, her shoulders and head tilted slightly forward. She'd begun to leave him behind again, and he had to exert himself to catch up.

Finally, over the crest of another ridge, Olwen drew up to what appeared to be her destination. A pond lay before them, the water a deep blackish-blue color and as calm as glass, the surrounding trees reflected in it like a mirror. At the water's edge, Olwen sat on a partially rotted fallen log, the innards a brownish-orange. A nurse log, delicate lady fern growing out of it, and a yellowish fungus. Nearby grew bracken nearly five-feet high, and shrub-like willow.

Pruitt sat next to her and idly pulled at the rotting wood, disturbing a black, yellow-striped millipede that hurried away. This end of the pond was marshy, with patches of skunk cabbage, cattails, and the usual array of rushes and sedges. Duckweed and small water lilies lapped at the shore.

From somewhere near the middle of the pond a ripple began, subtle, but enough to distort the reflection of shoreline and sky. Pruitt said, "Whoa! A ripple on still water!" He looked at Olwen. "Did you see that? No pebble tossed?"

Olwen smiled, wanly. "The Grateful Dead, right? But it's not what you're thinking. Watch." A few moments later she pointed. "There."

A beak poked up through the dark water. The top of a carapace appearing. A turtle lurking just under the surface. Good sized, maybe a foot across, it disappeared again, leaving an even more pronounced ripple this time.

Pruitt laughed. "It was still cool."

"Yeah, I like that song, too."

"You don't own the land your house is built on."

He thought he might have disarmed her with this knowledge, but all she said was, "Nope."

"A man named J. Michael MacClinton does."

Olwen sat with her legs pressed together and her elbows resting on her knees, slumped forward, her hands in prayer mode with the tips of her fingers under her chin. "I've seen logging trucks with that name on them. Same guy?"

"That's him. He give you permission to build on his property?"

She dropped her hands back to her lap. "There's no call for meanness."

Pruitt sighed. "That wasn't my intent. It just makes no sense to me, building a beautiful home on property you don't own. What possessed you to do it?"

She picked up a pebble and hurled it into the pond. "It wasn't planned," she said. "That's for sure. I was hiking when I found the spot. The vibes were good, so I camped for a few days. Then I put up an army surplus tent, decided to stay for a few weeks. One thing led to another. I'd been accumulating building skills over the years and I just wanted to try a few things out, you know? The garret went up first. It really got out of hand. And if you're asking did I think through the consequences, the answer is obviously no. I just did what I felt was right to do."

"Eventually," he said, "what you've built is going to come down." When she only continued staring at the pond, he said, "Doesn't that concern you?"

Olwen said, "I'd walk away from it as easily as I walked into it. Money, houses, clothes—it's all just maya. No more real than the images reflected in that water in front of us. Those sorts of realities come as easy as they go."

Pruitt regarded her a moment. "That's bullshit, Olwen, and you know it."

⊕

For his provocation Pruitt got nothing more from Olwen Friday than the silent treatment and another power-walk back to her house. Then the weekend began, which quickly turned awful, starting late Friday night with a grisly traffic accident that claimed the lives of two high schoolers who'd been celebrating Elkhorn's first basketball victory of the season by chug-a-lugging a fifth of vodka on the drive back from Ocosta. Saturday afternoon the Menlo Store got held-up, and then Sunday night a brawl broke out in downtown Elkhorn when three ANGER members tried to order margaritas in a bar off-limits to anybody but timber people. Pruitt himself had worked the periphery of the bar fight and, among other duties, had escorted a plaid-shirted, pony-tailed young woman to his cruiser. "Rough me up a little," she'd whispered. "Make it look real." His undercover. And he'd played it up "Watch your head, goddamnt!" he'd barked as he shoved her into the back. "You're under arrest!" he'd added. *Dang*, he thought, the DAU had sent him a helluva team.

After as emotional and draining a 48 hours as he could remember, Pruitt needed badly to feel like his life had some normality in it again. Monday he gave his pal, union president Dale Slater, a call and slipped into the old International Woodworkers of America Hall for a nooner. They'd not had a proper computer mah jong tournament in nearly two months; before Black Bear Ridge they'd been used to playing twice a week, so Pruitt just called him up and said, "Screw it, Dale, fire up the PC. I'll be over in twenty minutes to whip your ass."

He stopped by The Torchlight for two "Pruitt specials" to go—because while not a vegetarian himself, Dale didn't mind having a meal without meat if Pruitt were buying—then walked over to the union hall carrying the sacks of food: sweet and sour tofu, fried rice, and vegetable chow mein, everything in small waxed boxes he and Dale forked into directly.

Dale said, "Given the tenor of the times, playing a computer game feels more like sin than harmless diversion."

Pruitt said, "No kidding," and hesitated to set the sacks down. Was Dale trying to say that they ought to reconsider? Wolf down the food and get back to work?

"So given that we know this is probably a wholly irresponsible thing to do," Dale said, "are we going to let our guilt stop us?"

Pruitt smiled and said, "No way." He began parceling out the little boxes while Dale cheerily brought up their game.

⊕

Yet the excellent Torchlight lunch couldn't fully lessen their guilt at having some fun in the midst of an ongoing crisis. The food didn't seem to have the same renewing quality it usually did, and he and Dale's banter felt forced, as if they were striving for a good time rather than allowing a good time to happen. The games, too, seemed to have been rigged in such a way as to make sure they were both disappointed. He got under seventy tiles only once in four tries, and Dale hadn't done much better.

Dale said, "I think the computer game gods are messing with our brains. 'Getcher pimply butts back to work,' I think they're saying."

Pruitt said, "You may be right." He was scraping the sides of the take-home box for the last of the sweet and sour sauce.

Dale said, "I really am up to my neck."

Pruitt said, "Yep, me too," and looked to see if any fried rice remained.

"And I hate it. It's like I don't have a life anymore. I mean, look at me. I stuck with college long enough to earn an MBA, and I could have gone on and worked for IBM or some multinational and made the big bucks—but did I? No. And why? Because I wanted to have a life, you know? Move back home where everybody knows me and I know them and things get done, but at a pace that makes everybody feel good. We work hard, but we know that remembering who we work *for* is just as important as the work we do for them. Am I right?"

"In a small town," Pruitt said, "it's the whole point."

Dale Slater sighed and ran his hand over his immense belly. "You want I should start another game?"

Pruitt said, "Nah."

"Criminy, we only played half-an-hour."

"Better than not at all. At least I know that some of what I used to do before Black Bear Ridge is still out here."

"G'wan, then, Gavin. Keep the streets and by-ways safe for us, will ya? It's your job, damnit."

Pruitt said, "Let's try again next week, okay? Just to keep our hand at it."

"The game or a normal life?"

Pruitt said, "Both," and gave his bud a pat on the shoulder before he walked out the door.

⊛

He stopped for a sip from the water fountain in the hallway, then poked his head into the main office to wave good-bye to Evie Demaris, the IWA secretary, but she'd gone out for lunch. He raised his arms over his head and had himself a good stretch right there in the hallway, then strode to the Plexiglas front door and pushed his way through. Just as the door was closing, a tremendous rumbling engulfed him from behind, picked him up and carried him out onto the sidewalk, where he tumbled into a ball and rolled into the street.

A passing car, too, seemed to have gotten engulfed by the same immense energy. Either that or it was trying to avoid Pruitt, its horn screaming as it swerved and jumped the curb and the two steps leading up to the entrance to the Elkhorn Apartments building, where it smashed into the door, glass shattering everywhere.

His ears felt like a bubble of air was ballooning up inside his head. When the wave of energy that had carried him along passed over and finally abated, Pruitt found himself on his back in the street gutter opposite the IWA Hall, whose roof was spewing a plume of black smoke. Under the plume, orange and yellow flames jittered and licked—though Pruitt heard nothing but an eerie silence.

He tried to get up, but was unable to raise himself from the cold gutter. He swallowed, which cleared his ears enough that he could hear the crackle of the fire, if nothing else. Why was nobody responding?

Yet as soon as Pruitt had the thought, he could hear sirens in the distance, and a sound that made him think of a stampeding herd of animals, wildebeest or zebra, which he realized was actually the pounding of shoes on pavement. People running from all parts of Elkhorn in the direction of the IWA Hall, which had by now taken on a bizarre appearance. The back and front halves were still standing, but the roof over the middle section had caved in, the ceiling joists as they had cracked and fallen having taken some of the side walls with them. The plate glass of the swinging front door had scattered over the sidewalk, and thick, dark smoke roiled out between the twisted steel door frames.

Then the pounding of shoes faded and faces appeared around and above him.

"Jesus, you all right, Sheriff?"

"What in the name of chrissakes happened here?"

"Anybody still in there, Sheriff?"

Through thick lips, Pruitt croaked Dale's name, and suddenly none of the faces were looking at him anymore but turned instead to the burning hall. Somehow Pruitt managed to say, "Help me up," and was assisted to the sitting position.

A couple of men ran across Prospect Street with the intent of plunging into the smoke-spewing maw that moments before had been the union hall's front entrance. The smoke, thick and acrid, turned them back.

The county's Medic One van appeared, but the paramedics were no more able to get into the hall than had the men before them. Finally a fire truck arrived, and two gas-masked fire fighters dashed into the mouth of the building. It looked like Casey Adams and Janet Coles, but it was hard to know for sure under those masks and laminated slickers.

A wave of nausea forced Pruitt to cross his arms over his knees to steady himself. More police arrived, and more onlookers—the sidewalks full of people now. Finally the two bug-faced fire fighters emerged from the smoke dragging some strange mass behind them. At first denying what he saw, Pruitt imagined it as any number of strange things—a gunny sack of squashed tomatoes, a flank of meat. He wanted to believe it to be anything other than what it was: the trunk of Dale Slater, legs missing beneath the knees.

As his head drained of blood, Pruitt rolled from his sitting position to his side and began retching his portion of the lunch he'd just shared with his friend into the gutter.

CHAPTER SIXTEEN

The IWA bombing investigation technically fell within the jurisdiction of the Elkhorn City Police, as had the bombing of Pruitt's house. Yet the standing agreement between Pruitt and Elkhorn Chief of Police Dan Louderback was to turn all serious crime investigation—within or without Elkhorn—over to Lee Wilson, one the most well-trained forensics officers in western Washington State.

By late afternoon Lee was ready with his initial report, which he delivered in Dan Louderback's office just a few blocks away from the smoldering union hall. In attendance were Louderback and Pruitt, plus a collection of deputies— Raphe Jones, Ing Yen, Ethan "E.L." Laymont, and Walt Mero from the county, and Marvin Gates of the Elkhorn city police. Pruitt's ears were still ringing, and he had to keep turning his head to hear people.

Lee said, "I've found a bit of fuse, and I know the kitchen was the epicenter. Dale got torn up the way he did because the bomb detonated just on the other side of the wall from his desk.

"Problem is it's still pretty hot down there. I'm going to be a couple of days on this before I can give you anything concrete."

E.L. said, "If Evie hadn't been at the Dairy Queen…"

Chief Louderback said, "E.L., she *always* goes to the Dairy Queen for lunch."

"Actually," Pruitt said, "Dale usually does, too. Our routine has been to have lunch together at the hall only on Wednesdays."

"If the bomber knew the routines," Raphe said, "that means Dale's death might have been accidental."

"And they couldn't have known I'd be there," Pruitt said. "I'd only called Dale about half-an-hour before I went over. And we've never done lunch on Monday before."

"Sounds like those bastards in ANGER," E.L. said. "We ought to haul their asses in right now. Get to the bottom of this."

Raphe Jones said, "E.L., it could as easily have been that so-called Death Squad everybody's talking about." Raphe managed to strike just the right tone with E.L., firmly leading him back to objectivity.

Chief Louderback said, "You know it was dynamite, Lee?"

"For all I know at this point, it could have been plastique."

"We've got a list of licensed dynamite handlers, don't we?" E.L. said. "Because of the first bomb?"

Lee Wilson said, "Look E.L., before you go off half cocked, give me a couple of days to work up the bomb profile. I'm gonna collect more evidence, then make a run down to Portland, work with the ATF and their lab. If I can establish what kind of shot was used, it may help narrow the search— like if it was ditching or stumping powder at least we'd know a local was probably involved. If it was Semtex, it's an outside operator almost for sure. You see what I'm getting at?"

E.L. peered at Lee a moment, then dropped his head and pinched the bridge of his nose with the tips of his thick fingers to stem the flow of tears. "C'mon, man, you know I've been seeing Evie."

⊗

By the time the press conference was over it was quitting time—a concept that had no relevance whatsoever after a day like this one. Yet he was glad to go home. It relieved him to be home.

From his bedroom, he called Marion.

"I cannot believe this happened in Elkhorn!" she said. "*Dale* never did anything wrong to anybody. Ever!"

It was unfathomable, and they commiserated over losing their mutual friend before Pruitt asked her about chondrosarcoma, placing it in context of the John Carpenter murder investigation.

"This is all related, isn't it?" she noted.

Pruitt sighed. "Hard to imagine it otherwise."

"Well, as far as this form of cancer, John Carpenter could have lived a long time with it. As long as he kept on top of his treatments and checkups. Have you got his medical records?"

"Going after them as we speak. An oncologist in Portland."

"When they get in, bring them over. I can give you a better assessment then."

He thanked Marion, for the information, for the upkeep on the float tank, for being his friend. "It was my turn to clean it," he said.

"Consider it an early Christmas present."

After ringing off, he listened to his messages: one from Molly and another from his father. Both had heard about the bombing. He thought about returning their calls, but didn't feel up to it. Rather, he tossed his beeper on the bed and went out to have a float. But he cut it short. All he could think about was Dale, how he looked getting pulled out onto the sidewalk. Pruitt was afraid he would throw up again, right there in the float tank.

Back in his kitchen he made an attempt at fixing dinner, but the peppers and onions reminded him of alien things, and the eggs he cracked to make an omelet nearly made him sick. He dumped them down the disposal and put the vegetables back in the crisper. He didn't know when he might eat again, or if he ever could.

When he caught sight of Richard Emmett, the Seattle news reporter, walking across his back yard, the thought flashed through his mind that he would just open his back door and pop him in the mouth. It would feel good to rid his body of some of this anger. But common sense prevailed. "Look, Richard," Pruitt told him, "this is not a good time."

Emmett said, "I understand, but I've got some stuff I want to run past you. A little historical information I want to be fair with you about."

"Some 'comrade' of mine come forward? What did he tell you, that I once saw bats the size of eagles?"

Emmett smirked. "Not exactly."

At which point Angela Caracitto began yoo-hooing—in her inimitable style—from Bill Logan's back steps. "Good effing Christ, Gavin, what kind *brain*-dead *red*neck motherfreaking *ass*holes you got living in this town?"

Emmett, like Pruitt, had turned to look at Angela. "Neighbor?" he asked, his tone wondering just how often women with spiky black hair wearing black teddies, Doc Marten boots and little else on shivering cold evenings screamed obscenities at the sheriff from the house next door.

"An old friend," Pruitt said.

"Friend?" said Emmett. "No, this is what is called local color. Serious freaking local color." Barely giving Pruitt a final glance, the reporter began searching for the most direct path to Angela. Over his shoulder he said, "You mind if I catch you later?"

"Gavin," Angela yelled, "you want me to bring over some chicken soup?" Although speaking in a pitched voice, her underlying concern was surprisingly heartfelt. "Bill must have a thousand cans of it. I swear all he eats is chicken rice soup and deviled ham sandwiches."

Richard Emmett had crossed Pruitt's back lawn and stood now at the low picket fence separating Bill Logan's property from Pruitt's. "Pardon me, Ma'am. Have you got a minute to talk with the press?"

Angela didn't even glance at him. "Gav, this hack's looking for a tits-and-ass angle. You want me to get him off your back?"

⊕

Pruitt supposed his face must have told Angela all she needed to know: yes, he did need some help here. And as good friends often do, she stepped up for him, inviting Emmett in for a chat. It was behavior that reminded Pruitt of Angela's fierce loyalty. Once a friend of hers, always a friend. In their present circumstances, it was easy to forget they'd meant a lot to each other at one time.

As far as what she would say to Emmett, Pruitt wouldn't worry about it—nor could he. The reporter, if he was worth his salt, would use her for corroborative background on the story he apparently already had, ready to scatter Pruitt's drug taking days all over front pages coast to coast.

Then his phone rang. It was his father, who'd been drinking. Immediately, Pruitt began assessing how much he'd been drinking. Level one, Jack Pruitt donned a contented smile and could be humorously sarcastic; level two, his smile broadened, but his humor got personal; level three, when he was good and tight, the smile vanished as he settled a person's hash once and for all—if they were man or woman enough to take it, or even if they weren't. Fortunately, this call was about the bombing, which Jack had just heard about. And while he'd irrefutably reached level three drunkenness, he was not angry with but concerned for his son. Was he okay? Could he do anything for him?

Pruitt said, "I'm fine. Really."

"I'll come up there. First thin' tomorrow, all right? We got this paper drive, Lion's Club, but I'll drop it like a hot potato."

"Dad, I wouldn't be here anyway. My days are 15-20 hours right now."

"It just scared me," Jack said, a sob cracking his voice. "That I couldn't do anything."

This was the part that killed Pruitt, knowing that no matter how much alcohol had impeded his father's parenting abilities, he loved his kids and had been the best father he knew how to be. Jack Pruitt had seen his children to a better place in their lives than his own father had seen him to—an epitaph Pruitt would be hard pressed to improve on for himself.

⊕

After ringing off with his father, he called his mother, who had not yet heard about the bombing and whose emotions ran from shocked to relieved to outraged in a matter of moments. She knew Dale Slater, too. Pruitt asked her if she would call his brothers and sisters. News of the bombing would hit the eleven o'clock report with a vengeance, and he didn't want them to worry, yet neither did he have the energy for any more phone calls himself. "Yes, of course," his mother said, then they talked about getting everybody together over Christmas.

Finally, he called Molly, who asked him if he wanted to come over, or if he wanted her over there, or could she bring him something to eat. Then she was crying. "Oh, my god, Gavin. Poor Dale!"

Then he was crying, too, bitterly, thinking of Dale and the mah-jong tournaments they would never have again. His friend taken from him by a dispute over owls and 2x4's of all stupid things. Why did people get so entrenched? Where was discourse? Compromise? It was just so ridiculous.

CHAPTER SEVENTEEN

He and Molly finally stopped crying. She asked again if he wanted her over. "Actually," he said, "right now I feel like a shower and some music and bed. Thanks for calling, Molly. Thanks for being there. I'll see you soon."

Then Pruitt put his machine on first-ring pick up and turned the speaker volume off. He wanted more than just to screen his calls, he wanted to have no knowledge that people were even calling him. If the county fell into anarchy and chaos between now, ten PM, and tomorrow morning, the hell with it. Besides, if it did get that bad, they'd send somebody for him.

He took a shower, lathering himself from head to toe, then washing his hair with shampoo that smelled of green apples. Afterwards, he felt calmer, maybe a little hungry, but not enough to want to fix something. Maybe a sandwich later. What he really wanted was some music. He found his *Terrapin Station* CD. He didn't care what other Deadheads said about the studio albums, he loved this one: the counterpoint, the mix, even the orchestration on the title cut, despised by so many Grateful Dead "purists"—whatever the heck that was. He'd also been a big fan of the Music Machine and their 60's hit *Talk, Talk*, and it gave him no small amount of pleasure that Keith Olson, a member of the Music Machine, had been the album's producer. To get in the mood he turned off all the lights but one, laid down on the floor in front of his stereo system with a pillow under his head. Still in his soothing terrycloth bathrobe, he closed his eyes as the music cued up and began.

It was comforting there on the floor with his headphones and the Dead.

Then at about *Terrapin Transit*, a part of the suite of songs that ended the album, he heard some odd chiming that he did not remember hearing before. It took him a moment to realize that the chimes were not part of the music, but coming from outside the headphones. His front door bell, he realized, which made him instantly defensive. Not only was it after eleven, nobody who knew him ever announced themselves at the front of the house. He retrieved his service revolver, then eased towards the door, standing to the side, protecting himself with the studs of the framing.

"Who is it?" he demanded.

He couldn't quite make out the muffled reply.

Again, he demanded, "Who?"

Speaking up, the voice said, "Olwen."

What the hell? He opened the door, his pistol still held shoulder high.

"What are you doing here?" he asked.

Her gaze hopped from Pruitt's face to the gun and back. Though her mouth opened, she didn't say anything.

"Jeez, sorry," he said, lowering the gun and setting the safety. "I had a bomb thrown into my house last week," he said. "And today the union hall was bombed. A friend was killed."

"Killed?" Olwen said. "That's terrible." She looked at her feet. "My timing's so bad. I'll come back later."

When she began turning around, Pruitt said, "No, c'mon in. It's okay."

She turned back to him, a smile tugging at the corners of her mouth. "Hard to say no to a man in a bathrobe holding a gun."

Pruitt grimaced. "Sorry. Lemme put this thing away."

While in the bedroom, he quickly pulled on some jeans and a polo shirt. When he returned, Olwen was standing just inside the door, which she'd closed. On her head she'd tied a plain plum-colored wool scarf over a wildly-colored silk one. Her wool overcoat hid the rest of what she wore, but her legs were wrapped as usual in dark-red tights, and she wore the same pastel running shoes as yesterday on their impromptu hike through the woods.

Pruitt said, "What's up?"

Pools of tears had formed in her eyes. "I'm afraid."

He stepped towards her. "Afraid of what?" He hoped she was about to give up the name, or at least a description of some redneck in a pickup truck who'd threatened her and John Carpenter.

She wiped a tear away. "Of this," she said, and produced a sheet of paper from her coat pocket.

As a county sheriff, Pruitt immediately recognized a writ of eviction, this one drawn up by a law firm representing MacClinton Logging. They wanted her off the property in 90 days. *Crap!* he thought to himself. *What have I done to this poor woman?*

Olwen said, "I've been so cavalier."

She searched her coat pocket and pulled out her farmer's red handkerchief, on which she blew her nose. "This damn thing," she said, and removed the gold hoop that pierced her nose. After she put it in her coat pocket, she said, "It's my home. I don't want to lose it. All this time I've been so... 'Whatever will be will be' kind of crap. As if I really didn't care."

Pruitt was standing about four steps away and was experiencing extraordinary feelings. Guilt, of course, for having even brought her name up around MacClinton, yet something else besides. "You kind of got yourself in a pickle," he said.

"I've not come asking for help from anybody in so long." She sighed, her breath ragged. "Can you help me?"

His mind admonished him that with the investigation ongoing, it was inappropriate for this woman to be here. Yet he was also thinking of a Dead lyric: *Crippled but free, I was blind all the time I was learning to see.* Was this that same culminating point? Was he just learning to see what was in front of him, this incredible woman? "Of course," he heard himself say. "I'll do whatever I can."

She uttered a cry, almost a yelp, her hand reaching to cover her mouth, as if to suppress another such outburst, her eyes terrified.

Pruitt crossed the few steps between them. Somewhere inside him a voice was yelling that he was being spectacularly foolish, but he could restrain himself no longer and enveloped her as he had been aching to do, realizing as he did so that the ache had been there not in just the last few moments, but from the first time he'd laid eyes on her.

Yet even with his emotions tumbling over themselves, his first intention had been only to console, nothing more. That noble sentiment gave way quickly to others, especially as Olwen wrapped her arms around him and gave up the whole of her body to his, thighs touching, hips. She smelled of cedar and damp wool. He placed his temple against hers, gently, letting the heat in his blood cool from boil to simmer. He kissed her cheek. He kissed her just below her ear and again at the top of her throat. Her breath had already gotten ragged, as had his own. Her breasts were imprinting against his chest. He placed his hand on her there, softly, reveling in the short gasp his touch elicited. He kissed further down her throat, whispering, "My god, you are so beautiful."

He found her arms suddenly in his chest like poles, pushing him away.

"Please," she said, "don't."

He liberated her immediately. "I'm sorry. I didn't mean—"

"No," she said. "It's not that. It's just—"

"We shouldn't be doing this," he said. "I know. Not now."

"No, it's just…I can't—"

"No, it's me. I've no right. I'm so sorry. I don't know where this came from."

She turned. "I've got to go." But she struggled with the door, yelping in frustration when it wouldn't give way to her.

"Here." He reached around her, catching the close-in smell of her again—sweet and cedary. He could have eaten her up. Instead, he got the door opened for her, allowing her to flee.

From her truck, a safe distance away, she paused to look back at him. She was nearly panting from emotion—though whether passion or panic, Pruitt wasn't sure. "I'm sorry," she said. "Please, don't think ill of yourself."

Pruitt wanted to argue with her. Of *course* he should think ill of himself. *He* was the idiot who'd visited this horrible event on her home; *he* was the idiot who'd read something sexual between them—but before he could give voice to any of it, she'd ducked her head into the cab and driven off.

The next morning Pruitt woke two hours earlier than normal. His sleep had been fitful, his dreams furtive. In one of them Dale was talking to him. It was natural, nice—and felt absolutely real. In another Olwen's smell was on him like skin, as if she'd been lying next to him all night. Awake he could feel the imprint of her body against his—nothing dreamy about it. He dressed and went in to the office, determined to resolve the unresolvable by hard work and sheer will. Yet for hours he floundered, unable to steer himself in a constructive direction, only able to think of Olwen, then Molly, then Dale, then Olwen again—the situation troubling him most. A woman comes to him for help with a property dispute and he reacts with lust? *Good god*, what had he been thinking! Then salvation in the unlikely form of Andy Messerit appeared at his door.

"You might want to take a look at this," the little bookkeeper said, then turned and walked back to his cubby-hole.

To get his mind off Olwen Friday, Molly Burkhalter, Angela Caracitto, John Carpenter, Dale Slater, et. al., Pruitt was ready to follow the lead lemming over the cliff and so rose from his desk and strode into The Swamp. He snorted when he saw that the always considerate Andy had already closed the door to the office that had been so generously availed to him.

Thinking what a rude little shit Andy Messerit was, Pruitt pushed through the door, ready to ream him out. Yet once inside, his ire was tempered by the impressive work Messerit had done. While not particularly less intimidating, the wild mounds of paperwork, reports, books, etc., had been tamed, neatly stacked and piled, yellow post-its identifying various areas of interest.

Messerit said, "Found this box of magazines," and flopped an eighteen-inch stack onto the half-cleared desk normally shared by Ing Yen and Raphe Jones. Pruitt thumbed through the titles: *Time, Forbes, Business Weekly*, small trade magazines for various industries, many of them aging.

Pruitt said, "You can buy these anywhere."

Messerit stepped forward to extract a *Forbes* magazine dated in the mid-eighties. A yellow post-it saved a place. "This is what's funny."

The page he'd opened to featured a picture of a smiling executive. It was a profile piece, though it was not the text or charts that were interesting but the drawing in the top margin. Done in the style of a ten-year-old, a gun was pointed to the executive's head, penis-shaped bullets zooming from the barrel, velocity hites indicating a terrible speed and lethality.

"Are there more of the same in these other magazines?"

Messerit said, "Enough it caught my eye. I marked each one I found."

"Carpenter had no children we know of, no nephews or nieces, so unless we can establish otherwise, we'll have to assume he's the artist."

Without comment, Messerit returned to his desk. In spite of the presence of an expensive rack-mounted stereo system hiding behind the smoky glass doors of a walnut case, the room was unnervingly quiet. Pruitt thought a little background music might be nice for this kind of work, but realized the colicky Mr. Messerit probably enjoyed nothing but his own bad humor.

He sat down at the bit of space at the desk and examined a few more of the drawings. It didn't take an expert to see that the same person had drawn them all. He opened the archiving box containing Carpenter's personal files and began to study them again. As he read, he felt duty soften his edginess. His mind cleared, his goals refocused.

Within a half hour, he had Carpenter's diaries, his phone directory, the contents of his wallet, and other such items spread out on the desk in front of him, the scribblings and bric-a-brac that defined his inner workings.

One thing was clear, John Carpenter did not nurture personal relationships. None of his prose had been written about or to a lover, friend, or relative. Nothing even to Olwen, the woman he was in love with.

Pruitt corrected himself: the woman he was *allegedly* in love with. It appeared as if they were lovers, but they could have been something else. Co-conspirators, for instance.

Returning to Carpenter's dearth of personal relationships, Pruitt noted that the numbers in his phone book were those of book publishers, equipment wholesalers, photographic supply outlets, and institutions, foundations, and organizations dedicated in one way or another to ecological concerns. The names of people accompanied some of the listings, but almost to a one they were titled Mr., Mrs., or Dr. The man didn't even seem to have friends within the discipline he worked. Even Angela's entry had the stiff formality of a "Ms." preceding it— a woman with whom he'd had an affair. For all Pruitt knew, maybe a woman with whom he was still having an affair. He wondered if Olwen and Angela knew of each other.

Curiously, there were also listings that appeared incongruent with his work, those for corporations and businesses on the other side of the environmental issues John Carpenter championed.

Even as Pruitt was asking himself why such entries would appear in an ecologist's address book he was forming a hypothesis, one based on the psychology of a grown man who drew a boy's symbol of power and rage over authority figures.

"Andy, have you organized any sort of time-line graph of Carpenter's work up to but not including Black Bear Ridge?"

The grumpy little clerk swiveled in his chair and rummaged through a stack of paperwork, producing a file he handed to Pruitt without so much as a glance in his direction.

Pruitt said, "Thanks, Andy."

Messerit didn't even bother to grunt back at him.

A while later, Pruitt looked up at the litter of Carpenter's life spread out on the desk. He was seeing it anew, and suddenly of interest to him was the bag of items taken from the ecologist's 4x4. They'd already been checked for prints—nobody's but the deceased—so no longer had to be treated delicately. He emptied the contents unceremoniously into a pile and began poking through them.

The first connection he made was with a midwest company that Carpenter had exposed in violation of Illinois toxic dumping laws. Fines and clean-up fees alone had totaled over ten million dollars. When the lawyers and unretrievable court costs were added in, it had cost the company its existence. Yet nobody would be shedding tears for them. They'd left a legacy of death for a small community south of Chicago—a midwestern Love Canal. Ominously, the report ended by saying that the toxic dump discovered was probably only one of many the company had created.

The report itself, however, as compelling it may have been, had not been what piqued Pruitt's curiosity, but rather the plastic barrel of the outlaw company's pen whose tip Carpenter had drilled a small hole through and strung with a fine gold chain. He noticed that many of the items taken off the rearview mirror stem of Carpenter's 4x4 had been similarly tooled.

Cross-checking, Pruitt found that nearly all of the items were in one way or another connected to companies that

Carpenter had gone to battle with and won. Finally, Pruitt referenced the pictures of chief executives in the magazines to see if any were the men in charge of the companies Carpenter had bested.

Bingo. A headhunter's cache of trophies. A double life indeed, just as Deputy Yen had said. Beneath that mild, professorial countenance was a hard, determined man; behind the adult facade a boy obsessed with revenge.

An additional cross-check of the information showed that the names and telephone numbers of companies in the ecologist's personal phone book were mostly the same ones that he'd beaten in court. Had he called them to gloat?

Then he noticed something just odd enough that he should have noticed it before but hadn't. One of those what-you're-looking-for-is-right-in-front-of-you things. Your lost keys in the middle of the kitchen table, your hat actually on your head.

In this case it was simply another phone number, a small red dot next to it, inconspicuous if it were not the only one so marked. There was no identifying name, but the prefix looked familiar.

On a whim, Pruitt picked up the phone, punched a one, the local area code, then the number. There was a hesitation, then it began ringing in the normal fashion. No intercept. That meant it was somewhere in western Washington.

On the fifth ring someone picked up.

CHAPTER EIGHTEEN

"Mac here," the voice said. "What do you want?"

For an instant, Pruitt was speechless. "J. Michael MacClinton?" he asked.

After a pause: "Who is this?"

"Sheriff Gavin Pruitt. From Willapa County. I was there the other day? We had crab?"

"Pruitt, how the hell did you get my private line? It's unlisted. Is this some cop thing you can do? Get anybody's number you want without approval? I'd have given it to you if you'd asked, but I don't like this other crap."

Pruitt said, "I found your number in John Carpenter's personal phone diary."

After a pause: "Carpenter's?"

"Yes."

MacClinton said, "Good Christ," then was silent.

Pruitt said, "I'm curious, Mac, why would John Carpenter have your unlisted phone number in his personal phone diary?"

"Beats me, Sheriff. Cranks seem to get it all the time, though. That's why I keep changing it." Then he added, "Looks like I'm going to have to change it again."

"Did you know him?" Pruitt asked.

"Of course," Mac said. "Everybody knew who he was."

Mac was lousy at being disingenuous. "He ever have reason to call you?"

"Me? Why the hell would he?"

"Well, I'm sorry to have bothered you. It was an odd coincidence, I guess."

"Ridiculous coincidence, you ask me. Get a little money ahead, every crank in the world's after your ass."

Pruitt apologized once more, rang off, then called the phone company. The operator misunderstood his request and told him that MacClinton's home phone number was unlisted.

"That's not what I want to know. I want to know how many times the number has been changed in, say, the last ten years."

"I have no idea, sir."

"Look, maybe if you could put me through to your supervisor?"

The supervisor balked as well.

"Ma'am, I've already got his number." He repeated it to convince her. "I only want to know how many times he's changed it in the last few years. It doesn't matter what the numbers were. This is for a police investigation. Do you want to verify who I am? I'll hang up, then you call the Willapa County Sheriff's Office. Ask for Gavin Pruitt."

The supervisor said, "No, that won't be necessary. I don't see how your request would jeopardize our customer's privacy. I've just never been asked anything like it before."

For a full minute or so, Pruitt could hear the muted tapping of her fingers on a computer keyboard. "Well, according to what's here, Mr. MacClinton has *never* changed his phone number."

⊕

With the governor's aide's help, Pruitt's request for MacClinton's phone records got rushed through. By the middle of the next working day Pruitt also had the search warrant he needed. With that in hand, he arranged for deputies Lee Wilson and Raphe Jones to follow him to Riverton in the Willapa County evidence van. At Mac's house, Pruitt had his deputies wait by the vehicles rather than accompany him to the door. He wasn't expecting the kind of trouble that needed the presence of three cops.

As before, MacClinton answered the knock himself, swinging open the massive doors dramatically, like the curator of an exclusive private library. "Pruitt," he said by way of a greeting.

"Hey, Mac." Pruitt shrugged. "Sorry to drop in unannounced, but I've got a few things I'd like to talk to you about."

MacClinton regarded the sheriff evenly. His were eyes that melded intimacy and intimidation in equal measures. Gray-blue and steely, they were eyes to fear if he wanted something from you, eyes to count on if he was attempting to obtain something on your behalf. But today something was amiss. Maybe not the eyes as much as how his face, in spite its ruddy complexion, was curiously pale.

"Can you make it quick?"

Pruitt held the warrant up from where he'd been keeping it by his thigh. "Actually, I'd like to come in and take a look around."

MacClinton peeked over Pruitt's shoulder at the vehicles and extra deputies. "What's this about?"

"It's about John Carpenter."

Pointing to it, MacClinton said, "Does that piece of paper mean I have to let you in?"

"I'm afraid it does."`

Finally MacClinton moved away from the door. Pruitt signaled to his deputies, who strode forward.

"Are your vehicles unlocked?" Pruitt asked.

"I don't need to lock them up here."

Hearing this, Wilson ducked away to the garage.

MacClinton drew up in the middle of the vaulted foyer. To Jones he made a motion with his hand. "My office is down the hall, second door on the left. That's probably where you'll want to start."

Jones tipped her hat and said, "Thank you, sir," then peeled off in the direction their host had indicated.

When Jones had disappeared, MacClinton said, "You'll join me, then, Pruitt?"

⊕

Once in the quiet, comfortable living section of the house, Mac said, "I've got coffee on, but I'm for something a little stronger. How about you?"

Pruitt removed his hat. "Nothing stronger for me, thanks."

Moving about his kitchen authoritatively, MacClinton got Pruitt's coffee, then bent to a lower cupboard and pulled out a bottle of single malt scotch. He poured himself three fingers' worth and took a healthy slug. Even at a distance its peaty aroma made Pruitt's mouth water.

MacClinton let it warm him a moment before saying, "What have you got?"

Pruitt pulled up a counter stool. "Among other things, records that show more than a few phone calls logged between your phone and John Carpenter's."

MacClinton took another sip of whiskey. "I should probably call my lawyer."

"No problem. As long as you use the phone here in the kitchen."

Rather than reach for the telephone, MacClinton said, "What're you going to do today?"

"Look for some items in your office. Run some tests on your vehicles."

MacClinton pursed his lips, mulling over the whiskey and what was in his mind. He walked to other end of the lunch counter from Pruitt, and also pulled up a stool. He swiveled so that the back of the stool was against the counter and he could rest his elbows on it and gaze out his window.

"This is a helluva deal," he said.

"It certainly has been."

"I guess it was bound to come out. Sooner or later."

Pruitt took a sip of his coffee, but could still smell the whiskey. "Were you going to make that call to your lawyer, Mac?"

MacClinton said, "Naw, don't believe I'll bother."

"If it's your intention to make a statement, I'd like to do Miranda first. And I've got a little tape recorder here to make sure we get everything accurate."

MacClinton said, "Why don't you go ahead and do all that."

Once the formalities were finished, he said, "The deal is John Carpenter's been in my back pocket from the get go."

His eyes not moving from the panoramic view out his kitchen, Mac spun quite a tale."The men in my business," he began, "know how to make money all right, but most are also short sighted. That's what growing up soft does. But not me. I've always had to think smarter 'cause I started with nothing.

"Back as far as the mid-60's I knew this environmental movement was going to impact the way forestry operated. My colleagues didn't. Wrote'em off as nut-jobs. But I say things change; they always do. The point is not to lose sleep fighting it, but to keep making money by understanding and exploiting it."

He took a more modest sip of his whiskey, contemplative now. "What I did was set up this company: The Rare Earth Foundation. Got the name from that band with that song *Get Ready*. Remember it?"

"Sure."

Mac chuckled. "I was getting ready, all right."

"What kind of company was it?"

"A company that funded environmental projects, my friend."

Pruitt gazed at him a moment. "You're kidding."

MacClinton grinned. "Remember when the Russians tried to bug the US embassy? A great idea that. Intel, Pruitt. I was going to have a direct conduit. Best way to best your competition is to know their next move. That was my plan.

"Which meant, of course," he quickly added, "that I had to keep my name out of it. Completely. Man of my reputation?

To use their own terms, the greenies would have freaked if my name was connected to Rare Earth. So I set it up in Chicago. When I pulled strings it was through a series of shell corporations. First thing I did was hire a couple of PI's to pose as intermediaries representing some mind-blown old kook, took LSD and now wanted to fund environmental projects." He chuckled. "Greenies were so greedy for a source of private income they bought it hook, line, and sinker.

"And I kept it simple, man. All Rare Earth does is review prospectuses for environmental projects. Identify good ones, send them through those channels to me, I approve'em or don't."

"It's seems ludicrous, a man in your position doing all this."

"Like I said, Pruitt, forewarned is forearmed. Besides, you can't believe what passes for an environmental issue. You know the first thing I paid for? An aluminum can recycling center. Within a year these hippies offered Rare Earth points of their net for a second grant. A year after that, they're making me money.

"That, Pruitt," he said, tipping his glass, "is the kind of good crazy shit that happens if you've got any vision at all." He took another sip. "I know a good business model when I see one and started having Rare Earth take points on other projects. Shit," he drawled, "the last ten years my personal investment's down to a trickle. The icing on the cake.

"Patience was the key," MacClinton said. With his free hand he made a snake-like gesture. "I just let Rare Earth weave itself into the fabric of the movement, man. It wasn't until the mid-70's that I started toying with things a bit, see what I could get out of for myself directly. About that time I got a think tank split off from the Rand Corporation to do a little research for me. You should see that report, Pruitt."

He stopped to chuckle again. "Well, I guess you actually could if you want to. It's back there in my office. The top twenty-five environmentalists of their day."

"Let me, guess," Pruitt interrupted. "John Carpenter was on that list."

Mac nodded. "Right at the top. And not just because of his pedigree. Which was superb, of course—bachelor's degree at the University of Washington, Ph.D. at some Ivy league school, blah, blah, blah. Lot of guys had that. But Carpenter was a loner, you see. No hobbies, no friends to speak of, only a marginal interest in women, but ambitious as a beaver. But the kicker? He was an only child whose father had abandoned him and his mother when he was nine.

"Oh, yeah. I knew my mark when I saw him: competent, driven, but also psychologically fragile, susceptible to manipulation. I didn't know what I might eventually get out of him, just figured getting him in my pocket would provide a windfall some day. And it absolutely did.

"But, of course, I had to get him in that pocket first. So I told Rare Earth to give him anything he wanted. They contacted him, had him write a grant, gave him the money, and off he ran. Been putting money into his projects ever since."

"Guy like Carpenter," Pruitt noted, "wouldn't be interested in a can recycling center."

"Absolutely not. He was all legit stuff, and, man, am I glad I had the final say on what he'd work on 'cause that sumbitch was a bulldog. He absolutely killed that company in Michigan dumping toxic waste. Some sort of Midwest Love Canal? You remember that?"

"I read something about it, yes."

"His report style? Every 't' crossed, every 'i' dotted. Meticulous. Unassailable. And without all those strings you have with government money, he moved like lightning. That company never knew what hit them. One day they're making a mint dumping that shit, the next day they're in court standing in a whole 'nother pile of shit, right up to their necks."

"You sound proud of him."

"Carpenter? Of course, I am. I mean, hell yeah. I admire that kind of toughness. He might have looked like a bookworm, but he had a spine of steel. A good man," he said, a soft catch in his voice.

"Are you why he was out here?"

Mac polished off his whiskey, but continued to hold the glass in his hand. "When the Hicksons put Black Bear Ridge up for sale, I knew what I'd been saving him for. With Carpenter writing the environmental impact statement? Game over. I mean, the man practically invented how those are written. Nobody would refute his findings."

"Which you were going to have him manipulate in your favor?"

"Absolutely. When he realized who'd been supplying his grants all these years it was like Ralph Nader finding out Ford and GM had been funding him. Once he saw the paper trail, he'd do whatever I asked. And what I asked him for was every frickin' stick of lumber up there on Black Bear Ridge."

"I might have one more of these." MacClinton rose from his stool and walked to the liquor cabinet.

Pruitt said, "Why wouldn't Carpenter just tell you to screw off? He hated men in positions like yours."

"Of course he did, but he loved his work more. Don't forget, he had no wife, no kids, no family. All he had was his work. It was his legacy. If it went public that he'd been funded all these years by someone like me every report he'd ever written would be suspect. He might have never gotten work again— nothing of any importance anyway. And he considered himself important."

"Exactly how was he going to make the deal work?" Pruitt asked.

As he reached for the bottle of single malt, MacClinton said, "Do his usual thorough job, but turn it all over to me. Then tell the world he found nothing."

"Nothing?"

MacClinton flicked his hand. "Next to nothing. A few owls, whatever else is fashionable. All gussied up in John's style, the charts and graphs? A done deal. Nobody questions it. Save a hundred acres, log the rest."

Pruitt said, "I see a problem. You still had to buy the property, which the Hicksons could sell to anybody. Didn't the Japanese about double all the other offers?"

"Very astute, Pruitt. The Japanese had to be dealt with, that's for sure. I explained to them what I had, that it was me who controlled that timber's destiny."

He poured himself another scotch. "Smart businessmen that they are, they listened. They could see how it was going to go. If they didn't work with me, I'd scuttle the bastards by letting Carpenter's real study out, let them take the chance not even a scraggly Christmas tree would make it off that ridge. On the other hand, play along and they get what they want. Through me, through the Hicksons—what difference did it make as long as they got it?"

"What if Carpenter really hadn't found anything? Wouldn't all this have looked pretty foolish?"

MacClinton took a sip of his fresh glass of whiskey, a grin-like crease to his mouth. "An acceptable risk."

Pruitt said, "Any chance someone else would make an offer as large as yours?"

"No. There were budget limits on what that stand was worth for everybody but the Japs and the greenies. The greenies, of course, saw it as priceless and would have paid through the nose for it. The trouble was they had no money. The Japs, on the other hand, coveted that timber like the Holy Grail. All that straight-grained cedar and hemlock? It's some of the most beautiful wood in the world—which the Japs respected. They were going to log and mill it to the most exacting standards you've ever seen."

Pruitt said, "I take it there was no sentimentality left on the Hicksons' part to keep it unspoiled in memory of their father, sell it to the environmentalists for less than it might have been worth?"

MacClinton said, "No possible way. Their daddy was shrewd, but those kids went through their inheritance like water. They wanted as much money as they could get, and I was in a position to outbid anybody out there."

From the earlier investigation into the Hicksons, Pruitt saw the fit. "So you buy it, you log it, you sell the timber to the Japanese. A little windfall there?"

MacClinton tipped his glass to him. "A mind like yours, Pruitt, you could have made a lot of money." Mac grinned at him. "Hell, maybe you have. I hear cops can do that."

Weakly, Pruitt smiled back. "Thanks, Mac. But I'd still like to hear the end of this deal."

MacClinton said, "My offer to the Hicksons was going to be a good one, but under what the Japanese had offered. The windfall was selling to the Japs for what they were already willing to pay—a price inflated way over what I could get for it stateside."

With that, MacClinton drained his glass of his whiskey, then made his way over to the sink. He washed out his glass and set it on the drying rack.

Pruitt regarded him a moment. Something was off. "Let's go ahead and finish it." He nodded to the tape recorder. "For the record, if that's all right."

MacClinton said, "Finish what? I just gave you chapter and verse."

"The details of the murder itself, Mac. So my forensic people can sleep easy again."

Still standing by the sink, MacClinton stared at Pruitt with look of dismay on his face. "Good Christ, Sheriff, why would I *kill* him?"

"Once you had the report, Carpenter's better off dead than alive. What would you have done if he'd had an attack of conscience? What if he'd kept copies of everything and turned it over to the courts? You couldn't risk that, so you killed him."

Impatiently shaking his head, MacClinton said, "No, no, no, no. I'm being ruined here."

Pruitt said, "Hey, you killed somebody. What did you expect would happen?"

"Wait," MacClinton said. "Wait." He raised his hands. "I'm sorry. I left something out."

Pruitt sighed. Another criminal caught red-handed and ready to lie through his teeth to save his skin. "What?"

"The riskiest part, actually." MacClinton sat back at the table, looking at Pruitt this time, not the view. "I put up my holdings as collateral for the offer money on Black Bear Ridge. If I don't get that timber, I lose everything. The people holding the paper call in their marker."

Suddenly, details flip-flopped in Pruitt's mind. "Are you telling me you don't have the report?"

MacClinton touched the side of his nose; he tried to smile but could only grimace. "I do *not*. I was supposed to have it. Weeks ago. He was done, he said. Then he was dead."

"You didn't kill him?"

"No!" Mac barked. He held up his hands again. "Sorry, sorry. It's just that…No, I didn't kill him. I might kill him with my bare hands right now if he walked in here, for all the shit he's putting me through. But, no."

Pruitt regarded MacClinton a moment. "If you've got the report, we'll find it. If we have to tear this house down, and your mills, too, we'll find it."

"Fine," MacClinton said. "Tear it down. You may as well, for all the good it's going to do me."

Pruitt held up a hand. "Wait a minute. You say you've already borrowed the money for the offer on Black Bear Ridge? What bank would make a deal based on blackmail?"

MacClinton laughed, but not from amusement. "You're getting it, Pruitt." He wiped a tear from his eye. "You ever read that book about loggers? *The Great Notion*, I think it was called?"

"Kesey. Sure, I read that."

"Remember how that union man said all he wanted was a fair advantage?"

"I do. Pretty funny notion all right."

"Well, that's how the people I borrowed the money from do business. They look for a fair advantage. And I gave it to them. If they don't get the timber, they get my mills, everything I own." He held up his hands. "You'll find the whole thing in my office. They weren't screwing around. They had to come out winners no matter what."

Pruitt said, "Who?"
"The Japanese, Pruitt. The goddang Japs."

CHAPTER NINETEEN

It boiled down to whether or not MacClinton had Carpenter's data. If he did, he was the murderer. If he did not, he would be the last person on earth to want Carpenter dead.

The bust had not gone at all how Pruitt had expected. He couldn't imagine the timberman's tale being an elaborate lie, and found himself believing it—or would until the confiscated files had been combed through. In the meantime, there was only one thing that might support or unravel the story. Leaving his charge under the supervision of Deputy Jones, Pruitt went out to the garage to talk to Lee Wilson, who was examining, or maybe just admiring, the 1956 baby-blue Bel Air.

"Anything connecting any of these vehicles with either the murder site or Carpenter's apartment?"

"Negatory."

"You think calling in the state's crime lab people would help? On this case, I could make a call, get that arranged in a snap."

Wilson let his gaze fall slowly across the four meticulously maintained vehicles: the Bel Air, a 1962 Corvette, red, and two brand new 1994 models: a BMW 740i, white, and a Jeep Grand Cherokee, black. "You want your t's crossed," he said, "I suppose it wouldn't hurt anything. But these vehicles look as if they'd been detailed by professionals. I'd say it would be a waste of time and money."

⊕

Pruitt used his cell phone to call in his request for a state forensics team to go over Mac's vehicles. Though he agreed with Wilson that it was probably a waste, politically it would buy some time, make it look as if progress was being made when in actuality another dead-end appeared to have been reached. The woman who had taken his call put him through to the director.

"You want a team, you got a team," he was told. "This investigation has the highest priority with us. Hold for just a second."

Within moments Lee Wilson was talking with the state's best forensic technician. While those two fell into argot, Pruitt strolled back to the house, taking his time, commiserating with himself. Currently, there was no physical evidence connecting Mac to the murder site. And while his alibi was weak—here at the house on the night in question—neither was it evidence, just suspicion. Mac's confession may have implicated him in white-collar crime, but not a homicide. Even if there had been white-collar crime, it had not taken place in Pruitt's jurisdiction, so it was out of his hands anyway. He needed the documents that Deputy Jones had driven away with to verify Mac's story and clear him of the murder, but more than likely the paperwork would get passed back to some other law enforcement agency.

Pruitt found MacClinton in his living room, holding the framed photo of his wife and baby daughter, the family members lost to him. More loss facing him now.

"I could easily justify taking you in," Pruitt said, "but you've been cooperative and I don't think you're going to run off. I'll be straight with you, a deal like this, I'm more worried about your frame of mind than anything else."

Mac said, "I'm not about to do anything crazy."

Pruitt couldn't help but glance at the mother/daughter photo, mom radiant, the baby's sweet head swaddled lovingly in the blanket, an edge turned out revealing the letters 'DM' in script. "Tragedies compound," he said, "even if they're years apart."

"This?" Mac said, gesturing with his free hand towards Riverton, where mills, his included, continued to pump smoke into the already smoke-colored Gray's River sky. "You think losing this is tragedy? Compared to them?" he said, wagging the photograph.

Pruitt said, "Of course not." Then again, quieter: "Of course not."

Mac held Pruitt's gaze a moment longer, then turned to look out the window. "I'll admit I'm worried about my boys. Whether they'll still have jobs. They've got college degrees, of course. Years of experience. Connections all over the world."

"Can you call one of them now and let me talk to him?"

"I'm fine, Sheriff, if that's what you're thinking."

The indignation in his voice led Pruitt to believe he would be.

As he drove down to the flatlands and on through Riverton back towards Elkhorn, that last image of MacClinton standing by the window contemplating the demise of his empire haunted Pruitt. He might normally have taken some pleasure in bringing down a rich industrialist, but not in this case. How could he when Mac's crime, ultimately, was trying to best an upper class of dubious morality by playing too vigorously at their own game? If this was Mac's downfall, Pruitt couldn't help but think that while the law would be upheld, the system undergirding it remained suspect—a recurring conflict in his life. Of course he understood the necessity of law and order—how could he not and serve as a cop?—but whose law was it, and what kind of order should be imposed?

He laughed out loud. His distrust of the establishment seemed to be as intact now that he had become the establishment as it had been when he had tried to live outside it. This feeling also partially explained why he continued to relate so strongly to the Grateful Dead, for whom integration into the mainstream brought similar ambivalence. Take their crazy foray into establishing their own record company. Serious discussions about product distribution centered around a fleet of psychedelic-painted ice cream trucks that would be dispatched to communes and hip record stores. Of course reality eventually set in and compromises had to be made—just as in Pruitt's life. But the intent to do things differently—maybe even better—remained. That's why, 30 years and counting, they continued to inspire him.

On Friday Pruitt told Andy Messerit to drop everything else and go over the documentation confiscated from J. Michael MacClinton. He told Messerit the story Mac had told him about his leveraging his holdings and asked the bookkeeper to verify it. At this point a full report was unnecessary, Pruitt just wanted to know if it was plausible. Especially important was whether Mac had Carpenter's report. If he found that, call him, and they'd run over to Riverton and haul Mac's lying ass to jail.

Messerit said, "Can this hold a few days? I'd like to get home to my family for the weekend."

Pruitt thought about it. "I don't see why not. Man's not going anywhere."

"I appreciate it, Sheriff. First thing Monday morning, I'll get to the bottom of it."

At his desk, Pruitt brought his notes up to date, quickly, not even bothering to take his jacket off. Then he left his office, informing Joyce he'd be out for the rest of the afternoon. "I've got an interview to conduct," he said. "Out in the county. Got my beeper if you need me," he added as he hustled out the door, drawn to Olwen Friday like a moth to flame.

⊕

He went home first, to change into some comfortable clothes. His green cable-knit sweater and a wheat-colored shirt, some soft cotton twill pants, and his pair of well-worn tan moccasin loafers. On the way out the door, he threw on his suede leather jacket.

After a stop at Rhea's Food Center, Pruitt drove east out Highway Six. The last few days had been dry, with sunshine, crisp air, and spectacular sunsets. The orange and red of the latest beauty shone behind him—the colors so alluring Pruitt was glad to find something positive in how much he'd been watching his back lately. That's how he caught sight of something in his rearview mirror that displeased him greatly, a familiar pickup truck. If it was who he thought it was, he was going to be furious. With the vehicle about a hundred yards behind him, Pruitt at the last minute swung his car off the main highway onto Oxbow Road and gunned it. The surge of power from the big V-8 lifted the chassis like an attempt at flight, Pruitt's stomach lifting along with it. A quarter mile down the road he stood on the brakes and did a four-wheel drift onto the gravel driveway that led to Wilma and Quinn Hudziak's spread. Old elms bracketed the entrance, and a short row of cottonwoods led to a turnaround. Pruitt didn't know what the Hudziak's would think if they were home and witnessing him squealing around the circular drive and heading back to Oxbow like a maniac—but neither could he worry about it.

He got back to the driveway entrance in time to catch the pickup that had been following him speeding down Oxbow. Having already opened his window, he slapped the suction-cup mounted police beacon on the roof and hit the switches for both it and the siren he'd had installed in his personal vehicle, then peeled out in pursuit of Mr. Earl Ruddell.

Fortunately for Earl, it wasn't a long pursuit. If he'd forced a chase, Pruitt would have booked him immediately and let him sit in jail right through the weekend. Smartly, Ruddell pulled over to the narrow shoulder along Oxbow as soon as Pruitt got up behind him.

Off-duty, Pruitt did not carry a weapon, and without the pistol on his hip, he felt one tool short of playing the pull-over by the book. To compensate, he dealt with the situation as hostile. Standing at the back of the truck, he ordered Ruddell out onto the road. When he hesitated, Pruitt yelled, "Now, Earl, or you're under arrest!"

As Ruddell's door opened and he stepped out, Pruitt yelled, "On the ground, Earl! Hit it, mister!"

Ruddell had gotten as far as his knees when Pruitt rushed forward and forced him down, chest to pavement. With a knee in a the middle of Earl's back, Pruitt frisked him harshly. Finding nothing, he hoisted him to his feet and shoved him against the side of the truck, facing away. With his mouth practically at the man's ear, Pruitt growled, "What the hell do you think you're doing, Earl?"

When Ruddell refused to answer, Pruitt grabbed a handful of his hair and used it to pull his head back. The man stank, as sour as a gym locker. "I am mad as hell, Earl," he said, "and I want an explanation."

"God's calling," he said.

Pruitt gave him a yank. "Not good enough."

"There's some woman Carpenter used to meet. I saw them once at the Spartan Store. You've been going out there. To see her, I figured. I want to talk to her."

Another yank. "About what?"

"About Carpenter. What he'd found. This whole charade has got to stop. That timber needs to come down."

Ruddell's sour smell had Pruitt about to gag, so he let go of Earl and stepped back. He forced himself to take a deep breath. Another. Standing back even six feet there were more calming aromas: the heat of the pickup's engine, the dust of the road, silage packaged like enormous sausages in rolls of white plastic turning sweet in the surrounding fields. He ordered Earl to turn around.

When he did, something besides defiance had finally found its way into Earl's eyes. An inkling of fear.

Good. Maybe he was ready to listen to reason.

Pruitt raised his finger. "You stay away from that woman! Do you hear me? This is called hindering an investigation, and I can put you in jail for it. And I will. Right now, if I have to. You got that?"

Earl remained silent, head drawn back and cocked, exposing a gaunt cheek, daring Pruitt to smite him, at which point he'd offer up the other. A real piece of work. Yet Pruitt was feeling something other than anger now. Earl had always been thin, but never undernourished, and never with such pasty skin. Pruitt lowered his finger. "Jesus, Earl. You look like hell. When's the last time you had a bath, or ate a decent supper?"

Earl regarded Pruitt a moment before he said, "I'll go home, Sheriff."

Good. He hadn't gotten so far into doing the Lord's work that he couldn't look out after his own welfare here on earth.

"You do that, Earl. And if I catch you following me again— even a yard behind me, mister—you're going to county lockup."

When Pruitt reached to take him by the shoulder, Earl flinched, but it was a magistrate's hand on him now, firm and directional. "Get home, now," Pruitt said, turning him towards the truck cab. "Have Laura look after you tonight. Think about how much that woman loves you, Earl. Think about your boys. Get things in perspective. Can you do that for me?"

Ruddell didn't answer him, but did a careful U-turn on Oxbow and headed back for Elkhorn at a legal pace.

Once he was out of sight, Pruitt sat in his car and pulled himself back together. He couldn't remember when he'd been so angry—or if he had *ever* been. He'd almost punched Earl. Jeez, what was happening to him? He was behaving in ways he didn't recognize—some peckerwood smokey on the take. As the Dead put it, he was feeling like a stranger—to love, to himself as a man, as an officer of the law. Yet given the circumstances—bombs thrown at him, friends killed, higher-ups intimidating him—maybe the only self-recognition problem he was having was recognizing that he was the kind of man who fought back hard when cornered.

He took one long breath, the silage wafting in through his opened window overwhelming everything else, sweetly pungent. He rubbed his forehead, his temples, his eye sockets—started to feel okay again. He put the car in gear and drove off, picking up Highway Six where it intersected with Oxbow and the original intent of his trip.

CHAPTER TWENTY

Without the full moon and cloudless skies it would have been dark as ink in the clearing that led to Olwen's home. But the moon shone iridescently over the bone-chilling cold, coloring the gateless gateposts a dark and eerie blue, shading the salmon finials into an almost lifelike appearance. And although a soft, yellow light spilled invitingly from the windows of the house, the doll-eyed frog atop the garret appeared ominous as a poled, shrunken head.

When Olwen opened the door, she was cradling her shotgun.

Pruitt said, "I swear I'm not peddling Amway."

"You just missed this bear," she said. "He keeps trying to get my fish. I shoot over his head and it scares the hell out of him." Her face lit up. "Roses? What a treat."

She invited him in, hung the shotgun on the rack by the door. "You look so different out of uniform. I was just making dinner. Wow," she said, "red wine on a cold autumn night." She smiled at him. "It sounds delicious."

☮

They ate at a small table, a glass vase between them with one of the roses in it, stem clipped short. Pruitt was not surprised that Olwen was a vegetarian, but she was surprised that he was—even with his lapses, the oysters and clams and a little white turkey meat on Thanksgiving.

"I'm not a bad cook," he said, "but *this* is great. I'd just be guessing at what some of these spices are."

"Nothing exotic," she said, "just fresh."

"Cilantro?" he said. "In the beans?"

"That was a good guess, all right. Plus parsley, and some crushed chili pepper."

After they'd eaten, Olwen whisked the dishes away. She washed in a steel basin, rinsed in another. She used organic castile soap and hot water from the kettle on the wood stove.

Pruitt asked her if she had a well.

"I tote in from the creek."

"It's potable, obviously."

She plopped the silverware in the rinse. "I check it regularly, just to make sure."

"There's no drain. What do you do with the water when you're done?"

"In the summer," she said, "I put it on the vegetables. Tonight I'll just pour it in the pond."

"Wash water?"

"This soap won't hurt anything. The organic material the fish eat, or it settles on the bottom."

"We need to talk," he said. "About why I came out here."

There, he'd said it. Since walking up the flagstones to her house, it had been sitting on his chest like a gorilla. For her part, Olwen remained silent, waiting for his explanation.

"I couldn't help myself, really. After the other night."

She lifted the rinsed dishes from the basin, setting them on a wood dish rack. "I don't know what to say to you."

Pruitt was standing behind her now, wanting to reach for her, put his arms around her waist. "Something was there."

"Where you are is where you need to be," she said, "and it's always changing."

Though the chore appeared finished, she would not turn around.

"So this is what," he said, "where we need to be, or something that's already changed?"

She placed her hands on the edge of the counter. "I don't know."

"You don't have feelings for me?"

She said, "I'm afraid of what I feel for you."

"Can we talk about that? What we feel for each other?"

"Don't you have someone?" she asked. "You must."

"Some issues have come up. It's in limbo."

She turned. "Limbo," she said, "is where we are, too. As close as people in limbo can get."

Pruitt looked away. *Good god, what was he doing? Was this what he wanted?*

"You're still grieving?" he asked, looking at her again.

Olwen crossed her arms over her chest. "It's less to do with John than you think."

"You were breaking up?"

"Not like you're thinking," she said. "Not like lovers. We weren't lovers, you see. We never were."

Pruitt crossed his arms, too. "You were just friends?"

"The best of friends," she said. "The best."

"But he was leaving."

"Yes. For South America. He was going to put all his resources into the rainforest. He wanted to take his work to the next higher level, a global level. He was ready."

"So his work on Black Bear Ridge had been finished?"

"Yes. He told me so."

"The thing is, we can't find his report."

"I don't know about that." She made a face. "Except one thing."

Pruitt said, "What thing?"

"In here," she said, and led him over to her stereo. "I don't know if this has anything to do with it, but John brought this weird CD with him the last time he was here."

"What's weird about it?"

"It's got a Crosby, Stills & Nash cover," she said as she kneeled over her collection and searched. "But when you play it there's nothing on it. Here it is." She held it out to him. "You can have it."

Pruitt took the CD over to his leather jacket, hanging on a hook next to the shotgun rack, and slipped it in the pocket. When he returned, Olwen was tending the wood stove, fitting two pieces of split cedar into the fire box. Then she closed the fire box door and took up the full lotus position on her futon chair. Light and shadows cast by the fluted oil-burning lamps played across her face.

Pruitt sat on the couch opposite her.

"You want something more than friendship," Olwen said. "Which I'm not ready for."

Pruitt remained quiet. Being honest, he would have said he had no *idea* what he wanted, really. Yes, she was beautiful— as beautiful a woman as he had ever stood in the presence of—and he lusted for her. Beyond that, he was clueless as to his motives. Maybe the prospect of breaking up with Molly had triggered a single man's mindset: that whole biological thing of passing on his seed to as many women as possible— an especially crazy thought when passing on his seed was the issue between Molly and him in the first place.

But he said none of this to Olwen, but rather stayed lost in his own thoughts until her voice startled him. "I know I seem a little strange to people, Gavin—you included—but I know myself fairly well. What I'm capable of, and what I'm not." She shrugged.

He leaned to rest his elbows on the tops of his knees. He rubbed his forehead. "I've been making a fool of myself, haven't I?"

She said, "No, not at all. I'm going to be me, and you're going to be you. This thing will play out the way it's supposed to."

Olwen was changing in front of his eyes—the fog of limerence lifting from his mind, his blood cooling. He'd not felt such a strong need to be with a woman—other than Molly—since...Well, since Molly. Had he been transferring his feelings for Molly to someone else out of fear for what

Molly wanted from him? Lyrics from the Dead song *Althea* rose up in his mind: *There are things you can replace and those you cannot,* and *the time had come to weigh those things, this space is getting hot.*

"Well," he said, and began to stand so he could leave, but stopped himself, stayed seated. He'd forgotten all about the excuse he'd concocted as an official reason for visiting Olwen. "Actually, I meant to run something by you tonight. Remember I told you about J. Michael MacClinton?"

"Yes. The man who owns this property."

"Did you ever meet him?"

She pulled a face. "When would I ever have had an opportunity to meet someone like that?"

"Because of something between him and John."

"Between him and *John*? What sort of thing?"

Pruitt told her the story. It took probably five or six full minutes, Olwen's gaze never leaving his, her face impassive.

"Well," she said when he was through, "that's absolutely amazing."

"John never hinted at it?"

"Never." She put her hand to her temple. "Finding something out like this, something hidden about somebody you thought you knew so well…It's upsetting."

"I wasn't trying to upset you…"

"I know you weren't. And John *had* begun behaving oddly near the end, so it fits. I thought it had to do with the project finishing up. His plans to move to Brazil. Those sorts of things."

"How was he acting oddly?"

"He was distracted. He was here physically, but not in spirit. Do you know what I mean?"

Pruitt said, "I do." And meant it, thinking about the last few months with Molly, how he should have sensed something important was on her mind. He rose to his feet. "How about I drop by again in a couple of days? Okay? After you've had some time?"

She rose, too. Smiled at him.

Good god she was beautiful. But was she also like *Stella Blue,* a woman Garcia lamented could not be held for long? Or in Pruitt's case, only once?

"Yes," she said. "After I've had some time to decide."

⊕

The next morning, Pruitt was having coffee in his kitchen nook when his phone rang and it was Molly.

"Gavin," she said, "I know we're supposed to be giving each other some space, but I can't help worrying about you. I know the papers probably make it seem bigger than it really is, but…I just wanted to make sure you were okay."

Pruitt held his head in one hand while with the other held the phone to his ear. "I'll tell you something I've never told you before. Or anybody, for that matter. When Olivia was a baby she had these little tee-shirts. With a kind of overlapping fold at the shoulders? The first time I did a load of laundry that included her clothes I took those tee-shirts from the dryer and was folding them and just started crying."

Molly was silent a moment before she said, "I never thought for a moment that you didn't know how I felt about this."

"I'm not saying one way or the other. Only that I get it. I really do."

"Gavin," she said, "There's something else. Why I really called."

"About having a baby?"

"No, about Angela."

Angela? Pruitt said, "Well, you know about her and Bill?"

"I figured it out. I dropped by to use the tank a couple of days ago and ran into her. She practically ambushed me when I was coming out of the garage. And she said some things that…Well, frankly, she frightens me. More than a little, if you want to know the truth."

"What she'd say?"

"Nothing she said as much as how she's probing. You know? Looking for information? She asked me if I knew a woman who dropped by your place the other night."

That Angela had been watching him that closely made him furious. To Molly he said, "That woman's not what you think."

"I didn't call to check up on you, Gavin. I'm not. I just don't trust Angela, and wanted you to know she's watching you like a hawk. I think she's up to something."

So do I, he said to himself. *So do I.*

⊕

An hour later Lee Wilson of all people showed up at Pruitt's back door, grinning like the Cheshire cat.

Pruitt was washing dishes and wiped his hands on a kitchen towel before opening the door. "Lee?"

"Never," said his chief investigator, "have I kicked more ass."

"I take it you've got something to show me?"

Wilson was toting two bulging plastic grocery sacks. "You got a place I can spread this stuff out?"

Pruitt led him to the sideboard in the living room, removing the 8x10 picture of him and his four siblings taken at a summer party in the backyard of his mother's house, the vase with dried flowers Molly had bought him a few years back, and the pewter candelabrum with burgundy candles— which had not been so much a gift from Molly as a overseen purchase. ("These candles pick up the color theme of your furnishings," she had told him. "Buy them.")

Pruitt fixed Lee a cup of coffee while Lee readied his presentation.

"I'm a frickin' genius," Lee said when Pruitt returned to the living room.

Pruitt winked and said, "That's what I've always told people, Lee."

"Well, me and my friend from ATF," he added. "We worked this up in Portland."

"I knew that travel voucher was worth every penny."

Wilson chuckled, and Pruitt noted that he and his lead investigator had now had two pleasant encounters over the course of only a few days—a record. Was Lee finally forgiving him for besting him in the election two years ago? He also observed the various items Lee had laid out neatly along the top of the sideboard, some in heat-shrink packaging, some in plastic bags, some loose.

"Here's what I found at your place," he said. "You got your bridge spike and your fuse, a bit of match taped to the fuse."

Pruitt inspected the items carefully.

"Over here's what I found at the union hall. A little bit of electrical outlet cord, and this male electrical connector. You see it's had something additional soldered to it. You got slightly different colors, more solder than you'd need for the wires that go to these…

"Which are chunks of a heating coil. And this is a hunk of wire with a clean cut end that connects to the heating coil."

Hefting the next item, Wilson said, "Now this bag's got some wire twists wrapped in black electrician's tape. Looks like the same kind of tape and the same kind of wrapping was done to keep that fuse on that spike thrown into your house."

Pruitt examined the piece. "Careful job."

"Very neat," Wilson said. "Our boy's very neat. And here we've got the leg wires off an electrical blasting cap. A nice bright blue, even if they are a bit scorched.

"But here's the one that killed me, man." Wilson picked up the item at the far end of the sideboard. "This just killed me."

He held up a scrap of plywood about a foot-and-a-half across, ragged edged and trapezoid shaped. He held it by trapping two edges between the palms of his hands. "What do you see?"

"Looks like somebody carved some hieroglyphics in it."

"It's an imprint. You got a little hash mark and a 50 next to it, hash mark alone, hash mark with a 40, then hash mark alone, then...Well, you can imagine what's next."

"Is this a coffee urn?"

"The next thing to it. It's the impression that a piece of coffee urn left in this piece of wood."

Pruitt looked closer. "What's this line alongside here?"

"I found this first," Wilson said, "and I had no idea. But after putting the whole package together I'd say that was the wire that ran from the electrical connection up the inside of the urn to the blasting cap on top."

Looking at Wilson, Pruitt said, "The bomb was snuck into the IWA as a coffee urn."

"Frickin' right. Frickin' huge-ass bomb. Which we already knew, of course. Probably had fifty pounds of shot in it."

"You're saying the sticks were unwrapped and the explosive itself used to line the urn."

"Exactly. Be like working with putty. Easy to do." Wilson shook his head. "Frickin' clever by half, our boy. Hide a coffee urn bomb in plain sight in the union hall kitchen."

"Where's he going to get fifty pounds of unreported explosive?"

"Easy. Let's say our boy's workin' with an outfit blasting a ditch, got a series of ten blasts, ten shots to a hole, he's the one in charge of the set-up. He puts nine shots in a hole. Who's going to notice the difference between nine and ten in a series blow like that? Now he's got ten sticks to take home.

"The other thing is they sell by the weighted case, not the stick. Got a variance of two-three sticks a case. Our boy does a lift now and then. If you're working around it, it wouldn't take long to get fifty pounds of unlicensed shot."

Pruitt gazed at the remaining items. "What did he use to set it off, a timer of some sort?"

"Right. That's what I've got here." The bag he proffered held plastic shards, some with raised numbers. "It's what's left of one of those 24-hour timed light switches that people buy to make it look like they're home when they go on vacation. Our boy wired up his bomb, hauled it into the hall, then plugged the whole thing into a wall circuit."

"I can see why Dale or Evie may not have noticed the coffee urn, but how could they have missed the timer?"

"That kitchen, you know how it was added later? Well, they did silly shit like leave an outlet behind a cupboard door under a counter. Which is exactly were it was plugged in. Under the counter, out of sight. Evie and Dale hardly used that kitchen anyway. Plus it was there less than 24 hours."

"Then it was no outsider. What was going on the night before?"

"Meeting. A big one. Potluck dinner, lasted until after midnight. You got a ton of ruckus. Boxes and baskets and shit in, boxes and baskets and shit out. Afterwards, everybody tired, nobody payin' attention to anything but getting home."

"We should start by matching the list of licensed blasters by who was at the meeting."

"Better yet," said Wilson. "I'm going to check on their shot handlers. Those pukes have nobody to answer to but the blasters."

"Good call," Priutt replied. And then was surprised by how quickly the chill between them returned. It literally felt like a window had opend to a cool breeze.

"Lee?" he said.

"Boss..." He hesitated. "The thing is I got offered a pretty good deal at the Training Center."

Pruitt knew Lee was referring to the Washington State Criminal Justice Training Center in Burien, where he already taught quarterly seminars in evidence preservation. "That doesn't surprise me, Lee—only that they waited this long. You've earned it."

"Yeah, that part's cool. But I also don't know if I want to do it. Live in a big city? I mean, I like the work, but..."

"That's a tough call, Lee. Living in Elkhorn's got its ups and downs, too. But whatever you decide, I'm on your side, man." Then he added, "Just one thing, though. If you do take this new job, and if we ever get something heavy like this Carpenter case again, I'd like to have your home phone number."

CHAPTER TWENTY-ONE

Like everyone else in Elkhorn, Pruitt felt the presence of the Japanese but rarely noticed them. They'd been there since the onset of the Black Bear Ridge controversy—sometimes as many as half-a-dozen, although lately only two or three—but their numbers never altered their demeanor. Whether a demonstration, town meeting, or press conference, they never drew attention to themselves, always remaining on the periphery.

Rooms at the most remote end of Elkhorn's best-kept motel, the Montcastle, had been all but leased for them since they'd arrived in town eighteen months ago, and their faces often changed, despite the constancy of their reticence and dark-blue three-piece business suits. There was a notable exception: Randy Yoshiwara, their spokesman and lone American of the contingent, was always around. He was also the only one of the group Pruitt really knew, so Saturday afternoon, Pruitt looked him up.

"I've been meaning to ask," said Pruitt, "are you representing one company, or is it a coalition?"

The Montcastle had a seldom-used lobby, two low-slung, deep-seated chairs around a lone end-table with a stack of outdated magazines. The innkeepers lived in back, and had apparently just had a lunch of fried onions and potatoes.

Not partial to the uniform of the men he represented except when they traveled en masse, today Yoshiwara wore a tweed sports coat over a white, open-necked polo shirt, wool slacks, and Hush Puppies. "A coalition, basically. The lumber industry in Japan is close knit and well-regulated."

Pruitt, too, was out of uniform, wearing jeans and a royal purple University of Washington sweatshirt. "Some people might define that as well protected from outside competition."

Also unlike his colleagues, Yoshiwara expressed his emotions easily, and he now bristled. "The companies I represent pour plenty of money into the American economy."

"What I was wondering," Pruitt said, "is if you've pulled your offer on the Black Bear Ridge stand, why are you still here?"

"Who says we've pulled our offer?"

"Let's just say a little birdy told me." The birdy in question was actually two birdies. One was Andy Messerit, the forensics bookkeeper, who had discovered that MacClinton was indeed up to his eyeballs with one of the Japanese timber companies. The other was the DAU agent who had, indeed, been able to get close enough to one of the Japanese businessmen—and surprisingly quickly—to confirm that something slippery was going on, though he didn't know what.

The muscles under Yoshiwara's face constricted, at the jaw line and around the eyes. "As any timberman would be, we're very concerned about the outcomes."

"I'd say especially so if you've done some maneuvering that makes your position strong." Pruitt looked at him coolly. "Maybe quite a bit stronger than anybody but myself and a few others think."

Falling back on the habits of the men he spoke for, Yoshiwara's face lost all expression. "I have no idea what you're talking about."

"When the documentation we've collected from J. Michael MacClinton is cleaned up and presented to the Attorney General, what do you think the charges will be? Collusion?

Some sort of racketeering? Maybe there'll be nothing illegal, but when all this comes to light, do you think the Hicksons would appreciate that kind of bad publicity?"

Yoshiwara said, "You have nothing we're afraid of."

"Maybe not, but I wonder if you may have something too hot to handle. Important data of Carpenter's is missing. Whoever has it committed a felonious crime to get it. Anything you may not be telling me in regards to such matters will be considered aiding and abetting."

"I believe this is called a bluff, isn't it, Sheriff?"

Pruitt stood. "Not if you're fucking with me, my friend."

⊕

As Pruitt walked away from the Montcastle towards his car, he self-consciously avoided looking in the direction of "John," the DAU agent who was now going to be tailing Randy Yoshiwara. With help from Olympia, he'd also gotten a tap on the phone lines coming out of the rooms rented by the Japanese staying at the Montcastle. He'd played the salient parts of the MacClinton interview to a Washington State Assistant Attorney General, who in turn hooked up with a sympathetic federal judge. They got the allowance in record time.

His next stop was David Spoor's, out on the Rutsatz. Alder was burning in the wood stove—Pruitt could smell it in the breeze that swirled the thin stream of smoke emanating from the stove pipe out over the yard and on towards the Nawiakum.

Spoor's dog announced Pruitt's arrival in no uncertain terms. Leashed to a line run, it couldn't get at anybody outside a twenty-foot arc, though his attempts to charge Pruitt were heroic and he made plenty of racket. Pruitt stood waiting a few yards outside the dog's purview.

When Spoor came around the side of the house, he was holding a maul. "Sheriff?"

"Got an update on the investigation for you, Dave."

Spoor silenced his dog and indicated the direction he'd come from with a nod. "I'm almost finished back here. You join me?"

While Spoor split wood—the ubiquitous alder, all but considered a weed locally—Pruitt explained to him the gist of the connection between MacClinton and Carpenter.

"The bastard!" Spoor powered the maul's flat end onto the head of the fro, the hunks of splintered wood leaping away from each other.

He wiped his brow with his sleeve. "I always suspected there was more to that sanctimonious son-of-a-bitch than he let on."

"There never has been any love lost between you two, has there?"

Closing off one nostril with his thumb, Spoor blew a mist of snot out of the other, then ran his sleeve across his nose. "No, there never has."

"The way he was killed, it would take somebody who knew logging equipment."

"From the descriptions in the reports, that sounds about right," he said, wiping his nostrils with a gloved hand.

"And if I'm not mistaken, before your conversion to environmentalism, you worked the woods. Up on the peninsula."

Spoor stood looking at Pruitt a moment. "Back to that whole thing again, huh?"

"You killed men in Vietnam. It takes a certain kind of man to do that, to kill for a cause. Your cause might be entirely different, but have you changed all that much?"

Spoor lugged another unsplit hunk of wood onto his chopping block. He hoisted the maul high over his head and brought the ax end down. There was a thwacking sound, but the wood block split only about halfway through, leaving the maul clasped in a tight embrace. He cursed and struggled to pull it out. "It's wet," he said.

⊛

Spoor's line, unfortunately, he'd not been able to get a tap on. Which didn't bother him much. Spoor probably assumed his line was tapped anyway. Besides which, Pruitt was only half convinced that the murder was connected to either the Japanese or Spoor—they were just all he had. Wire taps and surveillance at least made it look like progress was being made. The problem was the trail was getting colder and colder.

Yet Pruitt had his own problems to consider, too—and that trail wasn't getting cold as much as narrow, reaching a decision point he could not put off forever. Early Saturday evening Pruitt called his good friend Marion Jones at home. He wasted no time in getting to the point.

Marion said, "I think it's wonderful that you're thinking of another child."

"But I *wasn't* thinking of it," he said. "That's the problem. Jeez, Marion, you know technically if this happened I could have a grandchild older than my child?"

"You're not saying Olivia's pregnant, are you?"

"No, not at all. I just mean that I'm that old. It's…It's like hillbilly stuff."

Marion laughed. "Don't be so hard on hillbillies, Gavin. America was built on the resilience of hillbillies. I'm sure we've both got plenty of hillbilly blood running through our own veins. Besides, isn't this exactly the kind of thing you and I have been trying to convince the world of since the 60's? That there are other ways to live your life? Alternatives to the ways our parents expected us to live? Maybe better ways?"

"Yeah, I know. But…There's something else."

Then he told her about lusting for Olwen. "I would have slept with her, too, if she'd let me."

"Gavin, you've got to cut yourself some slack. In a situation like this, you're thinking all kinds of things, including wondering about a life without Molly. Testing it, you know? The real issue is she's part of the murder investigation."

Pruitt lightly banged his head with an open palm. "So unprofessional. I can't believe I put myself in this position."

"Do you think she murdered him?"

He said, "No, no, not at all." There were plenty of unknowns in this case, but that was not one of them. "There's a Dead song," he said. *"They Love Each Other.* The first line talks about looking for a shove in some direction. Maybe that's why I called. I was hoping you could shove me in a direction."

Marion laughed. "Sorry, Gav. I'd shove you out of the way of an on-coming car, but the shove you're talking about has got to come from inside you."

⊕

Talking to Marion didn't really resolve Pruitt's dilemma, but it had felt good to unburden himself, to talk out loud about things he'd been keeping in his head. He felt strengthened— prepared to deal with the consequences of whatever actions he took, and also to take those actions soon. Yet he could not sleep that night, so finally had a float, then fell asleep in the tank, something he never did. He stayed in over three hours and felt positively astral when he got out, his knees weak, his mind as blank as a new blackboard. By that time, it was five in the morning and he didn't feel like he'd be sleeping again any time soon, so he ate some breakfast and thought about going into the office. It was Sunday and it would be quiet and he could get caught up on his paperwork. But after the food he felt a little heavy, so he went to lie down on his new couch, pulled the afghan over his shoulders to ward off the bit of feverish chill that had suddenly clambered over his body, and promptly feel asleep fully clothed.

Dreaming when the telephone started ringing, Pruitt awoke momentarily confused, then stumbled into the kitchen.

"I got the bastard." It was Lee Wilson.

"Which bastard, Lee?"

"The bomber, the shooter—same idiot. He's ready to confess. C'mon down and let's do this thing."

⊛

Out in the hallway near the interrogation room door, Pruitt said, "How'd it come down, Lee?"

Wilson leaned against the wall. "Remember we were talking about blasters and handlers? Well, I took the list E.L. made after the union hall and just started calling blasters and found out who they were using as handlers. I suppose I should have alphabetized it and started from the top, 'cause there was probably 20-30 people on it who had either been handling shot recently, or were handling as a matter of daily course. But this little freak's name just jumped out at me, and so he's the one I started with."

Pruitt snorted. "I would have, too."

Lee thumbed to the room in which Skip Ekrem was being held for interrogation. "A regular arsenal is what he had out there. Assault rifles, sawed-off shotguns, survival food, mercenary magazines, porno rags. That whole paranoid scene."

"No trouble taking him in?"

"Got there at six-thirty this morning with E.L. and pulled ol' Skippy out of dream land. The freak answered the door buck naked. Started stammering and confessing to everything just at the sight of us."

"You Mirandized him?"

"Damn straight we did."

"That bruise over his cheek, that wasn't E.L. working out a little of his frustration over Dale and Evie, was it?"

Wilson held up his hands. "No way. He let us in and stumbled when he turned around. You know what a clumsy punk Skip has always been."

"He's the dog killer, the drive-by shooter, the bomber?"

"All of it. One doofus."

"He say what he had against Dale Slater to want to blow him away like that?"

"Said it was an accident. Said he had nothing against Slater personally. Thought Slater was out to lunch at that time. Which, to give him the benefit of the doubt, is usually the case. Slater and Evie usually did go to lunch together."

Pruitt turned his head, his eyes suddenly unable to focus. "If I hadn't called him, goddamnit," he said. "For a computer game," he added.

Lee Wilson said, "Hey, boss, c'mon. Some things just have no sense or reason to them."

"It's a hard thing to let go of," he said. "Really goddamn hard."

Lee said, "I'm only seein' it from the outside, boss, but it looks like it would be."

"You play it over…Again and again…If we'd have gotten together a day later, a day earlier." The smell on Skip that Pruitt had thought was fertilizer had been the residue of explosives. Why hadn't he thought of it?

"It ain't nobody's fault but Skip's, boss. The bastard. Thinking of himself as some kind of agent provocateur. Trying to push the greenies and loggers into a violent confrontation, thinking that when push came to shove the locals would kick ass on the greenies." Lee shook his head slowly. "It was just him."

"What about John Carpenter? Has he confessed to that?"

"No," Lee said. "Been adamant about not having anything to do with that."

⊕

They got everything out of Skip they needed. Served up on the silver platter of Skip's need to confess—though whether to assuage his guilt or clarify the details of his fifteen minutes of fame Pruitt couldn't tell. Either way, most of the pending cases related in some way or another to Black Bear Ridge got wiped off the board. The notable exception being the murder of John Carpenter. Skip had an alibi for that—which Lee Wilson would check—not to mention the MO's didn't match remotely. Nevertheless, it was a productive Sunday.

Monday morning Pruitt slipped the Crosby, Stills and Nash CD Olwen had given him Friday night from his leather jacket to his uniform jacket, slurped the last of his coffee, then rinsed out the cup and left it in the dish rack.

When he got to his back door, Angela Caracitto was there. "Going in to work?" she asked.

"Angela," he replied, "you've got some frickin' nerve, staking me out."

"Hey, I saw what I saw. You had a woman over, I happened to notice her. Who wouldn't: a hippie chick in a pickup truck. I live next door, remember? "

"That's something else: what the hell you're really doing over there with Bill."

"What's there to discuss? You ever seen Bill so happy in his life? He is a great guy—I'm not kidding you."

"Let's cut the crap. You're on my shit list."

"That's what I'm here about. That reporter, Emmett? I think he's got something on you. I just wanted you to know none of it came from me."

"Well, I appreciate that much, anyway."

Angela smiled. "That hippie chick the other night, has she got anything to do with this? Kinda lives a long way out in the boonies, doesn't she?"

Pruitt's blood darkened. "Stay away from her, Angela."

"Too late. I introduced myself. Olwen Friday. Quite a gal."

"This case has nothing to do with you. Take Bill and have your trip to Chicago, but cut this other shit out right now, you understand?"

Angela glared at him. "Are you telling me I've got to get out of Dodge, Sheriff?"

"I see you on the back steps in your underwear again, I'll run you in. I catch you in my rearview mirror in Bill's Pinto, I'm calling it harassment. The slightest provocation, Angela. That's all it's gonna take."

"You got any Dead quotes for this one, Gavin?"

Angela's eyes had gone hard as flint, and Pruitt didn't like what he was seeing one bit. "You stay the *hell* out of this investigation. You hear me?"

She remained glaring at him a moment longer, then turned and began walking toward Bill Logan's, the chains hanging from her black leather jacket singing like wind chimes in a breeze. Halfway across the lawn, she stopped and turned back again. "I hope when this is over," she said, "you and I can be friends again."

CHAPTER TWENTY-TWO

Unless he had a private meeting or phone call, it was Pruitt's habit to leave his office door open, and he caught sight of Andy Messerit slipping in about ten minutes after nine Monday morning.

"Andy?" he said. "Can I show you something?"

Messerit wore a charcoal gray London Fog overcoat and a matching gray cap to cover his thinning hair, an umbrella hung over his arm. Pruitt handed him the CD. "John Carpenter gave this to a woman who knew him." Making quotations marks with his fingers, he added, "She said it's 'weird.' No music. You make anything of that?"

The state's forensics bookkeeper accepted the CD. "No music. Well, give me an hour, I'll see if I can figure it out."

☮

Not twenty minutes later, the office still in a Monday morning lull, the call came in, a frantic voice crackling over the dispatcher's speaker reaching into every corner: "There's a shot man down here! I think he's dead! Holy Jesus, right in front of the store!"

"Where, ma'am?"

"Rhea's Market! This is Ellen Rhea! Send somebody now!"

Pruitt joined the hasty exodus out the door, jumped in his cruiser and sped down the hill in a full-blown, level-four fury, siren wailing, cherry tops blazing. Rhea's was only three minutes from the Courthouse Complex, but it seemed to take forever to get there.

The shot man was David Spoor, his body sprawled on the touch-sensitive rubber mat aproning the front of the automated sliding glass doors, which were attempting to close every few moments, a jerking movement. Willapa County's Medic One emergency vehicle had already arrived, the EMT's kneeling over him, administering first aid. "It was Earl Ruddell," one of them told Pruitt, not looking up. Spoor's shirt, cut away and laying in tatters around him, was sopped in blood.

"They were out here fighting over some damn thing or another," Ellen Rhea said. She was standing at the front of a knot of bystanders, paper signs looming behind them advertising sales on canned peaches and pork roasts.

"Earl just blew him away." It was Peter Johnson, an unemployed nineteen-year-old waiting for something to break at the mill. "They started arguing. Earl pulled out a gun and shot him."

"Earl drove off?"

Ellen Rhea said, "Like a bat out of hell."

Pruitt turned his attention back to the medics. "Is he going to make it?"

"With any luck."

"Remember anything he might say, all right? I'm after Earl."

⊕

The county issued Fords. Powerful gas-guzzlers with V-8's and plenty of horsepower, radial tires, and beefed up suspensions. They weren't much aesthetically, but they could get you where you needed to go in a hurry. Pruitt wasn't expecting to overtake Earl, even at the eighty and ninety mile-an-hour speeds he was traveling, but it was important to get to where he wanted fast. Judging from what he'd seen last Friday, Earl had gone and done just what Pruitt had hoped he wouldn't: thrown himself over the edge. He was certain the shooting had not been premeditated but had occurred in the heat of the moment, and that Earl would not be taking flight but barricading his castle.

At the end of a long drive-way off Tayler-Skees Road, Pruitt lurched his car to a squealing halt at the front gate to Earl's home, Raphe Jones and Ing Yen pulling in right behind him. As he got out he stayed low, keeping his car between himself and the house. Earl's wife, Laura, stood on the front steps in her pink bathrobe. Her long, dark hair hung in wild disarray, and she was pounding on the door, yelling for Earl to let her back in, what had he done, damnit, what crazy thing had he gone and done now?

Pruitt hand-signaled Jones and Yen to his side. Yen brought his shotgun, racking a shell into the breech. Jones had taken her service revolver from its holster.

"We've got to get her out of the line of fire," he told his deputies. "Let's get a visual, try to figure out where Earl might be."

From different points along the length of Pruitt's cruiser, the three officers peeked out and assessed the situation as well as they could.

Jones said, "There's somebody looks like Earl sitting in a chair by the back wall, looking at the fireplace. From that angle he can't see Laura or the front steps, or the front half of your cruiser."

Pruitt said, "Okay, let's see if Laura will cooperate." He raised up and peered at Earl's wife over the hood of his cruiser. "Laura?" he called. "Can you come over here and talk to me?"

She began pushing the doorbell, again and again, as if she'd just missed an elevator and was trying to force the doors open. "Damnit, damnit, damnit, Earl!" she cried.

Again, Pruitt called to her, but she was oblivious, pounding the door, yelling at Earl to let her in.

Pruitt squatted back down. "Earl still sitting in that same spot?" he asked Jones.

"He is."

"Okay, I'm going to grab her. Be ready to open that gate for me."

He took a quick deep breath, then bolted around the nose of the car and ran crouched to the picket fence, vaulted over and landed squarely on the hardening pre-winter ground. He raced to the side of the house and placed himself backside and flat to it. He pushed through the branches of waist-high rhododendrons, knocking over a ceramic bunny rabbit, but sidestepping a fat-cheeked gnome. At the side of the porch, which was three steps up, he remained flat against the house and tried to talk calmly to Laura Ruddell, who paid him no heed but rather continued rattling the door handle and pleading with Earl, furious with him, delirious herself, pounding, pushing, yelling incoherently.

At this point there was nothing left for Pruitt to do but to execute the plan he'd vaulted the fence with—as crazy as it seemed now that he was standing in the Ruddell family's flower beds. He stepped around the boxwood hedge at the edge of the stoop, placed one foot on the step just behind her and grabbed Laura around the waist. She was a slight woman, probably just over a hundred pounds, and Pruitt spun her up and over his shoulder.

He'd been thinking from the beginning that since she wasn't too big he could do this. What he hadn't anticipated was the strength rage and fear had given her. She beat his back with fists, the blows nearly knocking the breath out of him as he toted her down the walkway. Raphe Jones, sidearm still drawn, was crouching at the gate and flung it open as he neared. Laura fought them tooth and nail as they struggled to get her into Deputy Yen's cruiser. She managed to rake Pruitt's neck with her fingernails and land a solid kick to Jones' mid-section. The scratches Pruitt wouldn't feel until later; the kick elicited a mild grunt from his deputy but little more—a testament to her conditioning. Finally they managed to get the door closed, which only renewed Laura's fury. She began kicking at the windows, pounding at the handleless door and cage grate, her screaming now muffled but her eyes wild with despair. Pruitt and Jones left her to her madness and hustled back to their positions, staying hidden behind the cover of the three police cruisers.

Yen had retrieved the megaphone from his trunk and handed it to Pruitt, who caught his breath for a moment before pointing the horn towards the house. "Earl," he said, "c'mon now. He's not dead. It's not as bad as you think."

Raphe Jones said, "He's walking towards the window."

Pruitt aimed the megaphone at the shadow that now stood behind the lace curtains. "Earl?" he said.

The shadow figure seemed to be studying the scene. It was definitely Earl. Pruitt could tell by the shape and size of the head. "It's not what you're making it, Earl." Although amplified, Pruitt spoke in a restrained, conversational tone. "We can work this out."

Ruddell gazed at them transfixed, featureless in the weird back-lighting, a full-figured shadow tracing of the sort school children made for their parents, black profiles on white construction paper. A tableaux fixed in time. Laura had stopped screaming and a peculiar calm had settled over them all. The hot metal of the police cruisers was cooling, popping and pinging.

Pruitt set the megaphone down. "Earl," he said, speaking almost in his normal voice, "just nod if you hear me, okay?"

In one smooth motion Earl shouldered his shotgun and blew the front window to shards. Pruitt and his officers ducked completely behind their vehicles. Earl fired again, throwing a swath of shot over the top of their heads.

"Take him down?" Yen called to Pruitt from the other end of the cruiser.

"Man must exert his dominion over nature!" Earl yelled at them, hell and brimstone quavering his voice. "The true and righteous purpose of God's gifts, pursuant to His Holy Scriptures!"

Still crouched behind his cruiser, Pruitt signaled Yen to hold his fire, let the quietude settle in again, then shouted, "Put the gun down, Earl!"

"Everything must pass, as must Black Bear Ridge, beautiful timber God has graciously supplied us! We the People of Posterity obedient to the Laws of Almighty God, also known as Common Law!"

"You're right, Earl. What's meant to be will be. But you've done your part, okay? Now lay your gun down and let's talk this through."

Raphe Jones ventured a quick peek over the hood of her cruiser. "He turned his back to us," she whispered across to Pruitt.

Pruitt and Yen poked their heads up, too.

Under the now glassless front window, Earl was sitting on the sofa. Victorian-styled, camel-humped, it was upholstered in a pink and green floral pattern whose colors were echoed in the gauzy window dressing, the pink flamingos in the flower bed under the sill, and in the bathrobe that Earl's wife Laura was wearing at this very moment.

Pruitt said, "Earl? Can I come in there and talk with you? Just for a minute?"

Ruddell slumped over, his head bent as if in deep prayer or meditation.

Just before the shotgun blast threw his head back like a rag doll's, spewing a pink mist over the rhododendron bushes and dead-eyed flamingos, a flock of a dozen Canadian geese landed in the barren field adjacent to the Ruddell's home. The sharp retort that brought Earl's life to an end sent them skittering again for the hard blue skies from which they'd just descended.

⊕

Pruitt left Yen and Jones in charge of the Ruddell scene and drove Laura Ruddell to the Willapa Harbor Hospital. Her fury had passed. At the emergency entrance, he assisted her from the back of the cruiser, her hand nearly weightless, as fragile as thin china. "My God, Gavin," she whispered as she stared at the scratches along his neck. "I'm so sorry. I'm so ashamed."

"It's all right, Laura. I don't want you to feel bad. I'm okay. It's you I'm concerned with."

"He'd been so depressed, Gavin. So depressed."

"Laura," he said, "I've got to ask. Your alibi for Earl the night John Carpenter was killed—it was the truth, right?"

Her eyes teared over. She touched his scratches, mouth quivering. "He was home with me, Gavin. I swear."

For a moment, Pruitt considered sharing the lyrics of *Black Muddy River* with Laura, a song about passing over, one of the sweetest. A man walks alone by a vast, dark river, singing a song of his own making. Although but a small comfort to know Earl had been such a man, any comfort might have helped.

But then Laura's eyes rolled back in her head and she fainted, Pruitt catching and lifting her, arms limp at her side— arms that had pummeled him practically out of breath half an hour ago now as weak as dry twigs.

Emergency nurses rushed out and helped him get Laura on a gurney. They wheeled her in for treatment, Pruitt at their heels, though he was admonished, gently, to follow them no further than the lobby. At the admitting desk, he used a line to call Laura's mother, who gasped, stung mute. Finally, she gathered her breath and said she'd be right over.

When he could see there was nothing left for him to do, he dropped back down the few hundred feet of road that led from the flat top of the hill upon which the Willapa Harbor Hospital sat, heading to the County Courthouse complex and his office. Before he could get halfway to his desk, Andy Messerit intercepted him.

"Better come look at this." He turned without waiting for Pruitt's reply and strode back into his office, where he had John Carpenter's computer up and running. "Here's the CD you gave me this morning. There's no music on it because it's full of data."

"What kind of data?"

"That report we couldn't find. See this?" He ducked his head and put his finger on a button on a piece of gear in the stereo rack. A carrier tray appeared, displaying a disc Pruitt assumed was the one he'd delivered earlier. When Messerit pushed the button again the machine pulled it in like communion—plastic wafer, plastic tongue. "CD-ROM player," he said. "And a CD burner underneath it."

"CD *burner*?"

"He could make his own CD's."

"You're kidding? I didn't know you could do that."

"Well, it's not cheap. These burners run around $10,000. Some higher. But then none of Carpenter's electronics were cheap. This guy went first class all the way." Messerit typed in commands and a list of files came up. "This is the one we want."

The words scrolled up on the screen. As they read each screen, Messerit rolled up the next one. "This is Carpenter's Black Bear Ridge report." A couple of screens later, he said, "Oh, I hadn't seen this yet."

He swiveled in his chair, took the Crosby, Stills & Nash disc case and slipped the cover from its slot. Unfolding it, shortened strips of film fell out on the floor. Pruitt retrieved them, handed them to Messerit, who held one up to the light. "I think these are the pictures that will match the latitude and longitudes he's mentioned," he said.

Pruitt took the strip of film and held it up to the light. The images were too tiny to make out; nevertheless, their importance was apparent. He handed it back to Messerit, who said, "I'm no ecologist, but I'd say John Carpenter found a treasure-trove out there on Black Bear Ridge."

"So if J. Michael MacClinton had this in his possession, would he have been able to deliver Black Bear Ridge to this Japanese consortium?"

Messerit's brow furrowed. "Sure. If it was the only copy. He could amend it all he wanted, I suppose. Keep Carpenter's style intact, but make it say what he wanted. It would be some hard work, but doable. One thing for sure, with this deal he had going with the Japanese, without it he was dangling his putz in the wind."

☮

By the time all the reports were in on the Earl Ruddell shooting it was two in the afternoon and Pruitt had worked through lunch. "I'm going home for an hour," he told Joyce.

Back in his kitchen, he decided to make an omelet. He piled the ingredients on the counter—eggs, onions, and cheeses—then thought he'd better check his answering machine. The first two callers had simply hung up. The third did not identify herself, but launched immediately into a halting message.

"Gavin," Olwen Friday said. "You're not home. Well, damn. The thing is…I've reached some decisions I've been putting off for a long time. Don't think ill of yourself…You know, for anything I might do…Because of what you told me about John getting mixed up with that man. I love you…I think. In some way or another. Brother-sister maybe? Something good, though…Love…Wow. That's been a tough one for me. Anyway…What was it they used to say in those old war movies? See you in hell? Not you, I mean. Jeez, I'm not making any…You're a good man, Gavin. Sorry if this won't make sense to you. Don't think ill of me, either. Okay?"

Pruitt didn't like the sound of her voice one bit: that of a person putting their affairs in order. Too often, at least when law enforcement got involved, it meant something drastic was about to happen. Pruitt didn't know what Olwen was up to, but something was wrong and it put a pit of emotion in his throat. She'd left no time, but Pruitt's machine logged that automatically. He checked and saw that she'd called barely twenty minutes ago. Leaving his omelet fixings on the counter, he ran out to his cruiser.

⊕

He barreled up the all-but-hidden access road leading to Olwen's house, lurched to a stop in the clearing, and bolted from the car. Olwen's truck was gone from its arbor of brush and small trees. Pruitt began running up the path anyway. He had no idea where she might have gone and was hoping there would be something in the house that might clue him in. On a hunch he had called The Spartan Store, and sure enough Olwen had called him from there, using the phone in the back, but Elaine, the owner, had overhead nothing, nor had she paid attention to what direction Olwen had driven off in after she left.

As he rounded the arching pathway leading to the house, the frog atop the garret began tracking him with its bright doll eyes. Out of habit, he knocked at the door, then shoved it open. Called her name and when no response came, walked in.

He stalked the perimeter, living room to kitchen to bedroom. Empty as he had expected. He loitered by the tapless sink, got a drink of water from the ceramic cistern on the counter, struggling within himself with his two choices: walk away and let it play out, or toss her place to try and figure what that play might be. Her voice on his machine haunted him. Standing by just wouldn't wash. He did a thorough search of the house.

He found nothing germane. At least not on the main floor. Then his eyes fell on the narrow door that led to the garret. He crossed the room and found behind the door a set of spiral stairs, narrow as a medieval castle's. Pruitt's shoulders practically touched each side as he ascended.

Three-quarters of the way up he thought he heard a sound. He called Olwen's name again, but got no response. He felt a pang of panic. Had it been a creaking step or was somebody up there? If somebody was up there, who the hell was it? He remembered Olwen saying she worked at her kitchen table, not the garret, dismissing the tower out-of-hand as if it had nothing to do with her. If not her, then who did it have to do with?

He pulled his weapon and continued his ascent, placing each foot carefully.

At the top of the flight there was a door, slightly ajar.

"Olwen?" he said.

There was no answer.

He pushed the door the rest of the way open. Something caught his eye. He raised his revolver.

"Whoever you are, I'm coming in. Police!"

But it remained still as a tomb. Now he wasn't sure if he'd seen a movement, or just caught sight of something stacked on the floor. He waved the barrel of his gun across the sight line a person standing hidden behind the door would have. No response. No shifting feet or snuffling.

The garret room had a musty, unused smell. Though it wasn't dusty. The floor, in fact, was shining.

He took a step into the room—crouched, sidearm ready—but there was nobody there, only the stack of items that he'd mistaken for movement. A shrine or memorial. A small table over which was draped a frayed blanket. On it was an 8x10 black-and-white photograph, a framed needlepoint, and a book on a varnished wooden stand opened to a page featuring an illustration of a woman in an ornate robe.

The photograph Pruitt recognized immediately. A woman wearing a suit that would have been popular in the fifties, holding a baby swaddled in a blanket, one edge turned out with the letters DM exposed. The same blanket that the photo now sat on. J. Michael MacClinton's dead wife and daughter. Was Olwen the daughter?

Pruitt approached the memorial, his boots heavy on the plain shiplap floor. The needlepoint reproduced a children's rhyme, Monday's child, etc. It was Friday's Child that interested him. She was loving and giving. The storybook was opened to *The Wooing of Olwen*. It was five pages long and Pruitt scanned it quickly. A Celtic king unwilling to let go of his daughter tried to thwart the courtship of a suitor. In the story, the king failed as Olwen and suitor conspired to bring him down.

Olwen Friday. DM. D-something MacClinton. Mac's daughter, not someone else. Not dead. Pruitt had worked enough child abuse cases to know what this was about: a shrine to her innocence lost. More than likely sexual abuse. Like he'd suspected from the phone call, she was indeed putting her affairs in order, some sort of closure at hand. Pruitt hoped it wasn't retribution, but feared the worse.

☮

Pruitt used his cellular phone to make a call as he drove pell-mell from Elkhorn north to Riverton. He abandoned his code four when he hit Riverton's city limits, restraining himself, settling back into a quick but silent code two. Not yet did he want to draw the attention of the Riverton City Police. Under a brilliant blue sky on a crisp winter day, he instead drove as inconspicuously as a cop in a hurry could to the east end of Elm Street and the Grapevine, the twisting, yet meticulously maintained switchbacks that led to the Miracle Mile.

As he nosed his cruiser around the slow bend before J. Michael MacClinton's home, Mac's Grand Cherokee lurched incautiously from the driveway. Mac was at the wheel, alone but quite alive as he tore out onto the street and drove away wildly, fishtailing, the back end listing starboard as he lost, then gained control.

Pruitt resisted the urge to overtake MacClinton and pull him over. Instead, he kept a respectable distance. His hunch was that Mac was rendezvousing with Olwen Friday—or, as

Mac would be thinking of her, with Dorothy MacClinton, his daughter. Pruitt's call to Riverton High School had supplied that part of the puzzle.

"Just disappeared about halfway through her junior year," the secretary had told him. "We thought she'd gotten pregnant. But then she never came back, and nobody's heard from her since."

There was only one road along the ridge, and it twisted like a snake for the mile-and-a-half stretch, which made tailing Mac easier. Pruitt had only to stay one curve behind, just out of his sight. He needn't worry about the timberman slipping away down a sidestreet, at least not until the road dipped down into the valley again.

The immediate problem was that Mac was driving like a maniac. Again Pruitt had to resist the urge to pull him over— this time before the crazy bastard missed a corner and hurtled himself over the cliffside and took with him the answers to a few questions Pruitt wanted answered.

But Pruitt was wrong about the presence of sidestreets, because Mac abruptly flared on his brakes, sidled over to the thin shoulder, then swerved onto an unmarked, unpaved road, spewing gravel as he fishtailed back into control of the vehicle.

More cautiously, Pruitt made the turn as well. Tracking would be easy now, just follow the roostertail of dust roiling off the back end of the 4x4. Hang back enough to stay out of the roostertail itself, where visibility was next to impossible, just trail the tip of wake, letting the last mist of particles settle at the nose of his cruiser before he stirred it all up again.

He couldn't imagine what was up this stretch of road, though clearly it had originally been put in for logging. Barely wider than a truck, packed gravel, miles from nowhere—in Pruitt's world, these roads were as common as blackberry vines. So near to the Miracle Mile, no way were they still logging up here, even though the trees were at least forty or fifty years old and ready to harvest. Likely it was a road left to its own demise after the upper class began developing along the lower ridge in earnest.

Starting from the turn-off they climbed a steady grade, scaling the side of a long sloping rise through a series of slow looping switchbacks. Actually, the road was in surprisingly good condition—which made Pruitt wonder if maybe a glitzy subdivision wasn't scheduled for the near future. If the view on the lower ridge was tremendous, this one would be spectacular. Ahead, Mac was gunning it, shooting out of the turns and reaching speeds as high as forty-five, sometimes fifty—which felt like a hundred-and-fifty with the brush clawing at the side windows, pebbles and rocks pounding the undercarriage like a hailstorm.

Up and up they rose, the turns getting tighter, the switchbacks more frequent. Then Pruitt abruptly found himself in the midst of a storm of dust. Losing all visibility, he legged down on the brakes and went into a slide, felt the back end of the cruiser sway out behind him. The fusillade of rock and gravel under tires, the sound of Pruitt's own voice cursing almightily—for a moment it was like the end of the world.

Then the car pitched over the side of the mountain.

CHAPTER TWENTY-THREE

As if by sheer will he could stop the fall, Pruitt braced the steering wheel at arm's length. His whole body had broken into an instant sweat. He still had no visibility, only a shocking and sickening sense of vertigo. A scream was forming in his throat when he was thrown harshly into the seatbelt straps, the sound of metal crumpling, his head snapping forward, grazing the inside windshield molding. Scree and rock pummeled the driver's side door and window. The assault seemed to go on forever.

Then an eerie silence. Dazed, his head limp, he silently praised the seatbelt straps for their reassuring embrace. The engine had died, the scree and rock had settled—through which a brown, enveloping dust continued quietly swirling. A *Black-throated Wind*, all right. If not exactly what the song was about, the image of life passing like dew wasn't far off from what he was feeling.

He tried to breathe deeply, but the gritty air seeping into the car only made him cough, which hurt, through his chest, across his shoulders. Unable to see through the haze of dust, he surrendered to the security of the seatbelt, tight across his shoulder, like the hand of God.

His vision had closed down and narrowed, but now began to open up again. As the dust settled he could see that his cruiser had become wedged between two fir trees: one at the grill, the other at the back passenger door. Another godly embrace. Solid—ostensibly.

He had to get out of there. From what he was able to see, he figured the cruiser had come to rest at 45- or 50-degree angle. If he was careful, he could scramble up the side of the mountain to safety. Then he remembered why he was there in the first place and put his hand on his service revolver, irrationally thinking it might not be there anymore, though it was.

His radio was still on, squawking. He used it to call Riverton dispatch.

"Officer in trouble," he told the woman.

"Where are you?"

As best he could, for his tongue was thick and his words were coming out funnily, he told her.

"We don't have anybody anywhere near there," she told him. "It's going to take twenty minutes easy."

"I'm gonna try…to crawl out of here."

"If you're stable, maybe you'd better not. You might be hurt worse than you think."

"I don't know if it's…stable. I really don't."

"Just be careful, whatever you do."

"Going to try my door," he told her. "If I can get out, I won't be near the radio anymore."

"Officers are on their way," she said. "And a tow truck."

He let the microphone drop. It clanked against the radio, then fell dangling against the passenger side door from the angle the cruiser rested against the trees.

Though rather heavy because of the angle, the door opened surprisingly easily. Pruitt used his left leg to get it fully open and it stayed, yawning wide. He used one hand to brace against the dashboard and used the other to let himself free of the seatbelt. The shift of weight caused the cruiser to rock on its springs, which Pruitt interpreted as losing its placement and gave him an adrenal dump that felt hot in his loins and across his knees and nearly caused him to lose control of his bowels.

He cursed and held himself still a moment, not knowing which course of action was best, remaining still or making a mad leap. But the movement stopped as Pruitt did. He took a couple of deep breaths before turning, slowly, so that his knees were braced on the seat divider. Using the doorwell frame, he pulled himself free of the car. He sprawled across it and it felt solid. The mountainside footing was tenuous, but relatively free of scree and loose rock. Apparently, most of the debris that had rained down on the vehicle had been pulled off the rim when he'd careened over the edge. He had about fifteen feet to climb. Not that bad. He'd keep the cruiser directly behind him in case he started to slip backwards.

He was about to make his first step when the barrel of a pistol appeared over the rim above him, followed by the stony face of J. Michael MacClinton.

"Where is she, Pruitt?"

"For chissakes," Pruitt said, "put that thing down and help me out."

"Where's Dorothy?" MacClinton reiterated. "She said to meet her here."

Pruitt almost confessed that he didn't know, but stopped himself. "We've got a code," he lied. "She won't come out until I give the word."

"If she's up here, I'll find her."

"You couldn't find her up here to save your life, Mac. She grew up around here. She knows these woods like only a kid would. You gotta play it our way."

The timberman stared hard at Pruitt, the pistol still trained on him.

"If you want to see her," Pruitt said, "help me the hell out of here."

Finally, Mac lowered the gun. Without comment, he turned away. Alone again, Pruitt wasn't sure if his stew of lies and truth had worked until he heard the sound of Mac's Grand Cherokee gunning to life, the roof of the back end coming into view where a moment ago had been the man's angry face and the pistol.

A line dropped to Pruitt, who tested it, then climbed up to safety, only to find himself staring at gun barrel again.

"Jesus, Mac. This is ridiculous."

"Step away from there."

Pruitt did as he was told. Back on solid footing, he could see that before he'd gone over the cliff they'd reached the end of the road and a graveled plateau about 20 yards deep. There was still a last nub of hill over the plateau, forested. Pruitt wondered where the hell Olwen had hidden her pickup truck.

"Undo your utility belt and let it fall."

Pruitt did as he was told.

"Now pick it up by the buckle and throw the whole thing over here to me."

The belt with his revolver, speed-loaders, pepper spray, bullet pouch, and handcuff case was heavy, and it landed a couple of feet shy of Mac's feet.

Mac stepped forward, kneeled and took the revolver from the holster, shoved it behind his own belt, then tossed the rest over by his Jeep.

"Where is she?" he asked as he stood.

"We gotta talk first. I've gotta have some questions answered."

Mac glared at him.

"When you told me you'd lost your daughter," Pruitt said, "you didn't say she'd died. It's just what anybody would have thought. When did Carpenter tell you he knew where she was?"

"I can explain everything," Mac said, stepping back a pace. "If I could just talk to her for a few minutes."

"Did he try some sort of counter-blackmail on you? Did he threaten to take her to South America with him?"

"My wife stopped loving me, man! Can't you see what happened…?"

A touch of hysteria had crept into his voice; Pruitt didn't like the sound of it.

"She went cold, man. Stone cold. With Dorothy it was different. Dorothy loved me for me. Just for me being there, that's all."

Mac was one sick bastard, but it wasn't the time to tell him so. "It must have hurt when she left. But maybe she felt she had to."

"She couldn't have. It was the drugs. Those people she hung out with. Don't you see, it wasn't a selfish thing at all. Dorothy and I were good together. It was as good as my life ever got."

As well as circumstances allowed, Pruitt attempted to sound like Mac's friend and confidant. "Is that why you killed Carpenter? Because once you found out she was nearby, you couldn't imagine not getting her back? That must have been tough."

Mac didn't answer and Pruitt felt he might be losing him. "It's easy to understand how you feel," he said, forcing empathy into his voice. "I've got a daughter, too, remember? We talked about our daughters, you and me."

"Him knowing where she was and not telling me," he said as if he'd not heard Pruitt. "It was the worst thing that could have happened. Look," he said, "where is she? She said she'd be here. I need to see her."

"That'll happen, Mac," Pruitt said. "But you've got to answer some questions first. It's part of the deal. When did Carpenter tell you about Dorothy?"

Mac breathed deep. He wasn't exactly training the pistol on Pruitt anymore, but rather wagging it as he spoke, though it was still aimed in his direction. "It was about a month ago," he said. "Called up and said the deal was off. He didn't care if I exposed him or not, didn't care anymore about his reputation." He snorted. "And I knew right away it had nothing to do with frickin' owls. I could hear it in his voice. It was about Dorothy, how he'd found her, then somehow found out about the two of us. Some kind of shrine in a tower or some such nonsense.

"At first I played it cool. Only he knew where she was. I was thinking that if I just sat still a while I could get it all,

Black Bear Ridge, Dorothy. Then the bastard called me and said he was going to fly off with her." He shook his head in disbelief. "South America, for chrissakes!"

Pruitt said, "What happened then?"

"He accused me of things I couldn't tolerate. Had it all twisted. Made everything that had happened sound depraved. Like I'd done something *evil*. And I couldn't have it, somebody out there saying those sorts of things about me, especially if he was saying them to Dorothy. I caught up to him at his apartment."

Mac glanced away, then back at Pruitt. "He just laughed. I had the gun," he said, holding it up as if Pruitt hadn't noticed it yet. "He said go ahead, I'd have nothing. Not the timber, not Dorothy. I knew then it was going to be harder than I thought. Then I thought about that spot—"

"By Nallpe?"

"I'd sold that parcel a year ago. I knew they were logging it. So I tied him up. Drove him out there. The plan...It's funny how those things start kind of fuzzy, then clear up as you go along."

"And you got to the site and then what?"

"It came to me when I crested that knoll and saw the tin spar. I remembered the old days when I worked the woods and we joked all the time about stringing the crew bosses up, letting them dangle 'til their eyes popped out. It was perfect.

"Dragged him over, let him sit there in the dirt while I fashioned a noose with a slipknot, started hooking everything up. The sky was clear, a full moon, you could see fine. I figured as the situation started getting obvious—you know, as he saw the noose, what I was going to do to him—he'd start talking. But he wouldn't, so I took him up, just for a taste. When I brought him down he was gagging for air. And I ask again where she is and he *spits* on me!"

Mac took a deep breath. "Have you ever had anybody spit on you? It's like your mind goes blank, you're so goddamned mad. So I took him up again, a little longer. Brought him down and he was hurting. I told him all he had to do was tell me where Dorothy was, to hell with Black Bear Ridge, and he told me to go screw myself. So I took him up the last time…And that was it."

MacClinton stiffened, his eyes jittering. "He got under my skin so bad," he said. "Nobody'd believe it now, but I never would have killed him if he'd just told me what I wanted to know. The thing was, man to man, he was having me for lunch. This ivory tower nerd, of all people. That's what mattered. Black Bear Ridge didn't matter, Dorothy didn't even matter at the end. It was him against me. I'd said I'd kill him, but I wasn't planning on it. But when he called my bluff, I had to."

"Then you hit him with the piece of wood?"

"I got panicked after," he said. "Only thing I knew was I had to put the blame somewhere. I mean, motive was easy. Hell, motive was established the day John Carpenter moved into the county. Just had to come up with some evidence. So I conked him with the wood to have something to plant on somebody."

"Earl Ruddell?"

"Him, right, that quack. Called with the tip. Like I was a neighbor or something. With a guy framed, and nothing connecting me, I figured I'd done it."

Mac looked off towards the surrounding woods. "Had it all neat and tidy," he said.

"Okay, that's enough," said a woman's voice. "Drop the gun."

Pruitt could hardly believe his ears. Had twenty minutes passed already? Had the cavalry arrived? He hadn't heard a cruiser drive up. The voice, however, was not that of a cop, it was Olwen.

She'd emerged from somewhere to Pruitt's left, shouldering the shotgun she kept by her door to scare off bears, aiming it now at MacClinton.

"Olwen," Pruitt said, "this is not what you want to do."

Ignoring him, she spoke to her father. "Do you know," she asked, "how low you are?"

Mac turned to face her. "Baby doll, I did it because I loved you. I still love you, don't you see that?"

Pruitt was dumbstruck. All his heinous acts, from the original molestation of his daughter to the final brutal murder of John Carpenter, had been, to Mac, no more than a good father's expression of love. And now this sick attempt at playing the long suffering parent of the prodigal daughter.

"I never loved anybody the way I love you." MacClinton took a step towards her.

"Liar and bastard," she said. She peered at him down the long barrel. Like everything else she'd taught herself, she looked like she knew what she was doing with the gun.

"No, baby doll," he said. "It's how I feel. When your mother rejected me, you were the one. You stepped in and saved me. You were so sweet, so innocent, so—"

"Shut up!" she demanded. "You, you, you. All you think about is you. You're so blind to anything but yourself, you can't see other people except for what you can do with them. Make them jump, make them squirm, make them give you their money. You tyrannized my brothers, tyrannized my mother."

MacClinton said, "No, I gave your brothers jobs, reasons to live." He gestured to the river valley far below them. The smoke from the mills along the river were thin threads twisting into the sky. "See? I've been good to them."

"Olwen," Pruitt said, "make him put the gun down."

"Put the gun down, Daddy," she said. "Right now, goddamnit."

MacClinton let it drop at his feet. "The boys'll be glad to see you, baby doll."

"Make him drop the one in his belt."

"The other one, too," she said.

He complied, the second gun joining the first on the ground. "They've missed you," he said. "They're right down there, being good boys."

"Living out the hell you've put them in."

"Olwen," said Pruitt, holding his hands up. "I'm going to retrieve those guns now. Okay?"

"No. You stay where you are, too."

"I'm going to retrieve the guns; just let me retrieve the guns."

"I'm going to kill him."

"No, don't. Please. It won't be worth it."

"I'm going to."

"Olwen, wait. Think about it: this might be where you need to be, but what you *do* with this moment is up to you."

"Living for the moment was what saved my life," she said. "Not thinking about my past, because it hurt too much."

"If you kill him you become him. You don't want to become like him."

"Torturing John like a sick little boy torturing a cat." Olwen squeezed the shotgun stock tight to her shoulder, squinted an eye as she aimed.

"Please, don't," Mac pleaded. "I'm sorry. I'm sorry."

Pruitt said, "Let justice decide this, Olwen. You're not judge and jury."

Olwen held her pose a moment longer, considering, deciding. Then, as if the shotgun had become instantly searing, she threw it to the ground, at the same time screaming, her head flung back, the tendons and blood vessels in her neck straining. It was the roar of a beast, speared and in pain. Emptying, purging.

MacClinton took the moment to swoop down for his pistol, which he brought up firing, at Pruitt, who had crouched, preparing for action, the bullet whizzing over his head, its power nonetheless palpable for passing by invisibly.

There was another shot, and another, so close together as to be nearly indistinguishable. One of them hit Pruitt, who staggered backward from the force, his eyes locked on MacClinton, who was pitching forward, a surprised expression on his face, a reflection of Pruitt's own surprise, falling. Pruitt wondered if Mac was hearing what he was hearing: a deafening roar, an ocean echoing in his ears.

EPILOGUE

The bullet from the second shot Pruitt had heard struck J. Michael MacClinton, who himself was squeezing off another round, trying to kill Pruitt. Mac's getting hit had skewed his aim, the bullet from his gun entering Pruitt's upper shoulder. Although damaging only muscle, it had thrown him backwards and put him in shock. Though not exactly unconscious, he had definitely been out of it, in a sparkling, dreamlike zone. The first time he regained a sense of full consciousness, Olwen Friday was driving him down from the mountain in her truck, and Angela Caracitto was holding Olwen's red farmer's handkerchief to his wound, doubly red now from Pruitt's blood.

"Where's Mac?" he groaned.

"Mac is dead," Angela said.

"Which of you?" he asked.

Angela said, "I got him. The cocksucker."

"Where'd you get a gun?"

"Bill, of course."

Pruitt groaned again. "You and Olwen were together on this?"

Olwen said, "No," as she wiped away tears from her eyes.

Angela said, "When you took off like a shot today, I followed you."

"You went in armed," he said. "That's going to look premeditated."

"Bullshit. He killed John. He was capable of anything. I took protection."

A wave of incredible pain shut Pruitt up. He had an overwhelming desire to curl into a ball.

"There's the cops," Angela said. "Tell them to get the hell out of our way."

At the tip of a switchback a Riverton city police cruiser had angled to a stop, blocking their path. The officer must have just arrived because a cloud of dust was still settling and the cop herself only now spilling out the door.

Olwen angrily sounded the horn.

Angela rolled her window down and screamed, "Pig bleeding here, you numbskull! Out of our way!"

Before Pruitt passed out, visions of Olivia filled his mind. A collage of ages and circumstances. He didn't know if his body was trying to die on him, but if it was, he was fighting it. He knew now more than ever how much his daughter needed him, and he would not let her down.

☮

A panel looking into the matter found Carpenter's report meticulous, but either inconclusive or wholly accurate depending on who was doing the interpreting. He had found owls, but were they too few or too numerous? Too few would mean endangerment, and no logging could be undertaken. Too numerous would mean a healthy flock and some logging could begin. To a layman the guidelines seemed capricious, changing weekly. Yet in addition to spotted owls, Carpenter had found western pond turtles, the nests of marbled murrelets and bald eagles, and the den of a pine martin. He had also found a black bear sow and two cubs—the first black bears seen on Black Bear Ridge in over thirty years. All were listed as endangered, threatened, or sensitive, yet the question remained: which agency had the final say? The environmentalists claimed victory. The timberists vowed litigation.

Outside the legal system, reactions to Carpenter's report were just as varied. David Spoor, recovering from the gunshot wound inflicted on him by Earl Ruddell, nearly pulled his IV tube from his arm raising a clenched fist. About the same time, the logging community in Elkhorn, their numbers swollen by sympathizers and supporters state- and nationwide, held a wake for their economy, homes and lifestyles. A priest gave extreme unction. Women sobbed, tears formed in the eyes of strong men, and children were frightened by adult solemnity into silence.

Ultimately, the Hicksons, the heirs to Black Bear Ridge, could have simplified the issue by selling to the environmental coalition, but that offer fell far short of the kind of money they had anticipated. When they balked, most of the original players headed back to court to try and sort out who would be allowed to buy what parcels and for what price and utility. To complicate matters, the attorneys hired by Saginaw decided to dispute Carpenter's findings line by line.

Only one thing was perfectly clear. For the immediate time being, the flora and fauna on Black Bear Ridge could continue to exist as it had been for thousands of years—wild, primeval, sacred and dangerous—and, as the hoopla left with the media, the Willapa County and Elkhorn law enforcement agencies could get back to the police work they were more accustomed to. Though for how long either would be allowed to do so was anybody's guess.

⊕

Pruitt didn't see Olwen Friday much after the shooting. Briefly at a deposition, enough for a few words at a later hearing.

With a police escort, she and Angela had driven Pruitt down the switchbacks leading off the Miracle Mile and directly to the hospital. Based on Pruitt's testimony, and the forensic evidence at the shooting site that corroborated their stories, they were cleared of all criminal charges expediently.

Pruitt himself took the county up on its standing program of extending to officers involved in a shooting counseling with a therapist in Olympia who specialized in such matters. He wasn't required to because technically he hadn't been the one to shoot MacClinton. But he felt he needed it. The therapist had been a good man, a good listener. A fan, even, of the Grateful Dead, although not a Deadhead in the same way Pruitt saw himself. Once they got rolling, Pruitt had been glad to unburden himself. He had indeed felt vulnerable afterwards, at odd times finding his eyes full of tears, at other times angry enough to want to hit something. Ultimately, he was able to regard the experience as one that had given him a richer appreciation for life. For Olivia, for Molly, for Marion and his friends. If he hadn't already been the kind of man who reveled in the presence of the people he loved, he was forever more so afterwards.

On the tails of the shooting of J. Michael MacClinton, Richard Emmett finally published his story about Pruitt's drug-taking past. "Sheriff took LSD in College" claimed the banner in the magazine section of the Sunday paper. A former friend—now a member of an organization trying to legalize marijuana that used the militant gay activist concept of "outing" the drug-using past of public figures—had indeed come forward. One person whose quotes were conspicuously absent from Emmett's article were Angela Caracitto's.

"He didn't get dick from me," she had told Pruitt by phone from Chicago. "And I'll tell you something else: Bill says everybody figured as much anyway and who the hell cares."

Pruitt said, "I haven't seen Bill for a while."

Angela laughed. "And you won't. We're playing house."

"How long do you think that might last?"

Angela laughed again. "C'mon, Gavin, you know I don't think that way."

Bill Logan had been right. The story caused a brief stir, then died away—much to the consternation of Pat Crowley and other Willapa County Republicans, who'd been hoping for a stick with which to beat Pruitt to a pulp in the next election. Pruitt took some ribbing from his deputies and constituents, a few extra peace signs got flashed his way, then things got back to normal. Pruitt was who he was, and however he'd gotten that way, it seemed to have worked. If he was somewhat eccentric with his floating and his diet and his drumming, so be it. The county prided itself on characters and if Pruitt were one of them, they were proud of him, too. The prevailing sentiment seemed to be that if he did start having LSD flashbacks, would he really come across as any less a blithering idiot than most of the people in charge of government already? At least in Willapa County, nobody seemed to think so. Pruitt's detractors would resurrect the issue around election time, though whether or not it would be issue enough to defeat him he had no idea—nor was he going to worry about it.

⊕

Some two months after the LSD article, mid-February, Willapa County received its major snowfall of the season, a thick and quieting white blanket. Driving conditions became frightful, yet Pruitt would not be daunted from the rendezvous he had promised to make, even as getting the chains on his car turned into a real knuckle buster. Next year, he swore he would upgrade to something easier. Nonetheless, he got them on, after which he could drive the uncleared roads just fine—if slowly.

He didn't have far to drive and was not too late for his appointment. The Torchlight was fairly brimming with business. Apparently others, too, had gotten cabin fever and decided to brave the weather for a bowl of steaming oyster stew. Olwen had arrived there ahead of him and, in greeting, rose when she saw him. Pruitt walked up to her and hugged her. She hugged back, buried her nose on his chest, stifling quiet tears.

Once they'd sat down and ordered something to drink— coffee for Pruitt, herbal tea for Olwen—Pruitt said, "You look like you're feeling much better. At that hearing, you were awfully pale."

"I'd only seen the therapist Marion suggested once then," she said. "I've been going in twice a week since. Tuesdays with the therapist, Fridays with the support group."

"It looks like it's helping," said Pruitt.

"It is. A lot." Olwen smiled. "It's like I say: where you are is where you need to be, and it's always changing."

"One thing," Pruitt said, "about where you've been, if you don't mind my asking: where were you before Huckleberry Hill?"

"On the move," she said. "After Mom died, Daddy started getting out of control—you know, with his abuse—so I fled. I was seventeen. Kept hitching until I ended up on a commune in upstate New York. Changed my name there, then kept moving, westward, from one remote commune to another, never staying too long. I knew Daddy would be trying to find me, but I was off the grid completely. Nobody," she said, "not the FBI or anybody, could have found me."

"If you wanted to stay hidden, wasn't it risky living so close to him, just one county over?"

"It was different by the time I started building my home. I was at the point where it didn't matter anymore whether he found me or not. I was preparing to see him again, anyway."

"And you met John at the Spartan Store."

"Yes. We were both buying fudgecicles, of all things. To eat on the porch. We got to talking and I found out he was setting up his camp near Black Bear Ridge."

"With Earl Ruddell hot on his heels."

"And it just started from there," Olwen said, shrugging.

"I heard from Marion that your brothers deeded the land to you, that your house is yours, free and clear."

"Not just the land the house is on. A lot more than that." Olwen looked away. "They've been great," she added, her voice getting husky from emotion.

"Do you know that Dead song *Till the Morning Comes?*"

"I've heard it. Why?"

"There's that line about the morning showing a person the way they need to go. That it leaves no doubt."

"That's nice."

"It's you, Olwen. The morning's coming."

☮

"Did you see her?" Molly asked.

"I did. She looks good. Unburdened. Or at least in the process of unburdening."

"What a horrible thing she had to go through."

"Did you want to go for that walk?"

"I did before we got all this started, but now I don't know. It's so cozy."

Pruitt had driven slowly from the Torchlight to Molly's; it hadn't taken them long to get entangled lovingly on the couch in front of a blazing fire, covered now by a down comforter pulled off the bed.

"I'm thinking of *The Wheel.*"

"You are, are you? What's *that* one got to say?"

"That the wheel turns, of course, and brings you around, sometimes to new places, but sometimes to where you've been before."

Molly chuckled. "Well, this isn't *exactly* where we've been before. But I get it."

A Deadhead of long standing, Gary McKinney is the author of two previous novels: *If You Want to Get to Heaven,* and *Choosing. Slipknot* is his first mystery novel. He lives with his wife and children in Bellingham, Washington.